Praise for Lynne Connolly's
Richard and Rose Series

"Lynne Connolly pens stories that fascinate me. I was completely hooked once I started reading about Richard and Rose... Richard and Rose are characters that found a way into my heart and I could not release them, especially Rose."

~ *Coffee Time Romance*

"As Richard and Rose bravely face each obstacle thrown their way under the diabolical pen of author Lynne Connolly, we readers are skillfully drawn into a finely crafted tale in which surprises abound...Richard and Rose will keep us engrossed until the very end."

~ *Romance Junkies*

"There are lovely, intimate scenes between husband and wife, and their hunger as well as gentle feeling for one another shines through every scene. Even so, Connolly manages to keep a constant tension going about what is about to happen. The storyline is mostly unpredictable, from start to finish."

~ *Long and Short Reviews*

"There is so much going on throughout the story that you have to pay close attention to each of the details given. I must say that Ms. Connolly created a well plotted, suspenseful, loving story surrounding Richard and Rose and their everyday lives."

~ *Literary Nymphs*

Look for these titles by
Lynne Connolly

Now Available:

Triple Countess Trilogy
Last Chance, My Love
A Chance to Dream
Met by Chance
A Betting Chance

Secrets Trilogy
Seductive Secrets
Alluring Secrets
Tantalizing Secrets

Richard and Rose
Yorkshire
Devonshire
Venice
Harley Street
Eyton
Hareton Hall
Maiden Lane

Lisbon

Lynne Connolly

SAMHAIN
PUBLISHING

Samhain Publishing, Ltd.
11821 Mason Montgomery Road, 4B
Cincinnati, OH 45249
www.samhainpublishing.com

Lisbon
Copyright © 2013 by Lynne Connolly
Print ISBN: 978-1-61921-135-3
Digital ISBN: 978-1-60928-879-2

Editing by Sasha Knight
Cover by Kim Killion

First Samhain Publishing, Ltd. electronic publication: June 2012
First Samhain Publishing, Ltd. print publication: May 2013

Dedication

To everyone who followed Richard and Rose through thick and thin, through trouble and happier times, this is for you. Thank you.

Chapter One

October, 1755

A shiver shook me as I stood at the ship's rail. I wasn't aware that Richard had noticed until soft fabric slid over my shoulders and touched my forearms. I should have known better. These days, Richard rarely kept his attention far away from me. He was ever alert for signs of fatigue or discomfort, but that made me more aware, more jumpy, not less.

"Thank you." I didn't recognise the shawl, a delicate confection of light woollen material in pale blue, lined with silk, embroidered with tiny flowers. I turned my head so our lips were close. "This is lovely. When did you get it?"

"At our last port of call. I saw it in a shop window, and I wanted to see you in it. It said 'Rose' to me." Once he would have kissed me. Now he drew back and smiled, the signs of tension difficult to see. But I knew him too well by now. The tiny lines at the corners of his mouth deepened, freezing the smile in place.

He took his hands away from my forearms, although several layers of fabric lay between my skin and his. Every time he withdrew from my touch, I felt him drawing away from me. Every time he did it, he could do it that much easier, that much more naturally. His eyes held wariness new to us, and something else I shied away from defining, but in my heart I knew to be fear.

Fear that I'd leave him, fear that I'd die. When I'd lain in the throes of childbed fever, he'd watched while I fought for my life, held my hand, pleaded with me to stay with him. If not for him, I might not have come back.

I hated the weakness, and even though months had passed since the physicians had declared my life out of danger, I still felt waves of fatigue, even though I improved every day. More than anything else, I hated the way my husband avoided touching me. He did it now, his fingers barely skimming over the shawl as he withdrew from me.

I turned back to the sea, letting the fresh wind whip away my stinging tears. Tears caused by self-pity, brought on by exhaustion, with a good dash of frustration. I couldn't pin Richard down to explain or discuss our current dilemma. I'd have more success catching grains of salt. I wanted, more than anything else, for him to hold me while I slept. I wanted the caresses and the kisses that made my days complete. I wanted what we'd had until last July. I wanted my husband back.

I turned back to him and smiled brightly. "We should see the port soon."

The coast fringed our sight, a low, blue-purple edge to the grey, white-tipped sea. By now I could hardly detect the swells that moved our ship and brought us closer to our destination, hardly hear the slap of the sea against the body of the ship. It didn't hurt that we occupied one of the most well-equipped vessels in existence. The staterooms were so luxurious they wouldn't have gone amiss at Versailles.

This situation between us was driving me insane. The politeness and care from everyone, especially Richard, the perfection of everything I touched or handled, the way even the boards beneath my feet on deck were thoroughly sanded and scrubbed every day before I awoke—I wanted some good, old-fashioned real life. I wanted to smell the horse dung in the streets, hear the raucous voices of traders, see a room where the floorboards dipped and shifted from years of honest use. I wanted to smash a glass, destroy a porcelain plate, mar this perfection, but I couldn't. The yacht didn't belong to me, and while the owner, my brother-in-law Gervase, wouldn't object if I destroyed the whole of the grand dining room below, I couldn't repay his generosity that way. Our frequent stops ashore, ostensibly to explore the places we reached but in reality to rest, had come as a relief to the glorious perfection of the yacht and the way everyone treated me like fragile glass.

"You're tired. You need to rest." Richard drew the wrap closer around me, covering my already well-covered bosom, but when I lifted my hand to touch his, to steal just a little of the contact I craved, he moved his hand away, as if he hadn't seen my gesture. I knew better, but I said nothing. "We won't arrive in Lisbon for a few hours yet. Plenty of time for you to recruit your strength."

I couldn't deny my growing fatigue. "I would perhaps like to go downstairs for an hour."

"Are you hungry? Would you like to eat something?"

I shook my head. "No." I'd long tired of the constant pressure to eat and build up my stamina, but I'd lost a lot of weight, so I did my best to regain it. I could no longer indulge in pleasing myself alone. I had children to care for now.

I took his arm when he held it out to me, enjoying the feel of his hard muscles under the green wool of his coat. It was the nearest I'd been to touching him for some time. I took anything I could get these days, a beggar for contact with him.

I descended the steep stairwell below as if born to it. At first I'd found negotiating the yacht difficult, but I'd accustomed myself to the stairs, just as I'd grown used to the gentle but constant movements under my feet. The white-painted corridor led to a series of staterooms, and the gentle sound of a child's laughter drifted out to us as we approached. Our daughter, Helen, every day growing more enchanting. I would visit her later. And our other children, still babes in arms, who did not yet recognise me as their mother, but they would, in time.

Richard opened the door and ushered me into a spacious stateroom, which I occupied on my own. Before my illness Richard and I had never spent a night apart. Now we never spent a night together.

"Shall I send Nichols to you?"

Defiance shot through me. Why should I be the only one suffering? "No, thank you. You can help. You always said you knew your way around a lady's garments better than any maid." I smiled but received none in answer. Only a still watchfulness, his classical features set in an expression of repose. I tossed my new shawl on a chair. "If you could just help loosen my stays at the back, I'll be perfectly comfortable."

I unhooked my gown at the front, let it slide off my shoulders and fall to the floor. All I could feel behind me was a hot breath on my nearly bare shoulder. Just one breath. He stepped back.

I hoped the restraint was hurting him as much as it hurt me. After all, these days it wasn't of my doing. I waited, and then felt his fingers on the strings of my stays. Hard, viciously ripping at the laces, as if he wanted to get the task over with as fast as possible. When he touched my skin, his fingers skimmed past the stays to linger on my shoulder blades, and I revelled in his touch, however slight. He sucked in a deep breath, his gasp harsh in the near silence of the stateroom.

I wouldn't tell him I could have done it myself. These stays hooked down the front, the back laced to fit me. My maid Nichols would curse when she found the laces undone. She would just have to put up with it. I wanted to force him back into some kind of intimacy. Surely he couldn't keep this distance up for much longer.

I turned back and smiled, keeping it friendly. A sultry

invitation would have him running. "Thank you."

He spun around and dragged down the covers on the bed. The scent of lavender from the sheets wreathed around us. I'd come to associate that aroma with closeness. It perfumed our sheets, my private linens, and warmed from body heat, escaped when we undressed. But that was before my illness. Now it meant loneliness and solitude.

I loosened the outer petticoat and the quilted one I'd chosen to wear that day in place of panniers, leaving me in my stays, shift and under-petticoat. Then I kicked off my shoes. That should be enough to tempt him. My breasts were more exposed than hidden, my arms bare, the shape of my body easily visible.

Not that I expected it now, but constant repetition of this scene would weaken his resolve. I would not lose the battle to recommence the intimacy that had made both of us so happy such a short time before.

He forced a smile and glanced at the bed. "In you get. I'll have Nichols wake you in two hours."

I climbed in, trying to tempt without being obviously provocative. He tossed the sheets over me and left without a backward glance, without bending to kiss me. He hardly looked at me. I dashed away incipient tears and set myself to my repose. Although I didn't really need it anymore, I would take all the respite I required to ready myself for the fight ahead. The fight to get my husband back in my bed.

That same evening, we arrived in Lisbon. Wearing my new shawl over a blue silk gown that almost matched it for colour, I stood at the rail once more and watched the city as it came into view.

I had studied it on the map, and it appeared at first sight that Lisbon was the same size as Liverpool, a rapidly growing port in England. Lisbon, however, had a grace and stateliness that engravings of Liverpool told me it did not possess. Churches and towers of great buildings dominated the view here, but I couldn't tell which was palace and which cathedral at this stage. I knew both bordered the sea, presenting an impression of wealth and power.

As we drew closer, I saw that the architecture had an appearance the like of which I hadn't encountered anywhere else. Although I had visited Venice, Paris and other great cities, I had seen nothing like Lisbon. I couldn't quite understand why, and I concentrated on the view to see if I could discern what the difference consisted of. Small rounded towers, some bulbous shapes resembling nothing so much as an onion, some bearing the remains of bright paint. Several buildings gleamed in the sun, colours shining, and I guessed they were decorated with the colourful tiles Portugal was famous for. The exotic mixed in with the mundane.

Some seagoing ships, sails folded away for the stay in port, and other, smaller vessels, bobbed in the tide, the smaller courting the larger like maids-in-waiting. All the small vessels seemed to be heading for us. Our captain would have sent word of our imminent arrival, to bespeak our berth at the port, but I didn't imagine it would create this kind of fuss. We were personages of some importance, but not that much, surely. Lisbon was a fashionable place to avoid the rigours of the English winters and had many an aristocratic visitor, so we wouldn't be unusual.

Our ship creaked to a near halt, and the gentle sway of the waves against the planking grew more pronounced.

Richard walked over to join me. He brought the captain with him, an efficient man with many years at sea under his belt.

"Why are all these little vessels heading for us? Do we disembark on them? I thought we had planned to do that tomorrow?" For sunset was bathing the horizon in gold, and it seemed easier to sleep in the staterooms tonight, rather than go ashore.

The captain gave me his answer. "Some passengers do use the boats, my lady, but it's not that. I'm afraid we have to suffer visits from officials before we're allowed to disembark. They wish to assure themselves that we are healthy and are not smuggling undesirables."

I exchanged a glance with Richard and saw his brief smile.

"You told them who we were and where we are headed, I presume?" Richard asked.

"Yes indeed, my lord. I dispatched a messenger as soon as we were close enough for him to row to shore. I believe that increased their eagerness to ensure that everything was done properly."

I laid my hand on Richard's sleeve, and then withdrew it hastily. Now was not the time to put more pressure on him in our own, personal conflict. "I believe he means that they wish to see us for themselves."

Richard gave a cold smile, and I knew he sensed himself under threat. The more he felt unsure or endangered, the further he retreated behind the cold mask he had used all the time until we had met. "We are in the nature of a play for them, a rarée show of some kind?"

The captain reddened and glanced away. He should have dealt with this eventuality before now, and he knew it, or at least prepared for it. "We must allow a pilot on board, my lord. He will guide us into harbour. That is usual in any port." It was telling that he reverted to Richard's formal address, not the "sir" he'd been using throughout the voyage.

"What *isn't* usual?" Richard demanded immediately.

"More officials." The captain sighed. "Indeed, my lord, I apologise for the delay, but I have been informed in no uncertain terms that we must undergo the formality of an inspection before we leave the yacht for shore. Doubtless others will seize the opportunity to see as much as they can of such a fine vessel as this one."

"You may tell them that we will accept their presence in the morning. I will not allow them on board until then. Send them back."

The captain touched his forehead with two fingers in an informal salute. "But, my lord, they are waiting to embark."

"Let them wait." He turned away, the conversation obviously done.

The captain made a gesture of helplessness to the officials in the boats. Several lights glinted off the telescopes some were holding, so they could see his action perfectly well. He snapped out an order, and a man scurried to the rear of the vessel to send a message by using that intriguing combination of flags and gestures.

I watched as the man sent the message and someone in the boat waved wildly back. The response didn't appear as controlled. More furiously angry.

Smiling, I went below to join my husband for dinner. Very few people got the better of him.

After another night aboard spent in my lonely bed, I dressed, ate and visited my children before going back up on deck to discover if the small boats had reappeared.

Richard was already there. It was the first time I'd seen him that day. He studied me, searching, I knew, for signs of strain, but I had perfected my veneer of serenity since my illness, and I was sure he could see nothing untoward. In truth, I was longing to see my sister, and I wanted nothing to get in the way of that today. In her last letter to me, she said she would try to meet us at the pier, but she could not promise it. We had sent word, but she didn't usually reside in the city, rather, in her house a few miles distant.

I saw the hard edge to Richard's expression, the firm line of his mouth, and knew he was thinking of the safety of me and our children. We still had enemies, despite defeating two of them last year. Every great lord had adversaries, but because of family matters and Richard's zeal to further the cause of justice, we had more than most.

Richard appeared smooth, in control on the surface. He had dressed up for our visitors. On board, he had been at his most informal, preferring country coats and plain materials, often leaving off his formal wig to bare his golden hair to the sun, but today he had returned to being the leader of fashion, and he appeared at his daunting best.

Magnificent only began to describe his appearance. He looked formidable, in full command of his destiny, and for that matter, ours too.

He'd chosen to wear his favourite colour that matched the hue of his eyes. His clothes were laced with silver that glinted in the bright sunshine; he could challenge the King of Portugal himself for magnificence. The large faceted silver buttons on his coat flashed, echoing the ones on the hilt of his dress sword, which I knew for sure were real, all adorned with the Kerre family coat of arms. He'd applied some powder to his face, and a tiny black patch teased the corner of his left eye. He would cow the officials into allowing us a speedy passage into port today.

I would not even attempt to compete with Richard in his peacock glory, but I had dressed more formally than had been my wont recently. I wore my blue silk gown over a silver-grey petticoat, with blue ribbons in my hat and pearls around my neck and wrists.

My gloves were of fine kid, pure and clean, the kind I would have preserved carefully in my Devonshire days, but now I discarded them when I considered them worn. Sometimes I smiled at the grand lady I'd become, but I'd never lost sight of the reserved, practical daughter of the gentry. Richard used to say he loved them both and adored the differences, but he hadn't said that in a while.

Three rowboats approached the yacht. There must have been eighteen people aboard those small boats, if not more. It made interesting viewing, and when they came close enough, I could see how full they were, men jockeying for places, the wide skirts of their coats crushed between their bodies.

Next to me, Richard murmured, "I'll do my best to get rid of them. I have the stairs blocked so they will not get to the children without our permission."

"Good. By your dress, you could wear that coat at court."

"They want a show. I could do nothing but oblige."

I laughed, and some of the reserve between us melted. I could see it in his eyes as his expression softened.

But we weren't alone, and we didn't have the chance of being alone again for some time. In the company of other people, he would feel safer because he knew I couldn't show him the fondness I felt for him in more than conventional ways. I couldn't try to seduce him, undress for him or share intimacies.

However, he had unbent somewhat from the cold, restrained man who greeted me on my return to sanity after the fever broke. He no longer conducted himself like some kind of animated marble statue, but he was still far from accepting effusive displays of affection in public. I would take what I could while I could and be pathetically grateful for it. It would help to sustain me in the battle ahead. For it was a battle and would continue to be so until I had him back in my bed.

A middle-aged man led the way aboard, concentrating on his steps up the rickety rope ladder to the yacht, so he didn't look up until he had both feet planted on the wooden deck. Just as well really, because he nearly tumbled over the side when he lifted his eyes and saw Richard.

Totally in his element, Richard raised a brow, the rest of his face still and waiting. The man stuttered something, and one of the men with him murmured, in English, "The pilot, your excellence."

"Your lordship." Richard's valet and general factotum, Carier, had unobtrusively arrived on deck and stood between the pilot and my husband. "You address him as 'your lordship'."

The pilot bowed low but straightened and held up his chin. For that alone, I liked him. Richard hadn't dressed like this for him, an honest man doing an honest job, but the threatened officials, who arrived in the pilot's wake. They crowded on deck with their entourage, and chaos ensued, the noise from many feet shuffling on the wood and the conversation, jabbering in a language I barely understood, shattering the relative tranquillity that we'd had before their arrival.

Richard moved to stand in front of me, partially blocking me from their view and impeding their access. He glanced at Carier, who went to the captain and said something. The captain nodded and gestured to his men, who came forwards and effectively boxed in our visitors. We had thought our yacht spacious, but it didn't appear so now.

They wanted to see the English gentleman. Perhaps

19

Richard's reputation had gone before him, or maybe the magnificence of the vessel sailing into the harbour had aroused their curiosity, but I was sure most of the people had no right or reason to be here.

I felt severely underdressed when the port officials extricated themselves from the mob and came forwards to stand before us. One in particular wore garments that rivalled my husband's, although to my prejudiced eyes, neither so well fitting nor so beautiful, and not embellished with a coat of arms. However, his cocked hat bore braid and badges, but whether some kind of badge of office or the fashion of Portugal, I had no idea.

Another wore the sober black garb of the priest, his only adornment the heavy silver crucifix around his neck. His flat, broad-brimmed hat sat completely straight on his head, like one of those china figures used for snuffing candles, the resemblance more noted by the way he had his hands folded neatly before him. Another man, the one who spoke English best, as it turned out, dressed in what looked to me like ordinary day wear, neat but unremarkable. They all seemed to have at least three assistants or followers, though that could hardly be the case, although they milled around so much it appeared that way.

These men spoke English, one fluently, the rest in a variation that sounded charming but that I found almost incomprehensible. I spoke French and Italian well, but not Portuguese and certainly not this version of English. They barely spared me a glance as they goggled at Richard before bowing low.

For one moment I thought he'd present them with one of the graceful, mocking bows London knew him for. Richard was greatly renowned for his bows, the depths of which he calculated to a nicety. If he gave someone a bow far too deep, he was mocking them, and they often knew it. As we didn't know the intricacies of Portuguese behaviour, we couldn't be sure that they wouldn't take one of Richard's low bows seriously, and I guessed that was why he kept his response to a curt nod.

The plainly dressed man spoke. "My lord, my lady, I have pleasure in introducing to you *Señor* Antonio Alvares, our esteemed Magistrate of Health."

Richard raised a brow. "We have no sickness on board to my knowledge. We are all in positively rude health." He did not reveal the wave of sickness many of the crew had suffered since it had passed and would only have delayed us now.

The man relayed the fact to his compatriots and received a string of instructions in return.

Richard spoke perfect Spanish and could probably work out most of what they were saying, although Portuguese had a different cadence to my ears. Less musical than the liquidity of Spanish, but attractive. I couldn't understand a word, but I employed my time listening to the rhythms and imagining how it would translate into bars and staves.

Richard remained silent, his chin up, his eyes half-lidded and his mouth firm and severely straight.

The interpreter gave us a sketchy bow and an apology. "The magistrate says that everyone must appear on deck."

I glanced around, and a bright head of fair hair on one of the visitors caught my attention, though by the time I returned for a closer look, it was gone. I shivered.

Richard, being Richard, noticed at once and bent to me. "You are tired?"

"Not at all. I just saw something that recalled another time to mind. I'm fine, truly."

The sight had brought back what we'd left behind, and what we'd been forced to do to ensure our safety and that of our children. I would not let such memories affect how I behaved now. Dead people could not hurt me, nor could people half a world away.

Chapter Two

Señor Alvares refused to budge on his decision to gather everyone on deck, even though Richard stared him down. Any longer and we'd all freeze from the fresh wind whipping up.

"You wish to disturb our children?" Richard asked the inspector, his voice positively arctic. "You wish me to produce my children like a man parading his stock before a buyer? You are doomed to disappointment, sir."

The official spoke, and our interpreter reddened. "It will be sufficient if you allow *Señor* Alvarez and myself to see the children. We will go to them, he says."

"If you absolutely must, then that is the only way you will see them."

Richard lifted his hand. The lace fell back from his wrist as Richard gave a signal to Carier, who nodded and hurried below, ignoring the officials intending to block his presence. When the magistrate opened his mouth to protest, Richard shot him a warning glance that made him close his mouth, his words remaining unspoken.

"Only you two gentlemen. You understand? Then you all leave."

The magistrate bowed, flourishing his hat in what I would have considered far too deep an obeisance. Probably an insult, though I couldn't be sure. I'd have to ask Lizzie about the customs here.

The Magistrate of Health strolled down the deck, the crew parting before him like one of the gentle waves supporting our vessel. An uneasy silence settled on the men.

The pompous man sauntered around, occasionally pausing to take a man's hand and feel his wrist, perfunctorily doing his job. No doubt he had other tasks, like reporting back to his masters that we had the bare minimum of weapons—not counting the ones the captain kept hidden behind the boards on the lower deck, which the magistrate would not know about—and that a great lord and his family had sailed into port.

The news would be all around Lisbon by nightfall. I hoped we could be well away from the shore by then, although I didn't know Lizzie's plans for us in any detail.

Her husband, the Marquês de Aljubarrotta, owned a plethora of names, but we had learned to call him Paul. His English mother had retired to her native country after she was widowed, and that had ensured his visits to our homeland, where he'd met my sister and fallen in love during the course of a season. The happiness in her marriage was a constant delight to me, but I missed her very much. We exchanged letters as frequently as we could, but we hadn't met since the birth of her son. Or of my babies. She sent me letters full of laughter and smiles, letters that went a long way towards buoying my spirits after my illness.

This delay to our reunion irked me. For all I knew, Lizzie waited for us on the shore, and I was so close to seeing her that had I a spyglass handy, I could have used it to search for her. Or she might have sent a coach.

Weariness swept over me in an all-too-familiar wave, but I fought to show none of it, apart from clenching my fist in the fabric of my gown to aid my concentration. I blinked and heard Richard's murmur, "Not long now. I'll send them packing very soon."

It irked me that he could read me so easily, but it also sent warmth to my soul to think that he understood me as well as he did.

Knowing the game was up, with Richard at least, I allowed myself to lean on his arm a little more, glad of his support.

The magistrate returned to us, coming much too close for comfort. I could smell his breath, faintly tainted with coffee, and sense his body odour mingled with the pervasive perfume of camphor. He hadn't worn this coat in some time, then. He must have drawn it from its careful packing especially for us. Or maybe the king was planning to visit him. For now he'd have to make do with us.

We let him lead the way, the better to keep an eye on him. With Carier downstairs and the captain and crew watching the plethora of visitors on deck, we were as safe as we could be.

Richard turned before he left the deck and addressed the crowd. He hardly had to raise his voice, but a hush fell over everyone. "I want most of you gone when I return. Only those who are absolutely necessary for this inspection may remain."

He didn't have to threaten or promise anything. His orders would be obeyed, and his tone held only certainty and the absolute arrogance he could evoke when he wished.

We descended below deck to the sound of feet tramping over the planking above our heads as the crew ushered the spectators off the yacht.

Just past our room was a suite that we'd had converted to a nursery. The gentle chatter of the nurses wafted out as we opened the door, drowned by our daughter's delighted squeal when she saw us.

Before anyone could stop her, Helen pushed past her nurse and ran to me, and immediately I bent to kiss her. The fragrance of her hair and the way she nestled into me enchanted me every time she did it. I couldn't imagine how some parents would choose to deprive themselves of the sensation. She had begun to walk freely alarmingly early, and now, at the age of eighteen months, she toddled proficiently, something that drove her nurse to distraction.

"Good morning, my darling." I greeted her with a fond kiss, pressed to her forehead since she was already squirming against me. I laughed and picked her up.

All our nursing staff was present, the three babies held in their arms. Even the official softened, smiling when he saw the children. He spoke to the interpreter who translated what he said for us. "*Señor* Alvarez says you have fine children. He commends you."

Richard didn't hide his annoyance. Personal remarks from someone we didn't know were more than presumptuous, they were insolent. His face became a frozen, arrogant mask of disapproval. "I wish I could say the same. Ask him if he's satisfied and ready to leave."

The magistrate hadn't attempted to speak English, but he replied to the interpreter in Portuguese, his words stilted. "He says he has seen enough, my lord."

I had a feeling the official wouldn't push his luck and insist on seeing the rest of the ship, and I was right.

Richard nodded to Carier, who guided the officials out of the nursery, leaving me free to speak to the head nursemaid. My daughter squirmed and I returned her to the floor where she clutched my skirts and gazed up at me until I bent to her.

"I know better than to ask if you've behaved well, but I trust you haven't caused poor Whitehead too many headaches?" Smiling, I glanced up at Whitehead, her lace-capped dark locks smoothly fastened back in a way I envied, since it took all the skills of my maid Nichols to keep my hair in order. Whitehead was neat in word and deed, a most excellent nurse and now head nursemaid, although Helen remained her particular charge.

Whitehead smiled back at me and bobbed a curtsey. "She is speaking more easily, my lady, and just an hour ago she said, 'Mama come?'"

I hugged my child. "Would you like to see your brothers?"

Helen nodded and then turned from me, stretching her arms up. "Dada take?"

In time she'd manage "Papa", but since her first recognisable word had been "Dada", Richard encouraged her to continue to use it.

He bent to her, as I had, but lifted her in his arms as he kissed her cheek. "My lovely girl. Have you done your lessons today?"

It was a joke between them. Helen showed every sign of intelligence and escaped the nursery to visit her father whenever she could, which wasn't often. Richard usually took her on his lap and called it "doing her lessons" to prevent her getting into trouble.

His daughter could twist him around her tiny finger. If anyone had told me that the coldly formal viscount I'd first met, who stared at me without expression, would turn into this man, taking pleasure in a child's chattering nonsense, I'd have laughed them out of existence. But he had.

An awakening cry made my stomach tense in response. Even though I couldn't feed my babies, my milk having dried up during my illness, the response, like something understood rather than learned, pulled at me, furled my nipples and tightened my muscles. I had engaged the service of two wet nurses to feed the boys.

Three of them. Three boys.

For me, the horrors of their birth had faded, obscured by the joy of their arrival and my subsequent illness. Richard could remember every detail. Unlike the birth of Helen, when he'd waited downstairs as he was supposed to, this time when he heard I was in difficulties, nothing had kept him away. Defying the strictures of his mother and the expectations of society, defying everything but his love for me, he'd come when I needed him. And seen things he should probably not have witnessed.

Giving birth was a messy business and not something a loved one would want to remember. But I came through it, tired but triumphant. I only feared the experience had added to the fear he had now, so he couldn't see me without remembering my pain and distress.

A day later, after I'd fallen into a life-threatening fever, he remained by me, ignoring everyone but me. One of the things that disturbed me the most came later, when he failed to tell me how he'd felt during that time. He preferred not to remind me, or maybe he didn't wish to remind himself, but when I caught him watching me when he thought I wasn't looking, it was with a look of sombre desperation in his eyes. He'd come close to losing me, and it had shocked him more than he cared to acknowledge, I guessed. I had to guess because he wasn't telling me.

Raucous cries greeted us as our babies awoke, interrupted from their usual routine. Richard held Helen close, and I heard her chuckle as the demands of the boys became apparent. Richard—who we called Dickon—James and William already had their own personalities, and we loved them all. I had wanted to call my youngest son Lancelot, but Richard convinced me it would be unfair to saddle a youngster with such a name, so we had compromised and used Lancelot as a second name.

Dickon flailed his limbs against the nurse who held him, and I thought he smiled at me. Of all the boys, this one had the sunniest temperament. He would need it. Although as yet unaware of the fact, he was heir to one of the greatest peerages in England.

Family history led me to believe that I might have twins, but I hadn't expected triplets. Especially when they all lived. The youngest, William, was sickly at birth but possessed of a determination of spirit that saw him through the dangerous first month. Now he was gaining weight rapidly, although next to his more robust brothers he still appeared frail.

Wistfully, I watched the wet nurse offer her breast to Dickon. She had a child of her own, but he must be in her bedroom at the moment. By all accounts, he was a good baby, rarely protesting. And unlike my three, he was swaddled.

The vigour with which my son attacked the nipple gave me a sympathetic wince. Perhaps strained pear would be on the menu sooner than I thought. I glanced at Richard and his hand twitched, as if about to reach for mine. But twitch was all it did. I hated his restraint, the fact that he thought before he touched me.

I had learned other lessons since my days as a gentleman's daughter in quiet Devonshire, especially how to mask my reactions. So with a particularly brilliant smile I bent to kiss my smallest son and take him from the arms of his nurse. I could croon over him, that little piece of my husband I could caress and give my love to in full measure.

Will chuckled and waved his arms. I heard the nurse's slight disapproving tut but didn't let on, although I could be completely sure that Richard had heard it too, and that small sound could well cost the woman her position. Richard would not have me maligned in any way.

I glanced up and caught his fond gaze. Before he could look away, I smiled, exchanging the kind of intimacy I longed for. He smiled back, and his shoulders lowered a trifle, an indication that he had relaxed. A tiny breakthrough. I was beginning to think that we would achieve our aim by a series of little breakthroughs rather than one cataclysmic event. I would have to force patience on myself and not push him away by insisting on closer contact before he was ready.

But I missed him so much. He handed our daughter back to Whitehead and concentrated on watching me.

Directing my attention to the baby in my arms, I played with him until the wet nurse was ready for him. He latched on with a little fumbling, unlike his greedy brother, and I watched him, wondering if it was normal to grope quite so much. But every child was different. I, the mother of four, knew that now.

A touch on my shoulder made me shiver with remembered echoes. Richard murmured, his breath warm against my neck, "The officials should be gone by now."

I turned to him with a ready smile but lurched forwards into his arms when a crash shook the whole vessel.

Chapter Three

Richard uttered a muffled oath. "What in hell was that?"

I picked up my skirts and ran, fully aware that if he caught me, he'd make me stay below, and I had no intention of letting him do that. I'd been protected and sheltered to the point of complete inertia, and I would not allow it anymore. I hadn't heard wood splintering, so I doubted we'd hit an underwater rock or anything of that nature, but if we had, I wanted to be ready. I doubted we were in danger. It was some kind of accident, I was almost sure of it, and in that case, they'd need my help. I had a deal of experience in attending to the sick, especially as the result of violent accident, and I would not stand by if I could do anything.

If we were in trouble, I trusted the nurses to take appropriate action with the babies, and in any case, I'd be back down soon enough.

Shouts came from above as I scrambled up the stairway. I heard Richard calling my name with increasing urgency but decided to turn temporarily deaf as I gained the top of the stairs and saw a huddle of sailors and the half-dozen officials that were all that remained of our previous crowd, hovering on the periphery. They were gathered around something on the deck. As I walked towards them, the focus of their attention grew all too apparent.

Carier, his craggy face set into stern lines, glanced at me and then away again, showing none of the overconcern for me that his master habitually used these days. Rather, relief limned his features. By that I knew my guess was right, and somewhere in that huddle lay an injured person who might need my help.

The crew around the injured man shuffled back to let me through. The boy was painfully young, barely old enough to shave. He lay on his side, his face contorted in pain, his leg twisted. Unfortunately, it twisted the wrong way.

"How did this happen?" I demanded.

One of the sailors glanced up. I followed his gaze, squinting against the intensity of the light. A man hung from the rigging, on his way down, bright hair glinting against the dazzling sun. He scrambled like a monkey or a particularly acrobatic spider. As I stared at him, he glanced up, as if expecting to see someone higher up. Richard gave a sharp command. "Bring that man to me."

I looked back at the man on the deck—the *boy* on the deck. He lay moaning, his features paper white, blood gathering from several wounds on his body.

"How far did he fall?" I asked.

One of the men shrugged. "About fifteen feet, my lady."

I winced at the reply. I shoved my skirts out of the way, heedless of the delicate silk, and crouched on my haunches. I glanced up into Carier's eyes. He had squatted down by the boy's other side.

The valet reached into his coat pocket and produced a wicked-looking knife. "Do you have another one of those?" I demanded.

Someone held a razor-sharp stiletto knife in my line of vision. Richard's signature weapon. I took it with a murmured word of thanks. I didn't need to look around to sense the tension emanating from him. I'd ignored him and his warnings of danger. We would no doubt have a discussion about that soon.

Not now, though. While Carier sliced the clothing from the boy's arms, I took care of his breeches and stockings. I heard some sounds of protest, but not from our patient. He was too far gone to do anything other than moan. He sounded pathetically young, and I guessed that only pride was stopping him from crying for his mother. I had treated young people before, and the worse they were hurt, the more they wanted their mothers.

A commotion went on around us, another thump that shook the deck, but I didn't look up. One slip of that knife and I'd cause the boy further harm.

Shouts and calls of "Get him!" were followed by a splash and several curses. I decided to ignore them as I was busy probing and touching the boy, searching for injuries.

"Just a broken leg here," I said. "It looks bad, but it appears to be a clean break."

"Shallow wounds, my lady. Grazes and such," Carier reported.

"Then we can safely leave Carier to attend to the boy," Richard said.

"No." I heard the sharp intake of breath at my response to my lord's command. Not his, but the men standing around us. "Carier and I have this in hand. He'll need my help." For the boy's sake, I didn't elaborate what kind of help he'd need.

"It's not suitable for your delicate sensibilities, my lady," our ship's captain said.

Behind us, the Portuguese officials jabbered.

I snorted, not bothering to cast a glance their way.

The leg had broken below the knee. Sickeningly distorted, it shouldn't have lay at that angle. We had to act quickly, before it went dead and numb, but the task didn't appear impossible.

Sailors were resourceful men. They had to be when they

could expect to spend weeks at sea with no landings. Someone had found a strip of wood that would act as a splint, and someone else raced up with several strips of rags, the planks of the deck reverberating under my legs as he thundered towards us.

I felt Richard's presence all the time. He was waiting for me to show weakness, to faint or something equally visible, but I would not do it. I wouldn't show him or anyone else. I knew Carier would be watching too.

Richard exchanged a few murmured words with one of the men, but I didn't listen. If it was important, he'd tell me later. I would ensure he did. No more cosseting.

Closing my ears to the boy's screams, I probed the injury as gently as I could, then Carier and I straightened the leg and reset the bone into its rightful place. I wished the sailor would faint or that we'd thought to ply him with brandy before we began, but I wanted this done, and I wanted the crew to see I was more than the feeble aristocrat I knew they all considered me. The looks had rankled with me. Now I'd show them I was more than the pampered wife of a privileged man.

But that wasn't why I did it. I had always responded to people in trouble. I had seen a man injured in the fields once, watched him bleed to death because I didn't know how to help. On that day, I'd discovered that I wasn't as squeamish as I'd imagined. Since then, I'd refused to ever let that happen again, to lose someone when I could do something to help him live. So I'd set myself to learn and hardened my stomach in favour of helping the needy.

I held the leg perfectly steady until Carier fastened the last knot in the last piece of cloth. Then I sat back while Carier attended to the less pressing injuries, the grazes and shallow cuts the boy had sustained on his fall. Someone handed him a damp cloth, and he sat back on his heels to wipe his hands. I didn't need anything, since I'd only helped with the broken leg, not the cuts.

"He'll need new clothes," I said. It was likely this man had a change of clothes, but that was all. One set. I would ascertain he had what he needed. The warmth that new clothes and adequate bedding would bring him was essential for his recovery. "He must rest. Carry him below, but don't jar that leg. And if he becomes overheated, or if the leg swells and looks strange, come and get either myself or Carier. No excuses."

"Put him in my cabin," Carier said. "I'll watch him."

The men murmured agreement, and I watched as three of them lifted the boy and carried him to the stairway. The boy's screams had subsided to moans and groans. He had probably given himself a sore throat with all that screaming.

Richard helped me to my feet and we faced the officials, who hadn't done the right thing and left after the man's injury. The Magistrate of Health stared at us while he spoke, the man at his side translating rapidly. "The city of Lisbon is honoured to receive you as its guest, my lord. If you wish for any care or have any concern, please do not hesitate to contact me. Please go ashore at your leisure." Another man handed him some papers, but Richard waved them aside. He didn't handle such trivialities. The ship's captain took them.

As a statement of reconciliation, it lacked a little finesse, but I was only too glad to see the official gone.

He took his time, his stately passage irking me further. A sudden gust of wind took me off balance. I staggered a couple of steps under the onslaught.

I recovered myself almost immediately, but not quickly enough. Richard was there, his arm around my shoulders, his firm hold supporting me as he had so many times in the last three months. And before that, but I hadn't needed it as I did now. I bit down on my lip to stop a snappy response he didn't deserve, and instead spread my feet a little wider to ensure my stance.

"We'll go ashore soon," he said. "We'll have you ensconced in Lizzie's parlour with a pot of tea before you can think twice."

It sounded heavenly.

"But you will," Richard continued, "come down to your cabin now."

Not a request, but I wasn't averse to this command. Fatigue tugged at me again, although I hadn't felt it while I was tending to the sailor.

Richard didn't touch me on the way there, a short journey but a solitary one. With the door to my bedroom closed, Richard helped me to sit before he turned to his valet, who had followed us down at his signal.

Carier's rugged features took on an even sterner aspect than usual. Few people knew that a soft heart lurked under that tough hide, but I had seen it more than once. He removed his hat and held it in one hand, using the other to run through his grizzled hair. "It could be nothing, my lord, my lady, but we should consider a possibility arising from this event. A few things disturbed me, and I would be neglectful if I didn't bring them to your notice."

Richard touched my shoulder, very lightly this time. "You should rest, Rose. I could tell you later."

Or, if he thought it too upsetting, he wouldn't tell me at all. I stiffened. "I'm sure I can bear it."

"Very well."

Carier regarded us both with the calm neutrality of a well-trained servant, but his iron-grey eyes saw more than we allowed most people to witness.

"Will the boy recover?" Richard asked.

"He should," I told him. "We didn't find any complications."

"Your help was invaluable, ma'am," Carier told me.

A tinge of happiness warmed me before cold shame washed over to take its place. I shouldn't be pleased that a boy was hurt. I should be glad that the boy had escaped with the use of his leg and little chance of complications. But I was so avid for something to do, so *tired* of being treated like an invalid, I welcomed the diversion. It was a measure of how desperate I was growing.

Richard crossed the room to the bed and then back again, restlessly pacing. Although luxurious for a seagoing vessel, it wasn't a particularly large room. Six paces and he turned. "The boy might be young, but the captain made sure to employ no beginners. And that man in the rigging—I saw what you two did not. He didn't fall. He dived overboard and swam for shore."

"Several of the crew were ill." By his tone, Carier intimated what he thought of the illness that had occurred two weeks before. It had driven Richard into a raging fury of concern. An illness aboard ship could wipe out crews, and with infants on board, it could be fatal. From the day the first man had fallen ill, the babies had been kept in one area of the ship, and only named people had permission to touch them. We'd alighted at the next port and spent several days in an inn close to the shore until the danger receded.

The babies were guarded closer than anyone knew, except us and the men we'd set to guard them. Although we had lost some enemies recently, some still existed, and we preferred not to take unnecessary chances. At the time we'd put the illness down to bad food given to the crew, or one of those inexplicable bouts of sickness that appeared from time to time.

However, in light of the recent injury, it began to look as if there might, just might, be a pattern forming.

I said the word first. "A saboteur?"

"Too early to tell, ma'am." Carier glanced at Richard, who continued to pace, his shoes hitting the boarded floor with a decided clunk. "On the whole, I think not. Such illnesses aren't uncommon, particularly when the crew is relatively large. We have extra servants aboard, and the regular crew suffered quarters more cramped than usual."

"You've investigated already," Richard said. "You suspected it too."

Carier shrugged. "I merely offered my help. It is as well to remain on the alert." Very few people had the ability to put people at their ease like Carier. He could efface himself so people almost forgot his presence, or he could use his natural kindliness, which tended to unbalance people when they expected something sterner.

"What did you discover?" Richard rapped out.

"A lack of alarm, my lord. There have been no new cases, and nobody died of it."

"And the injury?" Richard snapped.

"That could be cause for concern, my lord. It could have been accidental. However, I don't recognise the man who was up in the rigging with him. And when you asked him to be caught and held, he got away. It indicates he didn't want to be detained."

I gave an unladylike snort. "You don't say. Not unlikely if he'd caused the accident, even if he did it by mistake. He'd probably rather take his chances than face us, especially if the boy had died."

"Ask the men. Discover who he was." Richard fixed Carier with a penetrating stare. "I have to make sure."

Our enemies had sent assassins after us before. "But if it is someone sent for us, it's a remarkably clumsy way of doing it," I pointed out. "Why would he push the boy off the rigging?

38

Attract attention before he'd done the job he was there for?" Which would be to kill us, if Richard's suspicions were correct.

I saw this as another attempt to swamp me, to overprotect me, but I also knew that we could not afford to ignore suspicious activity around us. He would have investigated this even had he not been worried about me.

Richard frowned then jerked his head in a quick nod. "Yes, you have a point. So an inexperienced person, or a sailor with a vicious streak, perhaps. Even a lovers' tiff. Or an attack on us that went wrong. I want to know which it is, and as quickly as possible. If you need me to exert a little pressure, let me know. If they sent someone for us, then they got through Thompson's and all our other observances. I will not have my wife and children put in danger. I will not tolerate any carelessness." I had thought us far away from the staff agency we'd founded in London, but domestic servants travelled all over the world, and we had some of Thompson's special staff with us—the ones who also acted as bodyguards and even extra eyes when we required it.

Carier bowed and left.

Now we were alone, the tension in the room thickened. I wanted him to hold me, just hold me. No, that was a lie. I wanted to feel his body next to mine. I wanted to make love, feel him hot and naked over me, under me, by my side. But that wouldn't happen for some time yet. I had to curb my eagerness, or I might make a foolish mistake and drive him even further away.

His anger filled the room, and I wanted him to shout, to explode in fury. Anything to break this icy reserve, the calm I couldn't bear anymore. Richard had a vicious temper, but he'd controlled it over the years, so now it emerged as an icy condemnation. I didn't want that. I wanted the hot fury.

"You didn't know what waited for you on deck after that

crash. Or who." The still, quiet voice. Oh hell.

"No, I didn't. But I haven't changed, Richard. I still want to face my fate head-on."

His voice remained dangerously low. "It could have been pirates, mutiny, anything."

I wanted to laugh at his outrageous suggestions, but one look at his face, his features as graven as a marble statue's, told me that would be a mistake. "It was one crash on the deck. I wanted to discover what it was, so I could protect my children. *Our* children. It wouldn't have been pirates, and I knew it wasn't an explosion. It was some kind of accident, I was sure." He couldn't keep up this cosseting forever. I would go stark mad, and why did he think to question me in this way? I got to my feet and whirled around to face him in a flurry of skirts and anger. "Don't you trust my judgment any longer?"

A tiny twitch at the side of his mouth alerted me. He was thawing. He looked away and bit his lip before turning his attention back to me. "I— Yes, I do. But I trust my own more, and I couldn't tell what that crash could have been. I *do* trust you, Rose."

My mouth twisted bitterly. "Then act like it. Richard, I might tire easily, but apart from that, I'm not an invalid anymore. We didn't need this trip. I could easily have weathered an English winter, especially with the pampering you give me, but I wanted to see my sister. And I wanted to get away. I thought it might help. I'm the same person, Richard. *I am.*"

He stood fully three paces away from me. I took a step towards him. "Unfasten me, please. I need to change." My skirts were bloody from the grazes the sailor had sustained in his fall, and they were sadly creased. I wouldn't go ashore like this. I was still wearing the stays that unhooked down the front, and I could easily get out of them on my own. But I wasn't about to tell him that, any more than I was the day before. Unlike yesterday, I wouldn't allow him to flinch away. This was a challenge. Would he accept it?

Richard never walked away from a confrontation. Firming his chin, he stepped forwards and put his hands on me. I quelled my shiver of response. It might deter him.

Although layers of clothing lay between my skin and his, I sensed his touch like a burning brand. He must have felt my shiver because he paused, his hands on my robings where they hooked into my stomacher. He dropped his gaze, ostensibly concentrating on the fastenings. My gown undone, he pushed it off my shoulders, and I let it fall to the floor. My stomacher remained, and when I turned around, he could loosen its strings. I caught it as it fell away and dropped it on the chair nearest to me. This was different to yesterday. He wasn't in control of his emotions. I had to push a little more, take the chance the unfortunate boy had inadvertently provided.

His hands fumbled at the cords of my stays. He'd always undone them deftly in our days of nightly loving and punctuated the unfastening with kisses and murmurs of love. None of that happened this time. He gave me a gentle scolding, controlled and careful. I would have preferred a clearing of the air, but he wouldn't do that. He'd stopped himself a few moments ago when he was quivering with fury. I was losing him again.

He gave me reason and common sense. "Sweetheart, we have four children now. They need their mother. That's why we brought them, rather than leave them at home."

"I am here." I put my hands on my hips to facilitate his action. Incipient tears blocked my throat, filled my eyes, but I wouldn't let them fall until he'd left the room. Not that I intended that to happen for a while. If we continued like this, so watchful around each other, thinking about every word, every touch, we would drift apart. I'd seen it in too many couples who had let love remain hidden until cordiality became a habit.

His scolding continued. I still loved his voice, the quiet cadence, the rasp hidden under his customary congenial tones that grew pronounced in the throes of physical ecstasy. I wanted to hear that again. So much. Feel the touch of his hands, hot on my body, the soft, moist movement of his mouth on my skin, the hard suction when he sucked my nipple—I had to stop. I could feel the moisture forming at the top of my thighs. I let his voice float over me, listening to the tone rather than the meaning.

"You have to preserve yourself, let me care for you—"

But I had to respond to that remark. I snapped, "Like veal in aspic?" I hated veal in aspic. Slimy and cold. "You want to keep me wrapped up against all danger? You can't, Richard, it's impossible."

A small pause, then, "I know."

His hands left my body and the stays fell away. I caught them and dropped them on the chair, then bent to retrieve my gown and drape it over the chair too. I unfastened my petticoats myself.

I stood in shift and under-petticoat, still wearing stockings and shoes and my hair pinned up in its knot on the top of my head. Keeping my gaze on his face, I reached up and took out the pins, one by one. I knew the action lifted my breasts. It would make the nipples press against the thin lawn fabric. I would force him to suffer.

Because of my earlier thoughts, my nipples had peaked, and as I moved, the extra sensitivity made me shiver. He stared at me, his eyes cool but a small frown furrowing his brow. At least I'd had some effect. Desperation filled me.

"Do we stay like this forever?" I asked. "Do we draw further apart until you can't bear it anymore and search for something outside the marriage bed?" He opened his mouth to protest, but I wouldn't let him speak yet. "It would be meaningless, and that's what you'd tell me when I found out. Because I *would* find out, you know that, don't you? There are people longing for it to happen, for you to stray, people who will run to me to see how I'm taking your betrayal. And I'll have to smile and pretend I don't care, just as other wives do. You'll be sparing me, you'll say, stopping me from bearing more children, wearing me out with childbirth. During my time in society, I've heard it all, Richard, and the excuses, and I've seen the hurt in their eyes."

I couldn't keep my tears back any longer, and I didn't see the point anymore. I let them fall but didn't wail. Just let them trickle slowly down my cheeks, leaving hot trails behind.

"I'll never do that." He sounded sincere, his voice steady. He *was* sincere. But I knew he needed the closeness we had shared, if not making love, then intimate relations. I wanted the true involvement we'd had, the love and sharing, not just the making love. I wanted him to hold me. I wanted to wake up in his arms, to kiss him good morning. The lack of it was driving me insane.

I wanted to shock him into returning to me. I remembered something that had crossed my mind once, briefly. "And I'll be alone. After a surfeit of lovemaking, suddenly I'd have nothing. Richard, what if, one day, I see a man with your eyes? What if I grew lonely enough to turn to someone else?"

Shock forced his eyes to dilate and the lines around his mouth to whiten. But to do him justice, he didn't turn away. He must know I was close to breaking. I had shown him everything, only stopping when I could hold my voice steady no longer.

"You cannot. You know what sexual relations will mean—" Now his voice shook. "You can't fall pregnant again."

"It's an excuse." I knew several ways to avoid children, and

43

in any case, I'd had childbed fever. "The doctor told me that nine out of ten women who'd had what I had end the illness sterile. In others that might be unfortunate, but not in our case."

"There's always a chance. Always. And I can't lose you." He took my hand, stroking his thumb across my palm in a well-remembered gesture. "It's still me, sweetheart." His voice softened, gained that rough edge I loved. "I can't look at you without wanting you. Touching you is almost impossible because I want to do this—" He dragged me close. His arms locked around me, crushing my breasts against his chest, and his mouth collided with mine, needy and hungry. I welcomed him with everything I could.

Starved, I lifted one hand and pushed it under his wig, which fell to the floor with a thump. I threaded my fingers through his short, fair curls. Sleek to the touch, softer than the finest Chinese silk. He tilted his face to one side, taking my lips in a clearer, more complete melding.

I moaned and he responded, not breaking the kiss as he hummed. My tears dried from his body and the heat he was generating in mine. His erection rose hard between us, pressing insistently against my belly, and because I had undressed, I felt every ridge, right to the cap at the head. Oh God, I'd missed that. Those lover's touches, absent these last three months and more. It might as well have been three years, thirty years. A desert of longing.

His hands, up to now in hard, knuckled fists against me as if he still tried to resist, opened and spread over my back, encompassing all of my being. During our history together we had the truth that our bodies spoke to each other, never failing us in the tide of desire and togetherness. From our first kiss in the coach house in Yorkshire, we'd fitted like this. That kiss had persuaded my body that I belonged to no other, that I could give myself to nobody but him.

I opened my mouth, and his tongue thrust in, firm and possessive. I tasted him in return, boldly played with him, tongue against tongue, the sensitive buds tasting. He sucked at me as if he'd thought of nothing else, wanted nothing else, needed me to continue his existence.

When his mouth left mine, it was so he could kiss down my throat and find the sensitive hollow at the base. He teased me there, his grip loosening so he could stroke and then cup one breast through the fabric of my shift. Shivers racked me, and I gasped his name, pushing my body into his, desperate to feel his skin against mine once more. His tongue caressed and demanded, and I imagined all my nerves standing on end and screaming for his touch.

Emboldened, I palmed his balls, felt his hard, hot length. Something inside me seemed to loosen, just as he'd loosened my stays for me, and I gave myself up to him.

That was when he gasped, "No!" and thrust me away.

I took a step back, my eyes wide. I'd tugged at his shirt, which now flopped loosely under his waistcoat and over his breeches.

His mouth was slightly open, his breath coming in short gasps. "Now you see," he said. "*Now* you understand."

He turned and left the room, and a moment later I heard the slam of his stateroom door. I stared at the door linking our bedrooms. Other doors, other places, we'd never locked them, but this one we'd never unlocked.

I didn't understand at all. Not one bit.

Chapter Four

Considering the state of affairs on London's docks, this wasn't the most salubrious part of the city, either. I didn't hold much hope for our landing point, but even that appeared more respectable than Rotherhithe and the Isle of Dogs. The same type of rough man hung around, but they seemed not to have the air of menace I'd sensed at home. Or maybe my imagination gave the inhabitants of a foreign town a romantic glamour. Perhaps a Portuguese would give a similar connotation to our dockers. He wouldn't be entirely wrong.

The royal palace dominated the part of the quay that we approached. Gracious buildings with mansard roofs in the French style flanked a large, regular structure, framing a huge courtyard. I enjoyed the sight, with the autumn sun gilding the rooftops, and people coming and going about court business. We would probably make an appearance, if only to pay a courtesy visit to the king. He was out of the city at the moment, so we could postpone that visit, although I'd like to see the building in more detail.

We were to land at the brand-new quay, the *Cais das Pedras*, built of marble and very grand, standing adjacent to the palace. I ignored the wind whipping past my cheeks in favour of viewing the spectacle of our landing. The quay jutted crisply into the choppy sea, inviting us to land with its air of firm confidence.

Shaken from my recent encounter with Richard, I fixed the expression of interested welcome to my face and waited on events. We had the luxury of doing so. Other passengers from other vessels gazed around, bewildered and concerned, but I had the confidence of knowing that either we would be met, or we would procure a vehicle to get us to our destination. I never underestimated that and remembered what it was like to be alone, stranded and afraid and with insufficient funds or standing to obtain what I needed. It had only happened to me once, in Exeter years ago, but I had never forgotten the experience.

I saw all this as we approached the landing pier in a small boat rowed by some of our crew. We arrived at the base of a flight of steps, more like a ladder in truth. One of the crew led the way and then I went next, followed by Carier. It surprised me that Richard allowed Carier to take his place, but perhaps the manservant gave him little choice.

I was aware that Carier knew of my husband's qualms and care of me, and I also knew that he agreed with me, that Richard should relax his attentions. I only knew because I had learned to interpret his movements and expressions, and I am sure nobody else understood his opinion. My maid, Nichols, treated me as usual now and only gave me the care she considered I needed, for which I was grateful. I have observed that women frequently have more idea than men of how to treat others and deal with illness.

I climbed onto the bare planks that formed the pier and staggered. Carier quickly moved to place his hands on my waist from behind with a murmured, "If my lady will allow..." and then I understood why he had followed me up the stairs. He realized what my first reaction to dry land would be and acted to support me without fussing unduly.

Richard climbed up. He appeared remarkably and somewhat annoyingly steady. I repressed my irritation when he didn't stumble. I felt the pier move under my feet, but I was no longer sure if the movement came from my imagination or reality. Probably a combination of the two since piers were rarely completely unmoving. If I closed my eyes, I found it made the sensation worse, so I snapped them open again, and my gaze fixed on a figure at the end of the pier.

A woman stood there, leaning on the arm of a tall man. She was fair, wearing a fashionable gown and mantle, green and darker green. My sister, Lizzie.

I had missed her so much, and not until this moment did I realise how badly I'd desired her presence, someone I could entirely trust to talk to frankly. Despite my making some good friends recently, Lizzie remained my best and most trusted friend. Nobody else would ever take her place.

Richard dropped my new shawl over my shoulders and arranged it becomingly with a few flicks of his fingers. When he offered me the support of his arm, I could take it without stumbling, although I still had the sensation that I should move my hand an inch or two farther than I actually did. I gripped the coat, defying the fashionable do-not-touch demands the garment seemed to make, and essayed my first step.

Once I remembered to adjust my expectations and pretended that I didn't feel the earth move, I progressed more steadily. I would have run into my sister's arms if I could, and I saw from the broad smile she wore that she was ready to welcome me. In fact, I found it pleasant to watch her, to take in her expression, to see how much she had changed.

I could have said good-bye to her yesterday, for all the changes I perceived in her. Perhaps her bosom, swelling above the fichu tucked into her gown, was a little more pronounced, and her figure more womanly, but her face appeared as lovely as ever. Lizzie had always attracted more admirers than me, but not just for her appearance. Her lively nature drew people, and her lack of vanity, while still retaining a healthy respect for the way she looked, increased her attractiveness.

From her letters I knew that liveliness hadn't changed, and I was glad. Portugal and Spain had a reputation for being more staid and grave than England. It appeared that hadn't affected her, unless she curbed her natural *joie de vivre* in certain circumstances. For underneath, Lizzie had a more practical nature than I had ever possessed. She had always said that she would marry for companionship and the abilities she could offer a future husband, but when she met Paul, Marquês de Aljubarrotta, she had fallen deeply and irrevocably in love. Not instantly, as I had with Richard, but over time. She'd married him and moved to his home country.

And now I saw for myself how happy he had made her.

I took the last two steps at a faster pace and abandoned Richard to throw myself into her arms. I cared not that I should behave with more circumspection in public. Her warmth enveloped me, and I gave her a kiss on each cheek, which she returned. Then I stepped back to hold her at arm's length, laughing and crying at the same time. "You look so well!"

She opened her mouth and closed it again.

I smiled. "You don't have to say it. But I'm much better than I was and recovering all the time."

"You always wanted to lose weight."

I shrugged. "It's coming back."

"For which I am very thankful," Richard said from behind me.

Like most men, Richard preferred curves on a woman, but he would have to wait for me to regain mine. I'd had no appetite as I recovered, not surprising since I'd spent most of that time in bed, but with movement my hunger returned and I could satisfy it once again. Unlike my other hunger.

Lizzie gave me another hug and I turned to greet Paul. I had learned during his sojourn with his mother in England that his notions of correct behaviour weren't as rigid as some of his compatriots, so he was unlikely to condemn me for greeting my beloved sister before him. Richard grew up understanding the nuances of behaviour at the highest level of society, but I had to learn it, and I had discovered there was always something new to trip me up. Richard probably knew exactly how to address the King of Portugal, should we meet him. I had no idea. I relied on my sister to tell me.

Paul stood over six feet tall. He was dressed in dark, rich garments that contrasted amusingly with Richard's blue. But both had the air of the aristocrat, the disdain of the very air they breathed that only a lifetime's training could instil. They greeted each other with the reserve men who liked each other but didn't know each other very well showed. That at least I could recognise.

I curtseyed, and Paul tucked his hand under my chin to tilt it up. I smiled and he smiled back, his fine lips curving into an expression that transformed his face from the haughty lord to the amused man. A twinkle lit his eyes, and in that instance, he reminded me why Lizzie had fallen so hard for him. Once she'd met him and got to know him, nobody else would do, and he had since admitted that he was smitten the moment he set eyes on her. But unlike Richard and myself, they went through a courtship before they declared their intentions. And I had the word of my sister that they didn't anticipate the wedding day. Again, unlike Richard and me.

"We will help you back to perfect health," he assured me as he helped me steady my feet. "By the time you leave us, you will be fully recovered."

"I didn't have to come, but it seemed like a good idea. You have three new people to meet," I reminded them.

The second boat had arrived, the one carrying the babies. Each baby had an attendant, and they carried them towards us in a little procession. Although Helen could toddle, I had instructed her nurse to carry her. I would have carried her myself, but I had the feeling Richard would have forbidden it. He rarely forbade me to do anything, with the result that when he did, I listened. And he was right this time. The planks under our feet were uneven, worn and splintered, pale from the constant application of salt water, despite the magnificence of the design of the dock. But I was glad to see my babies safe.

At Lizzie's delighted laugh, I turned my head to meet her gaze and smiled. "I'm the mother of four. All alive, all healthy."

Only I heard Richard's fervent response. "Thank God."

I didn't let him know I'd heard his *sotto voce* comment. "Three boys and my beautiful Helen," I said.

I waved the nurses on. They paraded past us, an exhibition of our fecundity, but so much more than that. The babies' characters were forming already. I could have told them apart in the dark, just from the sounds they made and the way they moved. Lizzie and Paul gave admiring noises, and I knew that at least Lizzie understood my obsession.

Before I fell ill, I'd had time to touch and hold my babies. That, I think, helped to create a bond that went deep, so that even though I wasn't feeding them myself, I could tell when they were hungry, tell when they were uncomfortable, tell when they were bored and wanted to play. Helen had been more difficult to understand, or perhaps I wasn't as experienced in the ways of infants, but I understood my boys perfectly.

My mother-in-law had wanted me to leave one behind! Any one, it didn't matter, just one that would inherit if we all perished at sea. The woman was near to mad with her obsession with family and dynasty. Worse than any pharaoh. We treated her order with the disdain it deserved.

Paul and Lizzie led the way to a pair of handsome crested coaches. Paul had brought servants who would help Carier supervise the unloading of our luggage, and all we had to do was travel to the house. Richard had hired an establishment in the centre of Lisbon. Paul had selected it and assured us it would serve our purposes. Lizzie had wanted us to stay with them for the whole of our time here, but Richard would have none of that. It wouldn't do, he told me. We had to have an address of our own. While I didn't understand why, he did, so I was content to abide by his advice. He understood protocol much better than I did.

"It's a neat house," Lizzie told us as the coaches jerked into action. "A town house much like the one you have in London. But I would like to ask you a favour."

Richard raised a brow, but unlike most of our acquaintances, Lizzie did not allow his autocratic gesture to quell her sunny mood. Richard probably didn't mean it, in any case. He liked Lizzie.

Lizzie gave him her sweetest smile. "I thought you could see the house, rest there today and overnight, but I'd love you to come to stay at our *palacio* for a while. Sooner than you planned. The house is in the hills where the air is fresher. We have gardens and plenty of room."

Paul smiled fondly at his wife. "It is considered one of the most beautiful houses in the country. My grandfather built it. It is about twenty-five miles outside the city, maybe a little less. We can travel there easily in a day."

Richard gave him a friendly smile. "We would be honoured. Rose has missed you, Lizzie, and it would give you time to catch up." He exchanged a telling glance with Paul. "No doubt you'll want to discuss any number of matters with each other."

Lizzie's infectious giggle set me off, and I only stopped when I realised we were probably behaving more like schoolchildren than the grown women we were meant to be. I hadn't felt that way in a long time. Something lifted away from me right then.

Lightness of spirit returned. I didn't even know I'd lost it until I got it back.

The coach drew up outside the town house, and I sat back, gazing at the façade before I let Richard hand me down. By now the ground felt steady under my feet, but I took a moment to ensure it. If I fell now, or even stumbled, Richard might insist that I go to bed and rest. I'd seen enough of my bed to last me a long time, except at its proper hour.

I breathed deeply, taking in the air of this place. "I like it here." The air tasted slightly of brine. Although I'd lived inland at Devonshire, we weren't far from the sea, and the land ensured the tang of salt wafted over our estate from time to time. Only when I savoured it did I realise how much I missed it.

"You will recover well here." Richard placed his hand gently under my elbow, supporting me. "It was a good decision."

"Whose decision was it?" I couldn't remember, but the thought of seeing Lizzie again had buoyed me in the days when I was sad in spirit.

"I suggested it and you accepted it with alacrity," he reminded me. I had to take his word because I could remember little of that time.

A wide and airy hall decorated in light colours greeted us inside the relatively modern house. I detected the odour of fresh paint in the air, very faint, but my sense of smell sometimes seemed more acute than it had ever been before. A butler, housekeeper and two footmen awaited our presence, and to my surprise, I recognised our blue-and-silver livery. "Who arranged the costumes?"

Richard laughed. "Paul asked, and I supplied the details. I'm afraid I omitted to tell you."

He'd done it to make me smile—a recollection of our home

and something that reminded me of how very thoughtful he was. I found it so touching that if I hadn't smiled, I'd have wept. As it was, tears filled my eyes, but I blinked them away, not wanting to enter our new abode with any kind of sadness.

We inspected the house, followed by our little entourage. I was relieved to discover that the butler spoke serviceable English. The housekeeper too, but the other servants only had a few words. No matter. My maid would deal with them for the most part, although I wondered if we would need an interpreter. No, I would enjoy learning the words I needed. Something new stimulated the intellect, and after months of total ease, my mind was begging for something to do. The prevailing thought seemed to be that during times of physical distress, the mind needed resting too. Not something I agreed with, and in the endless parade of novels and sermons my attendants allowed me, I managed to conceal a few more demanding tomes.

Now I could read what I pleased and temper my usual fare with the accounts and histories that I felt heightened my knowledge. I had always read a mite indiscriminately, and I would prefer to continue in the same way. I was delighted to discover a well-furnished book room, with books and bound magazines, all in English, rather than carefully tooled and bound volumes of tedious sermons and the like. Some maps of the country made me vow to study them further.

Of course, Lisbon was the destination of many ailing British people. It had a reputation for mild winters. Our good friend Henry Fielding had died here last winter, a subject Richard had assiduously avoided mentioning recently. But people still travelled here to convalesce, so perhaps this house was previously hired by a British person, which would explain the library.

We had a suite of rooms. Two bedrooms, as usual, but Lizzie must have seen my face fall because she asked me, "Have we forgotten anything?"

I pasted on my brightest smile. "No, nothing. The bedrooms are beautiful. Facing the garden, and in colours I enjoy." This I knew was where the scent of fresh paint had originated because the room was decorated in an ivory and blue that would become me. "Were they orange before?"

Lizzie laughed. "Not far off. A strange shade of peach. But it was a small matter to change them."

"How thoughtful, thank you."

But Lizzie would not be put off by my effusive thanks. As soon as we'd finished our tour of the house and settled the children in the nursery, she bore me downstairs, back to the small sitting room attached to the bedroom suite, and ordered tea. The maid brought it to us, and I was charmed when she gave me a sweet "My lady," as she placed the tray on the low table.

"Paul will take your husband out of earshot," my sister assured me. "I've been watching him. He is so solicitous I don't know how you stand it."

I spun around to face her, my skirts whirling. "Exactly!" As usual, she had hit the matter dead centre. "He cares for me, Lizzie. Every minute of every day. Well, except at night." I hadn't meant to add that last comment. I knew how perspicacious Lizzie could be.

"Ah!" She paused, frowning, probably wondering how to broach the subject. But I knew what she must be wanting to ask.

Since our time here was limited, I made it easier for her. "We no longer share the same bed." I got up and walked to the window, staring out blindly at the street below. "He won't touch me intimately." The scene in the yacht came back to me in vivid detail. The memory was enough to heat my blood, though I fought to get the vision out of my mind of Richard kissing my throat. I was starved for such memories.

Lizzie broke the silence with an exclamation. "But I've seen you—" She bit off her words but not before I knew what she was about to say. She had unwittingly witnessed the extent of our intimacy, both before and after our marriage. She knew how close we'd been, how we slept naked together every night, made love with the abandon of illicit lovers, though she hadn't seen that part.

She wouldn't see it now, no matter when she chose to interrupt us. "It's only been four months. Three since the doctors declared you out of immediate danger."

"I know." I turned around again, my agitation making me as restless as I used to be. Silk swirled against my legs, and almost without conscious volition I straightened the skirts over my panniers with a deft twitch. "I've been patient, Lizzie. I've waited. I didn't expect to resume—" It was my turn to break off, more in respect for her feelings than for mine.

I could not share this information with anyone else in the world, not even Martha, my sister-in-law. I couldn't do it out of respect for Richard, but I needed to talk to someone so badly, and I knew Lizzie wouldn't tell anyone else, even her husband, unless I told her she could. "Not right away, anyway. But barely a kiss. As if he can't bear to touch me. His every touch is solicitous, and he doesn't linger. It makes me feel like a leper. I know he doesn't mean that, but every time it chips away at what we had, and what I want back. He won't discuss the matter with me, either. I've tried several times in the last month to talk it over with him. He won't. I'm at my wit's end, Lizzie."

She sat, her hands folded neatly in her lap, regarding me in the way I knew meant she saw right through to every nuance of what I was telling her. "What do you want, Rose? What do you *really* want?"

"I want him back in my bed. I want him to hold me like he used to, not as if I'm made of porcelain." The rest would flow from that. If we never made love again, I could bear it, if he gave me back some of what we had lost recently. "I'm afraid that if we don't get it back soon, it will become habit, and then it will never return."

Distress filled her heavenly blue eyes, but she considered, a small frown creasing her brow. "Yes, I see. You need to force him to take that first step, or his careful reserve will remain."

"You remember how it was when we met?" I swallowed, choking back the tears. "He took that step. One step, in the coach house at Hareton Abbey. That's all I need, just that, and a willingness to remain. That day he forced through the barrier he'd erected around himself. For me, Lizzie, he did it for me. He told me it was the first time in so many years that he didn't know if it could be done, but he saw in me his last chance to achieve personal happiness. He's throwing that away now. I don't even know precisely why he is keeping his distance, if he wants to preserve me, or if he wants to ensure I'm completely well. I need to know, and I need him to tell me."

"I can understand him caring for you enough to stay away, enough to ensure you're perfectly well before he shares a bed with you again." A wry smile twisted her mouth. "I can probably understand it better than you." She gave a short laugh. "You're very hot-blooded, my dear."

Heat rushed to my face, suffused my cheeks, but I couldn't hide from my sister. It would be a waste of time to try. "Yes I am. It's an important part of our marriage. It's part of what we are together. But it's more than that. We used to talk in bed, about anything, everything. You know, from politics to domestic details. I don't get that anymore, either."

I shook my head in despair. "He is afraid of losing me, I know that's part of it. His mother instilled in him a terror of childbirth. She had a hard time giving birth to Richard and Gervase, and she never allowed them to forget it. She went on to give birth again, but I don't think she intended to have another child. I don't think she allowed her husband back into her bed after Georgiana was born. It accounts for her coldness, the way she appears to be solely reason and behaviour, with no inner life." I paused, and the silence lay heavy on us both. "Richard could get like that. If I let him, if I don't do something to change his behaviour. But if I try to do too much, too soon, I'll drive him away."

She stared at me, frowning. Then the frown disappeared. "I have an idea. You're staying here tonight. If you can manage two nights, then I'm sure I can arrange something for the *palacio* too. We will pretend that I know nothing of this, that I've noticed nothing, if you please."

So later, we informed our husbands that we needed to stay another night. Lizzie insisted on taking me shopping, to ensure I had the latest clothes and to acquaint me with the most fashionable areas of Lisbon. When her husband laughingly protested that we had only spent a matter of a month or so at sea, she responded, "Fashion can change completely in a month, *meu amor*, surely I've taught you that."

He held up his hands in a gesture of surrender. "I am content. I'll take Richard to the coffeehouses and introduce him to some people who, they inform me, are aching to meet him."

"Not all of them respectable, I hope," Richard added, smiling.

It was indicative of our new relationship that for a bare moment I recalled the ladies of the demimonde who never failed to cast their lures out to Richard. At one time he would have accepted, but recently, more secure in my relationship with him, I had stopped worrying.

Now that had come back. After all, as a red-blooded male,

his baser urges wouldn't disappear overnight because his wife wasn't available. My husband wasn't about to turn into a monk.

This had to stop, and quickly, before we became like so many other couples. I was learning that a successful marriage meant hard work. But it was so very worth it.

Chapter Five

The two nights remaining before we traveled to the *palacio* would be the last time I'd have at drawing him back without subterfuge. The door opened almost silently, and I saw his reflection cross the mirror before he walked forwards to where I sat. He'd taken off his formal wig and donned a light banyan instead of his coat. I could see that he'd shed his stock and neckcloth as well. A hint of bare flesh showed at his throat, and I yearned to taste it. I welcomed the informality, but I couldn't take it as a sign that he'd unbent. Not yet.

Nichols was unfastening my hair, taking the pins out and dropping them in the pretty china dish set on the dressing table. Nichols finished her task and reached for the brush. Her hand hovered over the handle for a telling moment. But no quiet command came, no, "You may go, I'll take over." Just silence.

She picked up the brush and began to disentangle my curls. Before the advent of Nichols, I had sometimes ended the day leaving my hair in its tangles, just gathering it back in a straggling bunch so I could sleep. No more. Nichols could turn my hair into a shining sheet of chestnut waves. So could Richard. I loved it when he brushed my hair, but he hadn't done so for a while. Perhaps because more often than not he would begin by using the brush but would end using his hands. And not only on my hair.

We tended to conclude the business in bed, or somewhere near it, too impatient to take the few steps we needed to get there. Richard had introduced me to making love on chairs, standing up and other delicious variations. Heat blossomed between my thighs at the remembrance, and I lifted my gaze to meet his, reflected in the mirror. He blinked, his eyes opened wider and darkened as the pupils spread. He'd recognised my arousal, and whether he liked it or not, it lay between us now as an unspoken challenge.

I hadn't meant to approach him before we arrived at the *palacio*, but my instinctive reaction had brought the issues between us into startling focus. I couldn't ignore it. Neither could he. But I would do my best not to drive him away, to push him into erecting a barrier I had no chance of breaching.

I had seen him do that in the past. Against people who had proved themselves his enemies, but worse, some who had treated me badly. His response had devastated them, and they had found themselves on the outskirts of him and the circle of his influence, which was much larger than some imagined.

I had revelled in his protective attitude in the early days of our marriage. I had needed it then—I knew very few people and stood in awe of persons I was only aware of by reputation. Richard ensured that I entered the centre of society and did it with little disturbance, as if I were entering a place reserved for my use. I was confident enough to find my own way in society, and while I appreciated the shield he and his family provided, I wanted more freedom to make my own choices and stand by them, even if they went wrong.

Until that moment I hadn't realised how deep our problem lay. But we *could* get past it. Energy returned to me with that decision. Vigour surged through my body, making me feel stronger than I had in months.

I tore my gaze away from his and gave my attention to Nichols. "Leave us, please. I'll do that." I took the brush from her unresisting fingers and caught a flash of approval in her gaze before she left the room. Nichols attended me as a good lady's maid should, in silence when I wished it, but if I asked her, she would give her opinion on more matters than just the way I should wear the latest gown. She had lived an eventful life, one I found myself drawing from indirectly from time to time. Her advice was worth listening to.

Now she left me to my own devices.

"You wish me to act as your lady's maid again?"

I rose from my seat and turned to face him before I responded. "There's no need." Nichols had already helped me off with my gown and into a light robe. Now I shrugged that off, and I kept his gaze while I unhooked my stays—at the front.

To my relief, a slow smile curled his lips. "Witch. Did you wear the same pair the other day?"

I nodded and smiled back. "Sorry." Perhaps I could charm him into it, but not by applying any false airs and graces, just by being myself and showing him what I required of him. "I wanted you to touch me."

"I touch you every day."

"But not like you used to."

He closed his eyes for a moment. "No." He opened them again. "I can't. I daren't." I saw something I'd never seen in them before my illness. Fear. And I hated it.

"Daren't?" I needed him to tell me. I needed to hear the words.

"I didn't leave your side when you were ill." He glanced away, then back at me. I finished unhooking my stays, not attempting flirtatiousness. This discussion was far too important for any games. We needed honesty. Although perhaps later, we might play. I still hoped, even though our discussion had turned grave. But I had to listen to him. It was what I had asked for, after all, and he had never told me before but left me to guess at the level of his pain.

"I watched you, prayed for you, wept over you. I promised that I'd never allow you to fall pregnant, that I'd never, ever put you in that position again. I can't bear the thought of you...leaving me." Even now he couldn't say the word. He didn't want me to die. Neither did I, come to that.

"You can't keep me wrapped up forever, Richard. There are any number of ways I could die. What if I were to slip and fall? What if I'd fallen overboard and drowned?"

"I know that." He turned away and tunnelled his fingers over his scalp. His short hair stuck up in unruly spikes, so unlike the Lord Strang the world knew. Only I saw him this way. "If you had, I'd have to bear it. I'd have no choice."

He faced me once more, anguish etching his eyes into blue flames. His expression seared into me, and I wanted to hold him, love him, make that look go away. But I did nothing, just listened to him. "But this I can do something about. This I can affect. If I can care for you without the temptation becoming too much, I can have most of you."

"Is that what you reasoned while you sat with me when I was ill?"

"It's what I thought of." And more, I'd wager.

"Then you're trying to preserve me rather than keep me. You don't want what we have, you're trying to make it into something else. I can be a wife to you, appear at balls and routs, go to the opera and court, and I can be a mother to your children. But I can't be your lover? I can't hold you at night? I can never see your body again?" I fought my emotions down. If I shouted, if I grew too upset, he'd leave me alone, I knew it. I couldn't let him do that now, erect another impenetrable wall for me to break through. One day the wall would prove too well built and he'd be lost to me. And to his children.

His face contorted in grief. "We can do it, Rose. We can learn to live like this. Then, perhaps, some gentle intimacies.

Other people do it, other couples."

It wouldn't work. "They aren't us, Richard. We can't live like that. You taught me to give myself to you with utter abandon, and now I've known that, I can't take it back."

He winced.

One person stood between us, and I would not, could not, allow her to win. "Your mother has brought you up to believe it's possible. She has made you afraid of a woman giving birth. You were beside yourself when I had Helen, so now, with the boys, you would have been frantic. You were, I remember that. And then the illness made it worse. But your mother is small, a delicate woman. Bearing twins would be hard on such a female. I'm a country girl, Richard. I'm tall for a woman, comfortably built, or I was, and I had childbearing hips. I gave birth with relative ease, even to triplets. And I bore them all alive." A point that still made me proud and I refused to deny it. "I didn't fall ill until a day after they were born. I was perfectly well until then. Wasn't I?"

"You were weak."

I laughed, sharp and high. "It would have been a miracle were I not. I've heard of women who rise from childbirth a day later, but I had three babies, and I had every intention of obeying my advisors and resting." I reached for him but dropped my hand by my side. He had to reach for me. I couldn't bear it if he shook off my touch. "I'm not weak anymore, Richard."

"Yes you are. A long day pulls at you."

"In other words I have to be completely myself again before you'll touch me?"

His teeth grazed his lower lip, in a way I would have done anything to emulate. My teeth, his lip. "Something like that, yes."

"You could be waiting forever."

At that, a sign of relief crossed his features. "I don't mind. I'll wait."

"What if I stay like this?" I had no intention of doing so, but I wouldn't tell him that now because I couldn't guarantee it. "It's only a slight weakness. Every other part of me is fine." I meant one particular area.

"It's not been long. Have you no patience?" I saw the irritation in his face, the way the muscles tightened around his mouth. Telltale signs he'd have hidden with anyone else. At least I had that. At least he was letting me back in that far.

"The midwife and the *accoucheur* told me that after two months I would be well enough to resume relations. Richard, it's been nearly four months. I'm not asking for a return to the all-night loving we once engaged in, but—couldn't you just touch me?"

No longer able to resist, I reached out and laid the tips of my fingers against his right arm. I held my breath. Would he accept me?

He stared down at my hand, then, very slowly, lifted his left hand and put it over mine. His warmth suffused me, flowed through me, bringing my senses to life. It had always been that way between us. He raised his gaze from our hands to my face. The blaze of arousal seared me, but I was returning it.

"This is why," he said, his voice husky with desire. I had missed that sound, imagined it in the long, lonely nights. "I can't touch you without wanting you. Keeping away from you makes it worse, but I don't know what to do about that. It's what we have now and what we have to cope with. You look so damned fragile, I hardly dare touch you."

"You've known thin women before. It doesn't make them fragile. And now I'm moving around and taking exercise again, my appetite is back and I'm regaining my curves. I thought perhaps this shape didn't appeal to you, that you couldn't like it." Just one of the concerns that had kept me awake at night.

He was quick to reassure me. "No. I would want you however you look. You could lose arms and legs—God forbid—and I'd still want you. But the fragility unmans me."

"Could you try?"

He glanced down, but I couldn't see his state of tumescence because his banyan covered his groin. "I could. I want to throw you to the floor and take you like an animal would."

My mouth dropped open. "You never told me that."

His laughter echoed around the room. "You expect me to confess something of that nature? It's shaming, especially when you were so ill. But that isn't the reason I won't take you now. It's fear, pure and simple. I can't lose you."

"I could—"

He interrupted me with an impatient, "Yes, I know. Drown, fall from a high place. It doesn't seem to make any difference to the way I feel."

"It's not just that. It's holding you, talking to you, being with you." I stopped there, tears clogging my throat. "Don't shut me out, Richard, please. Leave a way through."

He released my hand but only to place his hands on either side of my waist and draw me closer. I went so willingly and nestled against his chest with a sigh of relief. Now I could feel his arousal, hard and strong, burning through to me as if it rested against my bare flesh. Remembered tingles returned, coursing my body with a delicious invitation. I knew better than to continue, as once I would have done without a thought. I had to take care, or he'd move away.

"I promise to try," he murmured.

I tipped up my chin and met his blue gaze, so close, so

beloved. I sank into him, willingly gave everything I was to him. "Thank you."

He took a breath, his nostrils flaring. "God, I've missed this. Your scent, so unique. I could remember it, but I could never replicate it. But I can't, sweetheart. Let me take it slowly. You know how difficult I find intimacy. You and the children have helped, but I fear I will never lose that reserve."

"You shouldn't. You wouldn't be you without it. And you helped me so much, when I needed to develop a shell. But not with me, Richard."

He gave me a tight smile. "Not you. But I can't give you everything you want."

Feeling his erection pressed hard against my stomach, I thought he probably could. I hungered for him. He could nourish me as no food ever did, give me what my soul needed. Always. "You try too hard."

"Maybe I do." He sighed, his breath sweeping over my cheek, raising the small hairs on my neck. I wanted him so badly. "But here's the truth, the real reason. Are you listening, my love?"

To hear the words "sweetheart" and "my love" came as a balm to me. He hadn't used them so much recently. "I'm listening, Richard."

He closed his eyes then opened them again, fixing his gaze on mine. They blazed with barely restrained passion, revealing his desires to me for the first time in months, and I knew hope.

"I thought to kill my love for you, or at the least mute it. Just to preserve you, to preserve *us*. I thought I could do it. But I can't. God help me, I can't. I love you, adore you as helplessly as I ever did."

His hands shifted, slid over the slippery silk of my robe, his fingers caressing my back, tracing the line of my spine. "I can't see you turn away from me, treat me as many wives treat their husbands. As friends, partners. We have that as well, but so much more. But I can't make love to you. Not yet. Please believe me. And because of that I can't share your bed. I can't sleep with you and not want you, not love you. I'll try, but don't press me too hard. We'll find a way, my love. We have to. Before the birth of the triplets, I had one consolation. My mother doesn't consider females important, so I could have left Helen in the care of Gervase as her guardian, where she would receive a loving and careful upbringing."

My stomach tensed. I had a feeling I knew what he was about to say, but I didn't want to anticipate his words. He had to explain in his way, and I had to be strong and listen to him.

He gave a wry smile. "You know what I mean already, don't you? This isn't sentiment speaking, it isn't hyperbole, it's the raw truth. If you died, I would have ensured I died too. There would be no reason to carry on. I could arrange it so it appeared to be an accident, so no opprobrium would fall on you or the family."

I whimpered, an involuntary sound, and he stopped, touching his lips to my brow in a featherlight kiss. "I have seen much, done much. But without you, it would have no point. I'd join you. You made me promise to live on, once, and I planned to beg you to withdraw it. Then you shocked me by giving me three sons. Three, and they all lived."

I knew for sure what he'd say, but I wouldn't make it easy for him. I lifted my head again and met his gaze. The little muscles around his jaw tensed, but he didn't look away. "I love the babies, as I love Helen. I can't leave them alone or in the care of Gervase because my mother would never allow it. She'd expose Gervase without a qualm, destroy his happiness in order to get her hands on the boys. Then she'd give them the same childhood that Gervase and I suffered. I can't have that, my love. I can't bear the thought of my children having their humanity beaten out of them, being told that family means all, individuals nothing. In time, she'd remove Dickon from the others in order to give him the special treatment that an heir deserves. Not a child, but an heir. I fear William might not survive the kind of treatment my mother is capable of meting out."

"You told me. I agree. We can't allow her to get jurisdiction over the boys." The words choked me, but he was right. Most aristocratic families brought up their male children with the training they would need to become leaders of men, heads of huge family concerns, but few did it with the cold-blooded ambition of Richard's mother. She tried to rip the humanity out of both her children, but most particularly Richard. He had looked for love elsewhere, with disastrous consequences. At fourteen, he'd become a father. Not that he knew it at the time because his mother spirited the woman away before he knew she was pregnant.

After that, when Gervase ran away with a male neighbour and revealed his true inclinations, once the affair ended, they refused to allow him back. He left, and the brothers, previously so close, spent over ten years apart. *Ten years.*

Richard was right. If we gave the children into Gervase's care, she would move heaven and earth to have them returned to her. Or she'd take Dickon, the eldest. I could allow my sister-in-law and brother to care for them, but the Southwoods would get them back. The law was too strongly on their side. There was no easy answer, no way I could reconcile Richard to the possibility of taking the children away from his mother's influence, short of her death.

Richard would never forgive his mother for dealing with matters after he got the maid pregnant, and for turning her back on Gervase. Lady Southwood removed the maid before

Richard discovered the pregnancy. Later, she rejected Gervase so brutally it could have destroyed him.

Neither would I forgive her. Despite Gervase returning home wealthy and in one piece. During his absence, Richard had turned into a cold, calculating man, capable of infinite cruelty. He'd wreaked his revenge on society, participating in *affaires* that were less love, more physical, destroying reputations, before moving on to the next victim. I couldn't call them *affaires du coeur* but *affaires du corps.* Only Carier had forced Richard to retain his humanity.

He could return to that if I left him. If I died. I had always known that if I died first, I would be the fortunate one, but I didn't have the pressures he'd suffered. I'd had a loving childhood, and I could pass that legacy on to my children, lose myself in them. I had other people I loved, my family, my best friend back in Devonshire, but Richard had nobody, except perhaps Gervase, and their years apart had damaged their relationship.

Now that Gervase had found himself a partner to love, even more distance existed between the brothers. So for Richard, I was the person he lavished his love upon. I had hoped that children would expand that circle, and it had, but I should have known better than to imagine he'd remove any attention from me. Yes, he loved them, but not as he loved me. He loved nobody as he loved me, wouldn't love anybody that way ever again.

To know that brought me great joy, but also terror. Richard would one day become the Earl of Southwood, a man who controlled many lives and many fortunes. As he was now, he'd prove a wonderful earl, but as the Richard I'd first met, he would have dispatched his duties with diligence but no heart.

"So one of us has to live," he murmured against my temple.

"*Both* of us will live." I wouldn't think of any other outcome.

But neither would I live a half-life. "But I won't live in the expectation of death, either. It will come, my love, whatever we do."

He swallowed. "Not too soon."

"No. I nearly died, but I recovered. A miracle, some might say. Do I repay that by withdrawing from the part of life that gives me the most joy? I think not. I won't, Richard. I won't give up, either. I refuse to hold you at a distance. You hear me?"

He stopped me the only way possible. He kissed me.

I leaned forwards, deliberately pressing my body against his, making him support me. One arm snaked around me, cinching me into him, as his mouth opened, coaxing my response. He didn't have to coax very much.

I separated my lips under his, and his tongue plunged in, taking possession. I flung my arm around his neck, holding him as close as he held me, locking him tight. His scent wove over me, inviting me in, an aroma of the citrus cologne he wore, mixed just for him, and his own male essence. I wasn't imagining the musky aroma of his arousal, although I had imagined it so much recently I had become adept at invoking it, but this time it was real. I breathed deeply, giving everything I was to him. Liberated, I gloried in him and forgot any warnings about pushing him too hard. I wanted him. Now.

I moaned into his mouth, responding to his voracious hunger with my own. His muscles flexed against my hands, and he tore his lips from mine. His arms tensed, holding me. Staring into my face, he released me, put his hands on my waist and paused. "Have mercy, my love." His voice sounded harsh but edged with concern, not anger.

"I—I don't understand." At that moment, I didn't. Dazed with passion, I knew only one thing. How much I wanted him.

"Give me time. Space. Please. I can't sleep with you tonight, but I will, I swear it."

"When?" I made no effort to hide my anguish. A tear rolled down my cheek, and he reached out to smooth it away. He held it on his thumb, looked at it as if it were the finest diamond. It sparkled for an instant before he brought his thumb to his mouth and licked it off. He closed his eyes as if savouring the most delicious nectar.

"Soon." He looked at me, regret and pain to match mine clear to see. "I swear it. But please, if we can, I want to start slowly. I don't want to hurt you. I don't want you to hurt me. We plunged into an affair, dived into marriage, but this time I want what we do to be considered and timely. Please."

I opened my mouth to claim that it was an excuse, but closed it again. I couldn't think of anything to say that wouldn't break what we'd built tonight. But oh, it hurt to watch him turn and leave the room. The door closed behind him with a decisive click. He had gone. I had it all to do again.

But I would, I decided. By all I held holy, I would do it.

Chapter Six

I thoroughly enjoyed my shopping expedition with Lizzie the next day. Lisbon was a beautiful city, with varied thoroughfares and lovely public buildings. Lizzie told me it was the Moorish heritage that made the difference in architecture, which gave the city an appearance unlike any other in Europe. It excited me. The colours were perhaps more vivid, the buildings. I savoured the sights and sounds, even the scents, and was determined to pin down exactly what I was experiencing. I could discuss it with Richard.

At least we had that back.

I'd seen him at breakfast, where we conversed as easily as we used to on the current topics of the day and how the advent of new alliances would affect Portugal and maybe the coming war. Richard was convinced war was coming, and unlike our close neighbour at home, the politician William Pitt, he deplored the necessity. "Expensive and wasteful," Richard called it. Not to mention the heartbreak suffered by the widows and children left without a breadwinner.

We went to visit our children. I left the nursery in excellent spirits, which only continued as Lizzie and I forgot all our troubles, in the manner of women from time immemorial, and enjoyed the sights of the city and the excellent shops. I returned with a pretty new fan, a few trinkets and the sense that my strength was returning. I decided to forego my afternoon nap in favour of a quiet hour spent studying the Portuguese language and learning a few key phrases, including my new address.

On our tour of the house I discovered a music room, and

while it didn't contain a pianoforte, a new instrument I was learning to use, it did have a harpsichord, and by some miracle it was in tune. With a brief thought to the tuner, who must have his job cut out as the air in Lisbon was relatively humid, I sat at the keys and looked through the music laid out on the instrument.

Someone had prepared for my coming. With a secret smile, I selected one of my favourite Bach pieces, something with measure and pace, and placed my fingers on the keys.

The first few bars I let pass. Mechanical playing, some errors and a mistake in timing rendered them horrendous, but by the time I reached the end of the page, I was involved in the piece. Before I could pause to turn the page, a hand appeared over my shoulder and performed the task for me.

I didn't need the sight of the rings on his fingers or that citrus scent to tell me that my husband had entered the room. Only my concentration had blocked out my usual sense that told me when he was nearby.

I continued playing the piece, and he moved to stand by me, so I could see him in the corner of my vision. He turned the page once more for me, then I was done.

He rewarded me with a sigh of satisfaction, and when I turned around to face him directly, I saw he was smiling. "Thank you," he said.

I raised a brow. "I didn't know you were there until you turned the page for me."

He grinned. "I know. I'm thanking you for any number of things, but right now I'm thanking you for giving me a respite from thinking."

He'd always said that about my music. I played well, but rather than assigning that to vanity, I can claim numerous hours of practice. Hard-earned skill was worth a little pride. I kept up my pastime, and I had sometimes played on bedsheets, books or flat surfaces while I was ill. I could hear the music in my head, and it had helped in the long, tedious hours of rest and recovery I had endured.

My attendants might have considered my playing eccentric but wouldn't say anything for fear I might hear them. My exalted position in society sometimes meant I could get away with activities that, if I had still been an unimportant member of the gentry, would have been remarked and laughed at.

I had a dummy keyboard brought on board the yacht, when I discovered that such an item existed, and spent hours working in silence. I wouldn't have a harpsichord on the ship, although Richard offered it, because the tuning would have been a nightmare. And I doubted at that time that I could get a decent amount of practice in.

I'd missed hearing what I was playing, missed the solace of making music. And it seemed that Richard had missed the solace of listening to it.

Another way in. I could reach so far inside him with the music because he loved it so much. I wouldn't abuse it—it had to remain something he could come to without feeling under stress—so it was yet another place where he had to approach me instead of the other way about.

"I can continue to give you that respite," I told him. "Moments out of time, just for us."

"I'd love that. Thank you." He held out his hand to help me up. This time he didn't let go as soon as I was up, but drew me closer and brushed a kiss against my lips. "Slowly, my sweet. We'll get there."

I knew we would. We had to. He was willing to meet me now instead of closing himself off from me. Suddenly, I didn't want him with such desperation. The edge of fear was dissipating, though it wouldn't go completely for some time. I

75

would always remember it. And although he was willing to try, he still wouldn't meet me all the way.

I wasn't working in such an empty space any longer. Gentle warmth filled me when I realised he wouldn't avoid me anymore, that he was willing to work with me to regain some of what we'd lost. I had a feeling it wouldn't be an easy recovery, even if my body was healing well. I quelled the part of me that demanded more, until we could share our passion all night without stint. Images of our past life, our bodies entwined, Richard introducing me to new and different positions, me delighting him with my inventiveness and my willingness to try something new. He taught me that lovemaking didn't mean the same thing. It felt different, could be achingly tender or furiously physical. And everything was wonderful, at least it was with him. Had been.

He drew me into his arms, and I went with alacrity. We didn't kiss, but held each other, taking comfort and solace. His body surrounded me in a benison of humanity, and I wanted to stay there all day. Eventually he released me with what I hoped was a happy sigh. "Thank you. You're everything to me."

I knew it. And sometimes it frightened me to death.

Before we left Lisbon for the country, we paid a visit to the man who'd been injured aboard ship. When I say man, in fact he was barely fifteen years old, but he had built a remarkable level of physical fitness for one so young.

Carier had found lodgings for him in a respectable house a mile or so from the one we had hired. The area appeared reasonably prosperous, and Carier, who accompanied us on this visit, assured us it had a good reputation. Otherwise Richard wouldn't have brought me. In previous times I would have insisted, but at this stage in our recovery, I didn't want to upset the apple cart too much.

But I was glad to go along. The landlady spoke no English, so Richard communicated with her using the Spanish he had refused to use with the Magistrate of Health. He apologised that he knew no Portuguese and had to speak slowly.

Luckily the landlady's Spanish was adequate. She told us that the boy, one Simon Crantock, was a good tenant and seemed to be recovering well. He had risen that day and dressed, with only a little help from another tenant, an English merchant called Barber with whom he was making fast friends. They played chess every day, and the merchant had decided to teach the sailor to read. I was glad to hear it. Maybe some good would come of the calamity.

"Barber," Richard mused. "I know that name." He glanced at the landlady. "Is he at home, by any chance?"

He was, and he entered with a glad smile and a bow. "I am honoured to meet you, my lord." He was a strapping man of perhaps forty, with a powerful frame and energy positively bursting from him. "The boy told me he was from your ship."

Only when he relaxed did I catch up with what Richard was thinking. The young man who'd escaped from the ship, the one who had been in the rigging with poor Crantock, could have followed him here and gained ingress, if he wanted to make good on his attempt and kill the boy. But this was not the man. Much taller, stronger and older. Even the small glimpse I'd had of the other man told me that.

Barber drew a paper from his pocket. "I have the honour of being acquainted with your brother, Mr. Gervase Kerre. We have entered several ventures together." He handed the letter over.

I peeped over Richard's shoulder. It was a standard letter of introduction, saying the bearer, one Christopher Barber, was a reputable merchant. I recognised Gervase's flourishing hand. It was undoubtedly his work.

Richard returned the letter to him. "I remember Gervase speaking of you now. I knew I'd heard your name somewhere."

"I've been in Lisbon for a month. If I can be of service to you, my lord, please don't hesitate to call on me."

"You've already been of service by taking care of the boy. Please contact me if anything happens, anything untoward."

Barber cocked his head to one side, a little like a bird. "You expect trouble?"

Richard shook his head. "Not really. Just a precaution."

Barber nodded. "Yes, of course." He bowed. "I'll leave you to talk to him. He's upstairs, first door on the right. Would you care for me to show you?"

"I'm sure we'll find our way," Richard said.

The boy tried to stand when we entered the room, grabbing the sturdy cane someone had provided for him, but Richard waved him down. "You are well?"

"Indeed I am, my lord." Like all the crew of the yacht, he'd been well schooled in how to address his illustrious owners, if they deigned to speak to him. "Thank you, my lady, for helping to care for me. I was too far gone when you helped, but I'll never forget it."

"Think nothing of it." I brushed his thanks aside, but not as brusquely as I would have done once, before I learned gracious manners.

"Perhaps you may help us in return." Richard broke off when Carier brought in another chair, this one for my use. He inspected it and glanced at Carier, who did everything but shrug to indicate it was the only one he could find. But I didn't mind. It seemed a sturdy piece of furniture. I sat down and faced the boy directly, although he seemed loath to meet my gaze.

"I'll do anything I can, my lord."

"The man who tipped you off the rigging. Did you know him?"

Crantock glanced away then back again before he shook his head. "No, my lord. I did not." He was lying, I was almost sure of it, or maybe his discomfort came from the fact that he was being visited by a lord.

"Did he push you?"

Crantock stammered and flushed. "I—I do not know, my lord."

"Stop calling me 'my lord'. Sir will do." Richard never stood on ceremony unless it was to his advantage to do so. Not above using his dignities, but not above dropping them altogether, either. "And don't prevaricate." He paused when Crantock's brow furrowed in confusion. "Dissemble. Play-act. I will have an answer. You've been climbing that rigging for weeks without accident. I've seen you, and you've always been sure and nimble. You're an experienced sailor, for all your relative youth, and the climate was good for such activities. No strong winds, no chill. You would not have fallen were you not helped. So tell us. I repeat, did you know the man?"

Crantock shook his head, swallowing. "No, sir. He wasn't a member of the crew." That last was true. He met Richard's gaze without a qualm when he said that. "What happened to him after the—the accident?"

"When I ordered him brought to me, he escaped and dived over the side. I presume he arrived with the mob who boarded the ship with the officials."

Crantock closed his eyes and breathed out in what looked like exasperation or frustration, but I couldn't be sure about that. "So he got away?"

"He did." Richard paused. "As far as I know. I am searching

for him. I want answers. Did you speak to him before he pushed you?"

"No, sir. He—he had a gun, and I hadn't seen him before, so I challenged him. As I made my way across the rigging to him, he caught me off balance and pushed me."

My blood ran cold. A moment's inattention and the attacker could have shot either of us. If Crantock was telling the truth, and I still had my doubts about that.

"What did he look like?" Richard rapped out.

Crantock frowned, as if recalling the scene. "Dark hair, grey eyes. About my age, or maybe a bit older. Yes, older. Not very brown."

Crantock was considerably tanned, due to spending so much time in the open. Even October in Lisbon was mild. But not tanned probably meant Crantock's attacker wasn't a regular sailor, or one who hadn't been at sea for a while. But the hair—Crantock was definitely lying about that, unless the attacker had been wearing a wig that was lost in the struggle. I saw the hair of the man glinting in the sun before he jumped. It was blond, as fair as Richard's.

The description meant little, but when Crantock recovered, he could help us further.

I glanced at Richard, and he nodded. "We will undertake to settle your account here. I would ask you, if you agree, to identify the man should we find him."

Crantock grinned. "Yes, sir."

One question remained. Crantock was right to have concerns for his life. The push had been, at the least, careless of whether he'd lived or died. After falling fifteen feet, the boy had been extremely fortunate to escape with bruises and a broken leg.

Richard sighed. "We shall take you into the country with

us. The air will do you good." And we could keep him safe so that he could identify the man for us and so we could ask him more questions. "Be ready tomorrow, at about ten."

Crantock nodded. "Yes, sir."

But he didn't come with us, after all. Richard arranged that he would join our small procession of coaches the next day. He'd allotted a space for Crantock in the servants' coach, with the story that the boy had done us a service.

We called at his lodging to discover Crantock in the throes of a heavy fever.

I wanted to go upstairs to verify the fever myself, but I was content for Carier to go after Richard demurred. I had to see sense. The fever could have been contagious, but if it had been so, we'd have it already, since we'd seen him the day before. Still, Carier could verify the report as well as I could.

Carier returned and confirmed the truth of the story. Our coach rocked into movement as he told us, "It's a fever, sure enough, my lord. I'd have said it was infection, but the wounds are still clean. I took a look at the broken leg as best I could, but it's heavily swathed. There aren't any marks on the bandages, though, and no sign of swelling. It's not the pox or anything of that nature, I'm sure of it."

I could trust Carier. "What do you think caused it?"

"I'm not entirely sure, my lady. It could be influenza, or a local fever, or even malaria. There's always a lot of fever about, and I don't think it looks too serious, if it's treated properly. No signs of markings that I'd expect to see in ordinary illnesses. His face is red, but then that's only to be expected. He is in no shape to travel today, though we'll send for him when he recovers."

Richard reached for my hand and gripped it hard. I was reminded of what I'd said the other day. Death comes unexpectedly, sometimes, and if the boy had something life-threatening that he had passed on to us, the deed was already done.

"We can travel back quickly enough," Richard said, "and I ensured we will have access to medical staff at the *palacio*. Was he in any state to vouchsafe any useful information?"

"Sadly, no, my lord. He babbled of illness, seemed to confuse it with the illness aboard ship. He has lost sense of time. His friend, the merchant, is with him, and he promised to send us word as soon as the boy recovers."

"Ah yes, Barber, his chess-playing friend."

"The man was genuinely distressed. He says he has a son of Crantock's age at home."

We had to remain satisfied with that for the time being. I could only pray that Crantock came through his ordeal.

My thoughts turned to our destination. Especially when we left Lisbon behind and met up with the rest of the vehicles, where Carier joined the servants' coach. Behind us rolled the coach containing Lizzie and Paul, and behind all, the servants. Most of our baggage had gone on ahead.

It sounded odd, to be living in a palace, but the word had very different connotations here. More like an Italian palazzo. At least, that was how Lizzie had explained it to me. "It's a good-sized house, but nearer to the size of our brother's house than it is to Eyton. That is much larger."

Richard's ancestral house, the place where I would likely live one day, was a great house filled with treasures, but in typical British fashion, eschewed the grand title of palace. I would miss our smaller house in Oxfordshire, but Eyton was a wonderful house. The thought of being its mistress one day had at one time daunted me, but now I anticipated it with more pleasure, apart from the inevitable death of my father-in-law, whom I'd grown quite fond of.

Already I felt the slight easing of tension between Richard and myself. Although he'd released my hand, he didn't separate himself from me completely. When our fingers brushed, he didn't jerk his hand away, and he leaned closer to me when he spoke.

Paul had provided an excellent vehicle for our journey, and Richard insisted I take the best seat. We travelled with two nurses and the boys, with Helen bouncing on the seat between us. She'd insisted, pushed her way in, and we gave her the indulgence. Another advance. Richard hadn't allowed the children to travel with me for fear they would tire me. This time I could enjoy the company of my husband and children and not be constrained by the strictures that I needed to rest. Together with Richard's new softening towards me came a resurge of the energy that I'd always taken for granted before my illness.

I knew better now, but I'd have chosen a less damaging way of learning that health was one of the greatest gifts we had.

The house came into view after nearly three hours of travelling through the countryside. The terrain was a little rockier than I was used to but foreign enough to be interesting and familiar enough to be unthreatening. I would enjoy noting it later.

I kept a journal, of sorts, nothing to compare with the way other people did. I'd seen women take out a notebook and scribble in the middle of a ball. I wasn't that devoted. But I would record this and my lord's relaxation in his vigilance of me.

And the house.

It stood on a peak, with a larger peak behind it, a step up but with something to protect it from the worst of the weather.

The most startling thing about its appearance from a distance was its colour. Pink. A deep, rich pink, the kind I had seen only once before, in a village looking over the Mediterranean at the foot of Italy. But this house was no cottage. The front contained large windows on both floors outlined in a rich cream that complemented the house's main colour perfectly. Each side of the house jutted forwards in two shallow wings, and a portico with stairs on either side of it showed the way into the interior.

As we neared the building and entered its grounds, I saw the topiary, green hedges cut into fantastical shapes, globes and pyramids, adorning the grounds. Although it was nearly November, the sun shone brightly, but with little of the heat Lizzie had told me about in her letters. I was glad of it. I disliked stifling heat, although it appeared that Lizzie thrived in it.

The rooms in this house would be cool in the summer. It contained large windows and balconies, to allow people to wander outside and the circulation of air between the rooms.

The large, cream-painted front door stood wide open in welcome, offering a tantalising glimpse of a cool interior, with the occasional gleam from something I couldn't quite identify. I felt a surge of anticipation, exciting in itself as a signal that I was coming back. That my real self was returning to the empty shell I'd been not so long before.

Richard alighted once a smartly liveried footman had lowered the steps for us, and held out his hand to help me down, instead of offering me the support of his arm in the more formal manner. I gave him a smile warmer and more natural than usual and took his clasp loosely, prepared to let him release me if he so chose. He didn't choose.

So we walked forwards, hands linked, his fingers threaded between mine, and his warmth coursed through my body. Lizzie caught my attention, and I gave her a brief smile. She knew. "This is lovely."

Her smile turned from conspiratorial to sunny. "I love it here. More than the grand estate inland, so we tend to spend more time here."

"If Lizzie is happy, then so am I," Paul said quietly. I loved that he'd taken to using the more familiar name we used within the family. He had called her Elizabet, which was charming, but Lizzie suited her better somehow.

The staff waiting at the door consisted of a housekeeper, butler and a couple of footmen. Both greeted us with bows, but I noticed the housekeeper's mouth twitch into a smile when she caught sight of the children. That augured well. I didn't let her know that I'd seen. Let it be her secret, that she liked children, until she chose to tell me.

To my relief Paul said that all the servants in the house spoke serviceable English. "It is a requirement for all my above-stairs staff," he told us. "I began it when Lizzie came, but my mother prefers it too." His English mother spoke excellent Portuguese, but I thought it a pleasant courtesy. I would like to have my wishes known without struggling for the words. I had no doubt that I would survive in Portuguese before we left, but so far I was finding the language difficult. In my experience, hearing it and using it would become easier in time.

I glanced at Nichols, who had travelled with the luggage coach and so preceded me, and her tiny sigh didn't escape my notice. She wasn't happy here, and I didn't know why. If I asked her, I might be inviting a familiarity both of us would find uncomfortable in the future, but her very unhappiness put me on edge.

My sister rested her hand on Paul's arm in the accepted, more formal mode. It was typical of her to prefer that to a less formal contact, even though she adored her husband with all her heart. Not, I thought, as much as I adored Richard, but I wouldn't contest her claim. I had never cared who saw my true feelings, but I behaved with restraint for Richard's sake. It was hard for a man brought up in extremely rigid circumstances to unbend. I thought I'd lost the inner man forever, but now I had hope that added warmth to the sunny but slightly chilly day.

I saw the cause of the gleam I'd noticed earlier. The moderate-sized hall was covered with the most beautiful ceramic tiles I had ever seen. The predominant colour was ultramarine blue, with rows and patterns reflecting and enhancing the effect. I stood, staring, until Lizzie spoke. "I hoped you'd have that reaction. It is lovely, isn't it? Strictly this is our summer residence, and the tiles help to keep it cool. The Moors began the custom for tiles. There are some most beautiful examples in the south of Spain, at the Alhambra Palace, but Paul's ancestors continued the tradition."

"I've seen nothing like it before."

I glanced at Richard, who shook his head. "Nor I. I really must ensure we see the Alhambra before we leave. Or on another visit. Especially if it's anything like this." It wouldn't do for England, where the weather was more temperate and damper, but for a hot country it was ideal. Beautiful.

Lizzie let us look our fill then took us through the hall to the stairs. We climbed them, getting a better view of the patterns nearest to us.

"How old is this house?" I enquired. The lightness of design didn't indicate age to me.

"Not very," Paul replied. "Possibly thirty years. My father had the tiles laid. I'm glad you like them. My country has some wonderful examples, but of course I consider this the best."

He would. So would I, were it mine.

Up another flight of stairs and along a wide corridor lay our rooms. I presumed that the larger passage immediately at the top of the stairs led to the staterooms. They would do so in an

English country house, and this smaller example contained the guestrooms. It gave us privacy enough but lay close to the main part of the house. Upstairs would be the servants' quarters, since this house only held two main floors, and a floor at ground level, which would, if the house were mine, have the offices and some family rooms.

I realised I was thinking in the way Richard customarily did. We were truly becoming one. I had gone into the house's plan so naturally that next I would be working out where everyone would exist. It was one of the ways Richard kept one step ahead of everyone else. Only *one* of the ways. His mind worked so swiftly that he could discover a multiplicity of facts before another person had worked out one. And it came naturally to him.

Lizzie led us into a large bedroom. The bed was equally large, heavy draperies at the head and foot, obviously intended to close, not merely for decoration. The predominant colour was an apple green, charming, and as Lizzie must have realised, one of the colours that went well with my hair and complexion. "Will this suit you?"

"Oh yes!" I dropped Richard's hand and took a slow stroll around the room. So pretty. The large windows opened on to a balcony that overlooked the gardens at the back of the house. Here, after a series of formal topiary gardens rare in England, I saw a massive fountain, dolphins disporting in a bowl of marble. The water was switched off. The draperies at the windows were also surprisingly thick, I noticed, when I turned my attention back into the room.

"Why do you keep the fountain turned off?" It must make a marvellous sight.

"We are approaching November, and it can get chilly at night. Sometimes we have frosts and occasionally ice. Ice would destroy the fountain, so we have it drained well before the frost comes." That sounded sensible from Paul, though I was sorry I wouldn't get to see the fountain working. Paul showed his supreme hospitality with his next statement. "Would you like me to order it filled? I should have thought to ask them to put it back for a week or two, but I didn't."

"There's no need," I told him. "It's beautiful as it is, and it has a lovely tranquil quality." And I couldn't bear if I were responsible for ruining such a lovely object.

"You've even provided Rose with a large chaise for her afternoon rests." Richard must have discerned that the large daybed set to one side of the windows was a new addition. I turned to study it, sure I could tell. I couldn't. Richard smiled and shrugged. "The moulding on the walls doesn't quite fit, and there's a small scuff on the floor. A smaller sofa or chaise sat here not long ago."

I saw it then, the slight difference in shading to one side of the daybed. Although it was upholstered in the same fabric as the window drapes, so I wouldn't have noticed. A matching chair stood to the other side of the windows, where someone could sit and read, or just rest. The polished floorboards bore two Oriental carpets in shades of green and pink. I would have liked this room at home, but the style wasn't one I customarily favoured, the baroque formality and the darker, polished wood not something I usually enjoyed. But it fitted well in this setting; it worked.

"You have separate dressing rooms, but knowing your...preferences, I had the bedroom on the other side turned into a sitting room and impromptu nursery," Lizzie announced casually.

So that was her surprise. To force us into the same bed but provide an alternative—the daybed—in case it didn't work out.

Chapter Seven

I felt Richard's stillness like a living thing. I didn't need to see it, but I turned to him anyway. He'd frozen, his hand on the high side of the chaise, his attention fixed on Lizzie. His easy smile firmed, stilled, and the animation I had been so glad to witness return to him leached out, leaving the great lord, the aristocrat I had rarely seen in private until recently.

"Thank you so much. It's a delight, having people who can anticipate our every need."

Lizzie swallowed. She hadn't missed his cool but polite response. She forced a smile. "I thought that if one of the children fell ill, God forbid that they do, but all children have little illnesses from time to time, you could let them sleep in the sitting room with the nurse so you can keep a closer eye on them. You did tell me in your letters that the third boy..." She groped for a name.

"William," I reminded her. I'd seen people behave like this before with Richard, turn into babbling brooks, but I wanted my sister to stop now. She didn't.

"Yes, yes of course. He is a delicate child, you said, and I thought you might prefer to keep him close. The nurseries are on the next floor. My father-in-law was a light sleeper, and he preferred not to be in earshot of his children at nighttime. Consequently, the main nurseries are on the floor above this. So I had the other room converted."

I was wrong about the servants' quarters then. Those steep roofs in the wing probably held more rooms.

I listened numbly to Lizzie's faltering explanation. Richard's reaction had shocked me, and pain held me in its thrall. I should be used to it by now, but I feared I'd never accustom myself to his reaction when forced close to me. In the old days he might have laughed and agreed with Lizzie. Not stiffened into the great lord, as he was doing now. His eyes, so full of life and love, had turned icy and dead, and he lifted his chin slightly so he could look down his nose at us, a pose based on defence.

As I watched, appalled, he took a deep breath. The bees and vines embroidered on his waistcoat changed shape, seemed to move as he inhaled, then returned to their original pattern when he breathed out. He smiled, and a little of the warmth returned. His hand clenched on the side of the chaise. "Of course. What a kind thought." He glanced down at the chaise. He would sleep there. My heart sank.

The servants would know, and since we weren't at home, where access to our private chambers was restricted, we could be fairly sure the household would discover it. While servants were always enjoined not to gossip, it was almost impossible to prevent them. Even the best of servants could let information drop, information that could be very useful in the right hands. We should know, we had maintained a company on it.

We had Thompson's men with us, as many as we could carry, but we had no network here as we had at home and in some other countries in Europe. I wondered if Richard had taken that into account.

Of course he had. With our principal enemies either dead or given up, or on the other side of the world, we could relax at last. The Drurys and John Kneller, Richard's estranged son, the one he hadn't known the existence of until a couple of years ago, weren't our only enemies, but they had been the most persistent. Gone now, or put out of action. I should feel safer, but somehow I didn't. My instincts were returning with my health, and I still felt on guard, wary.

We announced our intention of visiting the children in an hour, but Richard said he wanted to ensure that I rested. "After that," he told Lizzie, with his most charming smile, "we would love to see all of this delightful house. I can understand your enchantment with this country, Lizzie."

He set himself to please her so that she left the room with her husband more content. For an instant she had sensed the sizzling tension between Richard and myself, but he had dissipated it with a few words and the simulation of his normal self. He could do that so well, but I knew the difference.

Richard closed the door with extreme gentleness and turned to face me, but didn't come any nearer. "Did you tell her?"

Tears filled my eyes, and appalled at my weakness, I blinked them away. I wouldn't allow any more to fall. "Not all of it. She guessed some." I couldn't lie to him. I wouldn't give him the lack of respect that implied. "I'm sorry. But I hadn't seen her in so long, and she was always my best friend. Writing letters isn't the same thing."

He strode forwards and took my hands in his. "I've put you under so much strain. It only occurred to me lately that my reticence may have retarded your recovery. Has it, do you think?"

"You've taken the greatest care of me. I've never wanted for anything."

"You were right." His mouth twisted in a wry smile of acknowledgement. "I have swaddled you. We didn't allow it for our children. Too restrictive, we said. And yet I did it with you, didn't I?"

I nodded and kept my head down, staring at the pattern on his waistcoat, tracing the twining vines with my gaze. I would not cry. "I was more ill than I allowed. I would try to do something perfectly ordinary and fail miserably. I had to concentrate on recovering for some time, much more than I'd imagined I would. I've always been well, you see. Apart from an attack of cowpox when I was a child, and winter colds, I've been disgustingly robust. The smallpox that took my father and stepmother affected me but mildly. Being an invalid is new to me." I lifted my gaze to his face. I saw nothing but tenderness and concern.

I loved that he knew when to listen, and I had so much to tell him. I had stopped sharing my feelings with him when I became aware that he wasn't really listening, that he had decided what he would do and set about doing it. Now he listened. "At first I welcomed your concern. I hurt, Richard, hurt all over. Every time Nichols bathed me, she was so gentle, but I wanted it to be you. It wouldn't have hurt as much. I couldn't manage my new weakness, and it terrified me. What if I never recovered, what if I stayed that way?"

He paled. "That worried me too. I lay awake at night, my arms empty, and decided that I wanted you alive, even if it meant I could never share your bed again. After a while it became easier. I could block out the memories if I reminded myself of your appearance in your bed, so pale, so thin, so helpless." He closed his eyes. "Crying my name in your fever, pleading with me to make you better, and I couldn't." He opened his eyes again. "But I still wanted you. It shamed me."

I frowned. "Shamed you?"

"How could I want you under me when you were so frail? How could I even think it?" He released one of my hands and clenched his fist. "I was some kind of beast, I told myself. I deserved to be shot."

I shook my head and tightened my grip on his hand. If that was all he would give me, I would keep it. "I thought of it too.

Even at my weakest. I thought that if I died, I'd ask you to hold me as I went, then I realised that was too much. I couldn't ask that of you. But I'd have liked that. I shouldn't have been so maudlin—"

I didn't finish my sentence. He dragged me closer and folded me in his arms. "Like this?" His head descended, but instead of the hard, punishing kiss like he'd given me on the yacht when I'd provoked him so, he kissed me gently, as if I were made of spun sugar.

While that approach had irritated and infuriated me before, now I welcomed it because he wasn't kissing me like a friend, but like a lover. I tasted his longing for me before he pulled away. "I still can't promise everything. I need to take it gently. But I'll share the bed tonight. I won't use the daybed. It was good of your sister to think of it, to give me the option, even if it meant I had to stay in the same room as you, listening to you breathing. I didn't like the thought of someone else knowing, other than our body servants, but I should have known you couldn't hide anything from her."

I rested my head on his chest and revelled in his warmth.

"I could have said that you needed the space, that you were a restless sleeper these days. Nobody would have thought anything of it. I guard my privacy—our privacy—closely. Carier will interview the servants who have access here. Did you think my careful guarding of our private quarters was all because of our enemies?" The Drurys had tried to strike at us in our home, at the heart of our intimacy, by employing servants to spy on us. I knew that had alarmed Richard as much as it had angered him. "It's not just that," he told me now. "It's the thought of anyone sharing what we have. Carier knows, Nichols knows, and other people know a little of it. Your sister has seen more than she should."

I remembered Lizzie's shock. I hoped she wouldn't be as

startled now that she had a man of her own to love. The thought of her reaction made me smile, although I knew it should not.

Richard smiled too. "She knows better now, I'll be bound. Her husband looks after her well, I'm thinking."

"He's very handsome."

He gave a growl and tugged me close. "No looking in his direction, sweetheart. No looking in anyone else's direction. Just me."

He wouldn't have teased me in that way a month ago. We were both recovering.

Chapter Eight

A day later, I was sure this was one of the most charming houses I'd ever visited, and I knew I'd be happy staying here. While I remained to be convinced that I needed this treatment, I was content, or as content as I could be.

I chose one of my most frivolous gowns for dinner that night but took care not to make it too extravagant with lace and jewellery. I never felt comfortable dressed inappropriately, although Richard often did. He had the arrogance to carry it off, to make everyone else appear underdressed rather than appearing overdressed himself. So I chose the palest pink, with triple lace ruffles at my elbows and a lace overskirt to the petticoat. My favourite pearls, Richard's first gift to me of jewellery outside my betrothal ring, looked perfect. I put a set of pearl drops in my ears, and I was ready.

Richard rewarded me by pausing in the door to our room and looking at me slowly, up and down and back again. "When we first met, I told you that you'd learn to play the great lady in time. I indulgently thought that I'd teach you. But what I actually did was show you the way. You did the rest yourself."

I swallowed down my tears. My weakness overcame me sometimes. That had to stop. I couldn't spend the rest of my life with salt water coursing down my cheeks at every emotional moment. So I dipped a curtsey and blinked hard. "Thank you."

"And just as I told you, you have an innate elegance. It only needed someone to believe in you." He glanced at Nichols, and I nodded, dismissing her.

That was it, what I'd felt the lack of all these months. He hadn't believed in me. I told him I wouldn't leave him—I promised before I birthed the babies, and I always kept my promises. I smiled up at his dear face. "You believe me now?"

His lip twitched. "Nearly. Give me time, sweetheart."

I remembered that tone. I'd missed it. Warm, intimate, with a hint of desire. Desire held firmly in check, I guessed. Carier showed us the way to the dining room and dismissed the footman Lizzie had sent. I supposed he had something to tell us. One way of retaining privacy in an unfamiliar, large house full of servants was to keep moving, so we did so while Carier addressed us in a low voice. "The boy who was hurt on board the yacht, Crantock, is dead."

I blinked but took care not to tighten my grip on Richard's sleeve or give him any indication of my reaction. I wanted to hear this, and I wouldn't let them keep me out because of my weakness. "The fever?" I asked, taking care to keep my voice steady.

Carier shook his head glumly. "I fear not, although care was taken to make it appear that way. The unfortunate boy was strangled. Someone had tied a cloth loosely around his neck to conceal the marks of strangulation. Very neat. His friend Barber came to tell us immediately. He is still here. I took the liberty of offering him a bed for the night. You may question him if you wish, my lord."

Richard nodded. "I shall most certainly do so. He is a friend of Gervase's, but we cannot assume he is completely honest." He glanced at me. "I added a note in a letter I sent to Mrs. Thompson about the man. We should have more confirmation about him with her returning mail, but I fear that won't come for some time." He turned back to Carier. "Tell us more."

"Barber told me that Crantock had a visitor, a comely youth of maybe the same age as the boy, dark-haired with a smooth smile, not over tall. He spoke rough English, as if he were from the docks of London, and said he was a member of our crew. Barber had to go on an errand to pursue his business, but when he returned, he went upstairs and found Crantock dead. He thought it was because of the fever, but the landlady, in readying the body for the morgue, discovered ligature marks. They have informed the authorities."

There was something wrong there. Ah, I had it. The dark hair. The boy had said his attacker was dark-haired when I'd clearly seen blond, and now Barber made a point of describing the dark hair. Almost as if he wanted to put us off the scent.

"I think we should search the lodgings of both Barber and Crantock," I said. "The man who attacked Crantock had fair hair, not dark. Of course there might be more than one, but..." I shrugged. "It's best to make sure."

Carier gave me an approving smile and a nod. "It will be done, ma'am. I will send one of our footmen first thing in the morning."

One of our special footmen who had both discretion and intelligence. We had no reason to distrust the merchant, and every reason to trust him since he carried a letter from Gervase.

We had reached the bottom of the grand stairway and entered the hallway. A maid walked past us, not glancing at us, but maids had ears. Very big ones, and the servants here spoke our language. Carier waited until she'd passed, her sensible shoes beating a tattoo on the marble hallway, slowly fading into the distance. "The merchant noted some signs of struggle, he said. Bruises on the boy's forearms, for instance. He only searched for those after the landlady had informed him of the strangulation."

"A perspicacious merchant," Richard noted.

"We could have taken Barber into our confidence. He'd have watched the boy closer if he'd known there was any

97

danger."

"We weren't sure ourselves," Richard said, "and it shows a thoroughness of approach that not many villains would have used. Most would have merely made themselves scarce. His killer didn't want Crantock to identify him, which presumes that he is the same person who tossed Crantock from the rigging." He frowned. "What we don't know is why he wanted the boy dead. What had Crantock done that had meant he had to die? Or was it revenge because the man was sent to kill us and Crantock foiled the attack?" He made a small sound of distaste. "Ensure the boy receives a decent burial, and make sure his face is sketched before he is interred. We can at least inform his relatives and assure them of his identity."

I wouldn't have thought of that, but I'm glad Richard did.

"I would prefer to discover his killer quickly," Richard continued, "but I fear we don't have all the resources here that we can normally call on. We have to resign ourselves to the possibility that we won't have any success or that it will take longer."

I could see the sense in that, but the thought of aiding a man to escape his sins galled me. Richard touched my forearm, and I looked up into his face. "I know," he said softly. "It concerns me too. We will do all we can, if only for Crantock's sake. He could have saved our lives. The family has lost a son, if he has a family at all."

"Then I insist that we do our best to find out who did this."

Richard nodded. "I agree."

He paused before turning to Carier again. "I would prefer the merchant stayed here for the time being. Stop him from returning to the city. He could be in danger, since he too saw the man. And for the same reason, he could be useful to us."

Carier nodded. "I will see to it, my lord. I agree it would be unwise for him to return to Lisbon on his own. The killer may not wish him to survive."

The air seemed heavier from the knowledge. It wasn't a sense of being persecuted because we had been persecuted in the past and might be so in the future.

Richard had made many enemies in his roistering years, when he'd moved heartlessly from one woman to another, and we had one enemy in particular. We had every reason to believe he was half a world away, but we needed to make sure. And for the burgeoning closeness between my husband and myself, this threat could not separate us now, not at this sensitive time.

We met Paul's brother Joaquin in the drawing room before dinner. He rose to his feet when I entered the room. He was dressed fashionably, but not with the extravagance that Richard commanded.

Paul's smooth tones introduced us formally, and as I made my curtsey, I studied his quiet air of command and smiling good looks. "Joaquin runs the estate vineyards," Paul informed us.

"You have more than one?" Although Paul had mentioned it earlier, I hadn't thought of winemaking as a major concern to the Aljubarrotta estate.

Joaquin gave an indulgent laugh. "My lady, it is a large source of income." His accent was heavier than Paul's, but then Paul had spent a great deal of time in England with his mother and grew up speaking both languages as his own. For one reason or another, Joaquin had not accompanied his brother. I had to admit, I found the accent more than somewhat attractive in a way that appealed to my sensual side. But I didn't like the humouring tone of his laughter. I chose to ignore it, deciding that I would discover what manner of man he was before informing him that my question stemmed from not knowing rather than a lack of intelligence. "Portugal produces a number of excellent wines. You do not have *port* with your dinner?"

I couldn't decide if his emphasis on the word indicated indulgence or an insulting assumption that my female intelligence couldn't encompass the knowledge that wine didn't just appear, like water, from a well. "My husband prefers it. It is a little heavy for my taste."

I didn't have to look at Richard to know he had accepted my decision not to correct Joaquin's suppositions. "My wife prefers lighter wines. Paul was kind enough to send me a barrel of your finest port, and I have savoured it. My brother too sends his compliments." His light, inconsequential, slightly singsong tone told me he had decided to follow my example—to let the man think what he would. We would not masquerade as something we were not, but there was no need to tell him more than he needed to know. We had almost unconsciously gone on alert. The news Carier had brought us had alarmed us both. Just yesterday morning we'd heard of the poor boy's illness. Now he was dead, but not of what had ailed him.

Paul smiled and murmured his thanks. Unlike Joaquin, he knew something of our true natures. He watched us, his dark eyes wary.

"I would love to show you one of our vineyards, if you feel up to it. My brother says that you've been ill?" Joaquin asked.

"I feel much better now. I'm sure I could manage the journey." We were here for the whole winter. I'd need something to do if I wasn't to run a house and attend my usual duties. Or I'd go mad with enforced boredom.

"I hadn't realised your brother worked in your vineyards," Richard said, but he watched Joaquin rather than Paul as he made the comment.

"A very efficient manager," Paul remarked. "He has increased production and the quality of the wines in the five years since I put him wholly in charge."

I sensed an air of tension between the brothers, nothing like the friendly rivalry Richard sometimes engaged in with Gervase, but something darker. Joaquin glanced at Paul and smiled an instant later, but in that instant, a world of eloquence passed between them. I knew Richard had noticed too. But many brothers did have some tension. Not all were as close as Richard and his twin.

"Won't Mr. Barber be joining us tonight?" I didn't think they would deny a guest the family dining table, but the structure of society might be more rigid than we were used to at home. Still, it rankled that he might be refused a good dinner and conversation. He had done us a service by bringing the news about poor Crantock. If he was a friend of Gervase's, they'd probably shared a few meals together.

Paul assuaged my concerns. "He sent word that he regretted he could not join us. He says he has a cold and would not like to transmit the illness. I thought it enough to keep him away. After all, didn't the boy have a fever?"

I appreciated his thoughtfulness. "I see. I hope he is comfortable."

Lizzie smiled. "I have done my best to assure it. I sent him a meal to his room with our best wishes."

We went in to dinner, and Lizzie showed pleasure at my delight. The room had an intricate design of a vine and grapes twining around the ceiling and picked out with appropriate colours. The paintings were of the house and its various aspects, and the large, arched windows were uncovered.

"It's the winter dining room," she told us. "The summer room has a wall of glass windows that can be drawn back on fine evenings. I love it, but the evenings are too chilly now to eat

101

in the open air."

"We shall have to return one summer," I assured her, although I didn't know if the heat would agree with me. I had spent some of a hot summer in Rome on our honeymoon, and I'd found myself overcome, even though I was assured that it wasn't the warmest summer they had endured in recent years. Indeed, the weather showed some alarming instability of late, giving us sunny days when we should have had cold, and the spring had come late to England. At least it gave people a polite way of starting a conversation, but I have to admit I rarely discussed the weather. Recently I'd had much more to talk about.

Lizzie apologised for the uneven numbers. "But since Joaquin arrived after we did, I had no time to invite anyone."

"I didn't even think of it," I assured her, although I knew Richard would. His notions of formality came from his innate breeding, whereas mine were imposed.

They served us a light, refreshing meal consisting of two courses with half a dozen removes each, limited but delicious. Lizzie had included a few more substantial dishes, probably for the delectation of my husband and Paul. Despite his sometimes delicate appearance, my husband was a considerable trencherman. I could only assume that any avoirdupois he was in danger of gaining, he'd worried and exercised away.

I enjoyed what I ate, and Richard made sure I had sufficient. He would have helped me to more, but I waved my hand in a laughing gesture. "I really can't eat more. It was absolutely lovely. You have an excellent cook, Lizzie."

"Cooks." She glanced at her husband. "We entertain here from time to time. I have two here at present."

"Thank you for the lemon cream. It was quite wonderful," I said.

Lizzie smiled. "It was always one of our favourites." She glanced at her husband. "We used to badger Mrs. Hoarty's cook for it because we loved it so much. She did the best lemon cream in Devonshire."

"I did indeed. And Richard knows my preference for it." It was good to have my appetite returned, and I'd eaten a good amount of the dish. "But you didn't have any tonight."

"I ate more of the delicious beef. I left no room for sweet stuff. Paul knows I love lemon cream, and it was kind of him to ensure it was made tonight. It will keep for a day and I may have some tomorrow." Lizzie's smile broadened, and she let out a genuine laugh, not a polite society tinkling of bells. "Who would have thought this could have happened?" Without thinking, she reached out her hand and her husband took it. "One thing makes it all possible."

I knew what she meant—love.

Paul kissed her hand. "I can't take credit for something I didn't order."

Joaquin gave a shame-faced smile. I liked him better with a smile. A pity he didn't do it more often. "I have to take credit for ordering it. I know it's a favourite of Lizzie's. I did mention it to the cook this morning, when she said she had an overabundance of cream today."

Before I could speak, Richard chipped in. "A kind thought."

I shrugged, felt the edge of my fichu slip a little and resisted an impulse to hitch it up. Once upon a time, I wouldn't have hesitated to do so. Neither would I have worn such a delicate, almost transparent fichu with such ease nor had the confidence to state my opinion in such company.

"I have rarely seen such beauty in the same room." Joaquin lifted his glass and toasted us.

I was beginning to feel uncomfortable, a familiar sensation, but I hadn't felt it recently. It surprised me, but I strove to show nothing of it. I was out of practice at accepting extravagant compliments as if they were my due, but I did find Joaquin's compliments and solicitude a little...too much.

So I smiled. I thought Richard would suspect anyone who came close to me, especially recalling the events of last year, but I also knew he would feel easier in his mind if I allowed him to study Joaquin. I decided on some mild flirtation.

"I'm equally amazed to find Portugal so full of such good-looking men." Not that I'd seen too many as yet, but it didn't hurt to flatter. A lot could be discerned by relaxing a person, letting him feel at his ease, or even superior.

Joaquin gazed at me through lowered lids, his dark eyes glinting through the seductive veiling of his lashes. I had no doubt it was deliberate, but some men flirted as much as they breathed, and the instinct was just as natural. I wouldn't hold it against him. What Richard would do remained to be seen. He wasn't a jealous husband, because of his trust in me, but I had no doubt that if he felt threatened, he would reassert his claim on me. It might even do him good, give him a push back to sharing my bed.

It wouldn't do any harm. The only thing that would do that would be adultery, and I would never, ever consider such a course. To see me flirting might even amuse him, and God knew I was out of practice.

"You live here, sir?" I asked him. An innocuous enough question to give him an opening.

"No, my lady. I have a house not far from here, and another in the south, nearer to our other main vineyard. Charming residences. Nothing like the houses my brother owns, of course, but that's how it should be." He paused. "His two years'...superiority brought great riches." He paused before the fourth word, as if searching his vocabulary. A delightful affectation. I suspected he knew it.

"I have a brother who is older than me, but not by a great deal." I leaned back so the footman could remove my now-empty plate. The servants efficiently stripped the table of the remaining plates, flatware and the centrepiece, leaving us with the glasses and our wine. At this stage, Lizzie and I should have left the gentlemen to discourse and enjoy their port, which would be a considerable pleasure, from Richard's comments about the sample he and Gervase had received. But I was as yet disinclined to do so. I wanted to know more about Joaquin.

At one point he smiled and toasted me. "Who can doubt that a clever woman can't twist a man around her smallest digit?"

Finger, I nearly corrected him but stopped myself. It wouldn't have been polite. "Many women cannot. Many do not wish to."

"Oh, every woman has a little of the flirt in her. Do you not agree?"

If I disagreed, it would mean I had to provide examples, which would appear churlish. So I smiled and nodded. "You may have something in that, sir, but not every woman is adept at the art."

"Art?" He raised a black brow.

Richard took a hand in the conversation. "There is much to be learned, many skills that enhance the mere human exchange to that of an art." He lifted my fan and flicked it open with a sharp snap. "If a woman knows how to deploy this, it can be as effective a weapon as a sword—or a pen."

Laughter rippled around the table, but it wasn't of the natural kind. Richard handed my fan back to me and, without thinking, I twisted my wrist to flutter it before my face.

"See?" Richard said. "My lady knows that the mere lifting of the hairs at her temple, the stirring of the curls at her nape, makes a man think about touching it—" He snapped off his words abruptly, but the rest of his sentiments hung in the air. *Kissing it.* "Many women know how to flirt without prompting. Others see their mothers do it and copy them. Some will deliberately set out to learn. And a man cannot know the difference."

"You're right," Joaquin said, "that women flirt as part of their very nature. It's almost required of them, to attract a man. I believe your beautiful lady was born knowing it."

I bit my lower lip to stop myself from laughing, thinking of the way I'd run wild over the countryside when I could escape from my too-restrictive household, when I believed myself born to occupy the uncomfortable chairs set around ballrooms for the less fortunate to watch others dance the night away.

I had learned. I knew which angle to hold my fan for the best effect and how to hold my head to provide the most charming picture I could. Because I was setting out to enchant him. I had that niggling sense of not-quite-right that I never ignored these days. It nagged at me.

"You're most kind, sir, but I don't go above what is proper. I am extremely happy with my lot." I glanced at Richard then back at Joaquin, challenging him to make an alteration to that happy state of affairs. I didn't give Richard the warm smile I would normally have exchanged with him. I wanted Joaquin to suspect there might be trouble in paradise. Not much, just so we could discover more about the man. So I could understand that feeling, that instinct.

Richard joined in with alacrity. He leaned back in his chair. "I have no doubt my wife never trespasses beyond what is proper." He paused. "At least when I'm present to witness her efforts." That earned him a sharp glance from Joaquin. A clever man, my husband. If I took care, I could flirt with him while flirting with Joaquin. Or could I? Either way, it was a game we hadn't played for some time. We were overdue a command performance.

"If you were present more often, my lord, you might discover more."

If Richard hadn't been on show, he might have whistled through his teeth. As it was, he could barely suppress his intake of breath, which I noticed because I knew him so well and saw his waistcoat buttons glitter. "I believe I'm present at all the most vital occasions. Wouldn't you say, my dear?"

He only called me "my dear" in that superior tone of voice when he wanted to provoke me.

Joaquin gave an easy smile. "How would you know that, my lord?"

"My wife assures me that she doesn't lie." He took my hand, lifted it to his lips. "I wouldn't be a gentleman if I didn't take her word." Leaving room for doubt.

I repressed my shiver at the touch of Richard's lips. I could hope his reaction mirrored mine, but I saw no sign of it. Apart from a gleam in his eyes that could have been a trick of the light and the way he moved his head just at that moment. I gave Joaquin a full-bodied smile. He blinked and smiled back, his handsome face improved by the expression of surprised delight.

Had I given an invitation? Had he taken it? I rather thought he had.

I decided to stir the pudding. Or the lemon cream, since that had begun the discussion. "My husband isn't with me *every* hour of the day." We had gone far enough. I wanted to draw him out, not seduce him in reality. I had to pull back to see his reaction, so I picked up my glass of wine and studied it, the ruby depths glinting in the candlelight. I took care to display my hand to its best advantage. "This is very fine wine."

"I shall ensure you have a case or two to take home with you." That was Paul. When I glanced in his direction and thanked him, I saw bewilderment line his features, which I guessed must be from our play just now. And something else that I thought was probably anger. With whom? I knew when his attention turned to his brother and the glint became a spark.

I decided to start again with something innocuous, to gauge his response. "Your gardens are unusual."

"You like them?" Lizzie said, then laughed when I didn't reply at once. "Don't worry, it took me some time to get used to them. But I like them now. Fewer flowers, more greenery."

"And in such unusual shapes." I would have said more, but it would have been unseemly. The shapes reminded me of things perhaps they should not, and maybe my imagination was too vivid. Private matters concerning intimate relations between men and women, men and men, women on display. Richard's low chuckle told me he'd understood, and the heat rushed to my cheeks.

"Some people say," Joaquin chipped in, "that they were designed that way. To remind people of their origins and their reason for being. Rumour has it that in some houses, from a height, the gardens resemble other images."

"I've heard of some in England," Richard said. "Though I've never seen any for myself." He glanced up from contemplating his glass and flashed a hard smile. "I believe that if any had existed, I'd have seen them. My reputation isn't entirely spotless."

"I'd heard that." Joaquin gave him the same hard smile in return. "I have to admit, my lord, when I discovered that my brother was marrying your sister-in-law, curiosity overcame me and I...did a little research."

"I would expect nothing less." As Richard reached for the decanter, the brilliants on his waistcoat glittered, sending reflective sparks over the highly polished table. "I also researched Paul. Although I didn't research you. I only read that your family was wealthy and well-connected. We must look after our own, must we not? And once Rose married me, she became mine to defend and protect. As did the people who mean most to her."

As if I were a thing rather than a person. Although I knew he'd phrased that sentence to that effect, the sentiment still rankled with me. I should not concern myself with it, but it was a measure of my recent weakness that for an instant I allowed it to reach me. I opened my mouth to reply, then closed it again. I changed my sharp retort to something else. "I believe he researched me before he offered for me."

"In a way, yes, my lady. Though you gave me little opportunity." What could make me sound like a rapacious miss actually disguised his true meaning, and this time I didn't misunderstand him. It had been a source of constant amusement between us that I had seduced him, the philanderer, not the other way around. And it was true. I'd prepared the place I planned to do the deed and enticed him there, then made it almost impossible for him to leave. The remembrance of that wonderful afternoon made me heat. I could only hope I hadn't revealed my feelings.

I looked up, straight into Joaquin's dark eyes, and allowed my response to Richard's seemingly innocent remark show. I would let him misconstrue it if he wanted to. "I have always been more impetuous than I should be. My husband has had occasion to remind me of that."

Joaquin stared at me, his smile slow but calculating. "I consider impetuosity a virtue in a woman. It adds a liveliness of spirit that I enjoy." He glanced at Richard then back at me.

"Allow me to show you the gardens tomorrow. You might find that you like them, after all."

"I might."

Chapter Nine

"I saw your reaction to my claim on you. Are you not mine, sweetheart?"

Richard came up behind me and took the brush from Nichols. I caught her gaze in the mirror. She dropped a light curtsey and left.

He stroked my hair slowly, running his fingers through it, touching my scalp with caresses that made my whole body tingle.

I told him what lay in my heart. "I'm wholly and completely yours. For always." However long that would be. I only just cut off saying that I'd love him for the rest of my life. Not a suggestion I should make at this moment.

"You shouldn't say that." He swept the brush through my now-smooth hair. "I love doing this. I always have. You have beautiful hair, soft, silky, almost alive." I knew how much he loved brushing my hair for me, how sensuous he found the experience. That was why he'd avoided such little intimacies recently. I gloried that he'd relented.

"Like Medusa's?"

He chuckled. "I don't see it writhing with snakes. More sliding through my hands like the finest silk. If it were alive, it would consist of tiny, beautiful creatures. Or maybe those lovely, elegant snakes, ones that will coil around me and ensnare me."

I wasn't sure I liked that. "I never tried to ensnare you."

"You didn't have to try. I was yours from the first moment I saw you."

That was true, although I hadn't known it at the time. "As I was yours. But I had no idea. When you spoke to Gervase back in that dusty courtyard, I thought you were laughing at me."

"Appearances are often deceptive." He laid the brush gently down on the dressing table. "As we have learned and sometimes used before now. As we did tonight."

When I got to my feet, he didn't step back, as I'd half-expected he would. Instead, he took me into his arms. I leaned against him, my head resting on his shoulder, savouring the heat of his body.

He took a sharp breath. "My love, I know I've kept you at a distance. I know it has to change, but be patient with me. Let me take this at whatever pace feels comfortable."

"Yes." I was so glad to have him back and that he was making the effort to restore our relationship to what it once was. I decided on a light tease.

"Do you think I should let Joaquin escort me around the gardens tomorrow?"

"If you do, I'll follow you as a jealous husband should, so you won't be in any danger of falling for his charm." Amazing how a man as flamboyant as Richard could remain unseen when he wished.

"What do you think he'll do?"

"Try to seduce you."

I didn't like the calm way he said that. "Do you want him to?"

"What do you think?"

Without warning, he turned his head and seized my mouth in a savage kiss. I opened for him immediately, my desire as great as his, but his mastery too much for me to do anything except respond. But I remained wary, in control. I didn't want him to have an excuse to move away, to reject what I could offer him. I would tease him. By now I was desperate, and I tasted Richard's surrender.

His lips left mine, but he didn't move away. His breath skimmed across my lips when he spoke. "How far will you let him go? Will you kiss him like that?"

"I—I don't know. If he asks nicely, perhaps I will." I caught my breath at my own audacity, but we both needed this. The challenge, left open for so long, required an answer now.

His eyes gleamed with blue fire. Dangerous, exciting. "You will not."

"Should I let him take me in his arms?"

His embrace tightened, the muscles going taut in his forearms. "No. Not if you want him to keep them."

"I have to give him some encouragement."

"You will let him escort you in order to tell him who you belong to. You're mine, you hear?" This was not the time to remind him that he hadn't wanted what belonged to him. Not now. But I should have known him better. "I know, my sweet. I will try, I swear. Our current situation will change. It has to."

I raised a brow and shook my head as well as I could with it pillowed against his shoulder. "I won't hold you to anything. I won't ever do that to you."

His voice gentled, although his breath was still ragged. "Do what, sweetheart?"

"Betray you. You should know that."

"I don't deserve it, but I do know that." He kissed me again, this time his lips as soft as a kitten on snow. He drew away reluctantly. "Whatever we do, however I behave, never doubt that I love you. With everything I have. All I've done recently is because of that, and it's because of it that I will change."

113

"Because I want you to?"

"Because you want me to. Because I want it. Because I can't bear not to any longer." He gave a wry smile, the corner of his finely sculpted mouth lifting at one corner. "I made you a promise, and I intend to stick to it. Only you, as long as we both live. And probably afterwards too. I can't imagine being with anyone else now. I never want it." He kissed me again, like a man addicted, forced to against his will. Another sweet kiss, but I opened my mouth for him and touched his tongue with mine. He took my invitation and responded, caressing my mouth, savouring it. The quiet groan he gave reverberated through me.

Our bodies pressed together. I had removed my outer clothing and donned my robe. He was dressed similarly but still wore his breeches under his knee-length silk robe, and his shirt.

All our remaining garments were light, nothing hidden between us, so I felt his arousal harden against me and I loved it, welcomed it back. I wanted him so much, but I had to take care, say nothing, do nothing that would remind him of my weakened state, that would drive him away. I hated the necessity, but I would get my reward. Soon he would come to me as his right, would take me without hesitation, without taking overmuch care. I knew he'd look after me this time, treat me like porcelain, maybe, but I would have him whatever, however he wanted it.

He broke away, staring at me. There was no restraint in his gaze now. His eyes seemed darker in the candlelight but burned with a desire I recognised. If he stopped now, I would die.

"Rose, I love you. Now and always. You saved me, you gave me my life back, after I'd so nearly thrown it away. I was on the road to a fast death when I first met you. I'll do anything you want. But I'm afraid."

I knew that too. It took a brave man to confess his

weakness, a man sure of himself and who he was talking to. "There's no need. Remember, and keep telling yourself. We will make no more children." The doctor had told me solemnly, and I recalled the man's astonishment at my delighted response. I was relieved. After an ordeal like the one I had been through, I imagine many women felt the same but didn't express it quite so willingly. Who would want to go through that again? The difference was that I knew my husband would welcome it too. As he did now. His shoulder muscles lost a little of their tension.

"I know. That is what is giving me the courage now. After Helen was born I didn't want to put you through childbirth again, but you persuaded me. This time I will not do it. Never, ever again."

"I don't think I will."

"There is a chance. A very small chance, he said."

My heart sank. He must have asked him separately. "I don't think so."

"I consulted elsewhere to confirm it. The possibility is remote, but it is there." His voice lowered, cracked on the last word, but his gaze remained clear and steady.

He was persuading himself out of it. I wouldn't let him. "I refuse to believe it. Even if we did conceive, I can birth a child fairly easily. It was the childbed fever that nearly killed me, not the births." The fever hadn't struck until a day after I'd given birth and the doctor and *accoucheurs* had declared themselves happy with my state of health.

"Besides, it's the wrong time of the month." How many women had said that only to discover they were wrong? But I would use anything to keep him here, keep him passionate, keep him wanting me. There was one way to ensure that. Stop him thinking, keep him aroused and needy. I happily set myself to the task, and he didn't object.

When I moved the sides of his robe, a tantalising vee of skin revealed itself. Since he'd removed his stock and neckcloth, his shirt gaped open down to his breastbone. I leaned forwards, tasted his skin with a flick of my tongue and let him hear my moan. "You taste so good. I've missed that so much. Your taste, your texture."

I found the belt that held his robe together. It should have been held closed with the frogged fastenings at the top, but Richard often merely used a silk belt he'd had made, knowing it would come off soon enough, and the frogs could be an impediment that took too long.

He sucked in air through his teeth. "Rose, oh God, you can't do this."

"Can't do what? Touch you? Taste you?" I pushed his robe off his shoulders and tugged his shirt free from his breeches. I wanted it off. Pausing only to ensure he'd undone the buttons at the now-plain cuffs, his valet having removed the fine lace ruffles he'd sported earlier, I drew it up and over his head. He helped, running his hands through his tousled blond waves to push his hair back from his face. The shirt dropped to the floor, unheeded by either of us.

I kissed his chest, loved that hardness, the sheer masculinity of him. His chest hair was slightly darker than that on his head, reminiscent of the hair that surrounded his manhood. The thought of it made me moan again. I touched a nipple with the tip of my tongue, and it responded, hardening to the size of a small button, the kind that fastened secretly under a garment, the tiny, unseen ones that kept the whole garment together.

He cinched his arms around me again, pressing me against him, his powerful body shuddering with need. "God help me, but I can't hold back anymore."

"I don't want you to. Don't. Take me, Richard, just as you

used to."

Growling low in his throat, he bent and swept me up before carrying me the couple of strides that brought us to the bed. Nichols had already turned the sheets down, so he placed me on them and followed, lying beside me. That in itself felt good, but I would savour that later. Now was all about passion and need.

I let all my barriers down, all my yearning free. He could see anything he wanted, take what he wanted, but I would take in return. The time for waiting was over. Now was ours.

He bent to kiss me and I embraced him, slid my hands over his skin, the satin heat tantalising me, promising more. I loved the way his powerful muscles flexed, the changing textures poetry under my hands. He moaned as my hands mapped the beloved area so long lost to me. In truth I had not done this for half a year, as I'd grown very large with the triplets and I couldn't bear his weight. Or much else, for that matter. Now, down to my old self, or rather, less than that, I felt him like I was coming home.

But not in a comfortable, soothing way. That might come later, but not now, God, not now. I arched up to him, and he lifted off me, his legs bracketing mine. "I want to see you now. See what I have." He smiled. "You've changed, and I've not seen you properly."

True enough. He rolled off me and helped me with my robe, but I wouldn't let him remove my shift until he'd taken off his breeches and underwear. I feasted my eyes on his body as he exposed it for me, his taut, rounded buttocks, the dip above it always one of my weaknesses. I loved to shape it with my hand, feel the smooth curve with the leashed strength beneath. He groaned and half-turned his head, smiling at me. "Your turn."

I dragged my shift over my head and cast it aside.

I was never ashamed, afraid or shy with Richard, but this

117

time apprehension tightened my throat. I had changed, and not for the better. My stomach was now completely flat, if not concave, my breasts smaller, and I had hollows inside my hipbones. My collarbones were too prominent for beauty, and I constantly tried to disguise them these days with jewellery and fichus. I had few of those silvery marks that come as the skin shrinks back to its usual size after pregnancy, so I was lucky there. The hairs on my arms prickled as my self-consciousness increased.

Richard stared. We had retained the two branches of candelabra on the night table and the dressing table, and the candles in the holders above our heads were also lit, so I was too brightly illuminated for comfort. I had wanted him to fall on me, take me with hunger, but the pause while he removed his remaining garments had provided a natural break. Now he looked at me.

A smile spread slowly over his lips. "You are so beautiful. Always. I've missed you so much, missed seeing you, touching you." He hid nothing, his erection proudly displayed, the flesh darker than the rest of his skin. As I watched, a bead of clear moisture seeped from the tip. I wanted to lick it off, and my tongue touched my lower lip as I thought it. He groaned, low in his throat. "Don't, sweetheart. You'll unman me."

I wouldn't draw attention to my drawbacks, but I was in hope that now that I was taking regular exercise and returning to my old ways, my appetite would return and I could regain some weight. I wanted to alter my pose to conceal the points that I was less than proud of, but he stepped forwards and lifted his knee to rest it on the high mattress.

"You've changed. But you're always you, and you're the woman I want above all others." He knelt and swung his other leg up so he could join me on the bed, lying by my side but not touching me. He laid one hand on my waist, softly, as if afraid to touch me. "We'll get there, Rose. Between us, we'll have all we lost, and more."

"Yes." That sounded good to me. It sounded wonderful.

He gave me a little push. "Now lie back while I become reacquainted with your beautiful self." His smile turned more wicked, an edge of intent sharpening his gaze. I rolled over onto my back, and he leaned over me. "You, my dear delight, are still as alluring as ever, still as frighteningly seductive. Frightening because I find myself thinking of you at the most inopportune times and find it difficult to suppress it. Even when I was at my most concerned for you, the darker, deeper side of me wondered if anyone could ever compare to you in bed. The answer, in case you were wondering, is no. I can barely remember them now. I don't try anymore."

I felt secure enough to scoff. "And you with all that experience?"

"Experience is nothing." He punctuated each word with a kiss, dropping them on my mouth like morning nectar. "Not when we improve every time we're together, every time we touch. Knowing that, I had to suppress what I wanted to do, what I *needed.*"

"You don't have to anymore. Richard, my love, never do it again, please."

He bent lower so my nipples grazed his chest. By the increase in sensitivity, I knew they'd hardened for him. I yearned for more, wanted him to touch them with his hands, tease them as he knew so well how to do.

"Anything for you," he murmured, and as if unable to help himself, took my mouth in a deep, ravishing kiss. He explored my lips, my teeth, caressed my tongue like he'd never tasted them before. I answered. Now that I had permission to touch him, I wanted everywhere, everything. All at the same time. I wanted to saturate myself in him so that no part of my body

119

wasn't covered by his.

I sighed in sheer delight when he moved down to my belly and circled my navel lazily with his tongue. "It's like making love to a fairy," he said, the hum of his voice creating delicious vibrations on my skin. "And do you still taste the same?"

I tensed because he headed so slowly down that I thought I might go mad. He gripped my thighs when I wriggled, wouldn't let me lift up to hasten the tasting. His chuckle told me how much he was enjoying the tease. Without further warning, he swiped his tongue from front to back in one savouring lick. I squirmed and cried out, "Oh, God!"

He ignored my increasingly frantic protests and continued in his self-appointed task. He tasted me thoroughly, tracing his tongue over every part of my most intimate flesh. Prickles of sensitivity increased to shards of sheer sensation, making my back arch and my breath arrive in short, hard gasps. When he took the pearl of flesh at the front fully into his mouth and sucked, it was a matter of seconds before I screamed his name and exploded in sharp, violent pulses.

I lost sense of time and place. Richard spun me into a world I hadn't visited for some time, one I had yearned to come back to, one that belonged to us alone. And I went alone. I had wanted him to come with me, but next time we'd go there together. A place where colours were more vivid, touches more intense, where it was never cold.

He lifted, and I felt a momentary chill before the heat of his body covered mine. Then I was deliciously enclosed, surrounded by love, the hard muscle of his sex pulsing between us.

It pulsed a little more than it needed, throbbed against my stomach then came a warm, wet gush as he released his long pent-up desire for me.

With a groan, his head dropped, his damp hair tickling my forehead, his breath heating my cheek. "Ah my love, my love."

His regret sounded all too evident in his words. "I'm so sorry."

I swallowed my disappointment, which wasn't as great as his by the sound of it. "Don't be. Please. You've given me such pleasure already." I put my hands on either side of his head, urging him to look at me. His bright blue gaze bored into mine, but he said nothing. "We've begun. We have all the time in the world. We just left it too long, that's all."

He laughed, but I heard the tremor behind it. "You mean *I* did."

"No. Whatever we do, we do it together." I wouldn't let him take the blame he seemed so eager to shoulder. "You took time to pleasure me beforehand, and if you had just decided to pleasure yourself and try to take me along with you, it wouldn't have happened." I didn't know that, but I didn't care. "We may wake later."

He smiled, but I hadn't completely dispelled his concern. I could see it in his eyes and in the tiny crease between his brows. "We may," he agreed smoothly and rolled off me. I reached for the handkerchief Nichols always left by the bed and put myself to rights, deliberately keeping my actions practical and efficient. Then I performed the same office for him, cleaning him as I might clean a child, with gentleness but no emotion of any kind. I dropped the cloth over the side of the bed without looking, and before he could turn away from me or leave the bed, I curled into his arms.

I couldn't prevent my sigh of pleasure when his arms closed about me. I wouldn't have suppressed it had I been able to do so. I wanted him to feel my happiness. With the release he'd given me came ease and relief because of our togetherness. I had felt increasingly separate from him in the last few months, and it had scared me. Very much. I couldn't bear not being with him, but being with him and yet apart would, I realised now, be far worse.

He held me tightly, and although his tension remained, we would recover from that soon enough. I knew it. When I raised my head, he bent to touch his lips to mine in a gentle kiss. I lifted my hand to cup the back of his head and feel his hair, and I deepened the embrace, trying to show him how much I loved him.

The last of the tension left his body in a deep wave of relief, and I tucked my leg between his, feeling his strong protective embrace like coming home.

We slept.

I awoke a few hours later, when dawn had begun to seep through the darkness of night. I lay on my back and watched the sky outside, wondering what was wrong, what had woken me. We always slept with the bed drapes open and with the curtains open too, when we could, because Richard preferred it that way. I had learned to enjoy the sight of dawn on the occasions that I woke. I had missed the sight, for when I slept on my own, Nichols closed the drapes for me. That was one way I'd known when Richard visited me in the night, when I woke and found I could see out into the sky. I suspected he had sat in the chair by the fire and watched me, but he hadn't done that recently. Only during the first month of my recovery.

He could have closed them before he left, but I think he wanted me to know he'd visited me. Trying to keep some path open between us, afraid of closing it. Now I had him—I lay in his arms, mine encircling his strong torso—and we were together once more.

A stirring in my belly made me roll over and head for the dressing room. As well I remembered where it was in this strange place, because I barely had time to get there before most of my dinner returned.

I was kneeling over the pot, retching in the aftermath, when I realised someone was holding my hair back, gathering it out of the way. Richard. I must have been tremendously ill because I hadn't noted his entrance. "I'm sorry," I managed.

"I don't have the least idea what you might be apologising for." His tone of mild reprimand held tenderness too. He twisted the long rope of my hair so it would remain clear of my face, and I felt him slip something under it. He'd secured a ribbon around it.

The next wave of sickness arrived and by then Nichols had roused. Richard was holding my shoulders steady, and I drew back to accept the damp cloth Nichols held and wiped my mouth. Although Richard appeared perfectly calm, I felt his concern, and I feared it might turn into something worse, back to the state of extreme anxiety.

"I'll come back to bed in a little while," I told him. "But I would really appreciate something cool to drink."

"You shall have fresh, iced water," he said. "I will see to it directly." I knew he'd ensure the water had been boiled, to make it safe. I loved the way I could trust him.

When he'd gone, I heaved a sigh, but I didn't have much free time because another wave came upon me, and this time it was worse.

Nichols had fetched fresh pots. I needed both of them, and by the time I had done, I was shivering, despite the mild weather. Nichols threw a robe over my shoulders and went to the door when a gentle tap fell upon it. She murmured to whoever stood outside and returned with a can of hot water. "I've roused the kitchen and ordered a bath drawn, my lady." She crossed the room to the washstand and poured some of the water into the china bowl, watching carefully for any splashes. "But there is something else, first."

She put the can down on the floor. Steam wreathed around

the rim, and I stared at it while I sat on the stool, waiting for the next attack. Nichols put the used pots outside the room and came back in with more. Some poor soul would no doubt dispose of them. She reached into the pocket of her robe and drew out a small screw of paper. I eyed it with suspicion, and I was right to.

Nichols met my eyes when I lifted my gaze to her face. "Ma'am, I'd like permission to purge you."

I knew my maid—she wouldn't put me through this without reason. But I wasn't a child, here to take direction. "Why?"

"Because the way you were retching just now put me in mind of something else. It could be a simple matter of bad food—Carier is conducting enquiries in the kitchen," she said. I groaned. No doubt the whole house had roused. I hated the fuss, but it was too late to complain now. "I just remember seeing someone in a similar situation, ma'am, and even if it is bad food, the purging will help you to recover faster."

It would empty the bad food and prepare me to accept new. "Nichols, I feel tired and weak at the moment, but I won't stay in bed any longer than I have to. Do you understand?"

"I do, ma'am." She had seen much over the last few months, and while I wouldn't dream of complaining to my maid, she understood. At the top of her profession—and well able to care for me in other ways too, with her services as a bodyguard well established—I knew I could trust her decision.

"The bad food will not weaken me if I eat properly tomorrow."

"That it won't, ma'am," she agreed. "All the more reason to clean you now."

I prefer not to recall the following hour. Enough to say that by the end of it I was completely empty. Only then did Nichols allow me to drink a glass of water, which Richard had gone down to the kitchen to supervise the boiling and cooling of, and a similar glass stood waiting on the nightstand in the bedroom.

The bath came as a blessed relief, and I let Nichols do everything necessary until I heard the door click quietly and knew she'd let Richard in to see me. I schooled my face into a tired smile, hiding the exhaustion and the hint of fear deep inside. I would trouble him with them if my suspicions came to a firmer conclusion, but they could easily be a result of my overactive imagination, rather than have any truth. I needed to reassure him. I was his weak spot, so I had to be strong for him. And I did feel better, if somewhat feeble. My stomach ached, but it didn't feel queasy any longer. Bathed and my hair freshly washed, I went gladly into his arms and let him put me to bed.

"Carier has begun investigations," he murmured. "I may have to dress myself for a while." He sighed. "The sacrifices a married man has to make!"

I chuckled and drew back the covers on his side of the bed, remembering not to hold my breath while I waited for him. To my relief, he shed his robe and climbed in next to me. I wanted his arms around me and I got them. "That, my love, will be the day. Carier will be there for you tomorrow."

Chapter Ten

Waking up with Richard had a special sweetness to it, one I'd missed, a sweetness laced with a trace of excitement. We used to talk about our day, even if we were going our separate ways, on our own business, and we'd meet again before dinner to discuss how it went. The pattern of our days could be predictable sometimes, but the content never so, and after the turbulence of our lives recently I welcomed a chance to settle into a comfortable routine. But that extra touch meant we might choose to start our day a little later.

However he insisted I stayed in bed that day. "I wouldn't hear of you rising."

"But I feel perfectly well now. Just bad food."

He leaned up on one elbow and cupped my cheek. "For me. Stay here for me."

"Not all day, please." I groaned. "I've spent so much time in bed, I'm tired of it."

He sighed. "Let me see what Carier has discovered. It's probably just food poisoning. Since you feel so much better now it's more than likely. But I want to make sure." He paused. "Take Lizzie with you if you go to the gardens, not Joaquin, and stay indoors until tomorrow."

"Jealous after all?" I didn't want our progress to intimacy halted in any way, so I agreed to send word to Joaquin that Lizzie had asked me to accompany her.

He kissed me again. "No, merely concerned for you. Dress and rest today. I have promised you not to treat you with too much care, but had I been as violently ill as you were, I would certainly wish to rest the next day."

It took an effort to recall that he had always treated me with such careful concern and it wasn't a result of my recent illness. It had better not be. "I'll stay until you're satisfied. But I wanted to see the gardens today. I want to redesign the gardens of our London house. Perhaps I could do it Portuguese style."

He laughed, and I loved to see the sparkle return to his eyes. "With box hedges and bushes clipped into odd shapes? Not the whole garden, if you please, sweetheart. I'm fond of the flowers." The distraction removed the anxiety from his face, and as he bent to kiss me, I felt much happier. He would return to this bed tonight, or we would use his. Not another night apart, I was determined on it.

Truthfully, after such a violent bout of sickness, I was more glad than I wanted to admit to spend the day in gentle, indoor pursuits. But I felt much better, and I took that as a sign of my general return to health, not just a recovery from an unfortunate stomach problem.

The next morning, Lizzie brought me my breakfast tray, refusing anyone's help. "It was the only way I could get to see you," she confessed, dumping the laden tray on my lap. She ignored Nichols's stifled *tsk*s as she removed the tray and put it on a folding table she'd erected on the other side of the bed. My maid poured tea for two and placed a plate of toasted, buttered muffins within reach. My stomach responded, and I gratefully chose one and took a savouring bite.

"I thought you were close to death," Lizzie said. "But you look well settled to me now."

I glanced at Nichols and grinned. "My maid insisted on

purging me. It left me tired, empty, but recovered."

Lizzie choked and placed her hand over mine. I could have used it for my tea, but I let it lie for now. "I'm so sorry, Rose. You arrive in Lisbon to convalesce and the first thing we do is give you bad food!"

"Was it the lemon cream?" Only I partook of that dish, so I thought it likely, if no one else had fallen ill. And even in October, this weather was warm enough to turn cream. Unseasonably warm, even for Portugal, Paul had told us.

Lizzie bit her lip. "I'm so sorry."

"Unless you prepared it yourself, I don't think it could be your fault." I took another bite of the muffin, and after I'd swallowed it, wondered aloud why Nichols hadn't brought up some preserves to go with it.

"I thought we'd start plain, ma'am," Nichols replied, not in the least abashed. I never expected her to be, but I preferred her straightforward care to Richard's fussing. Or rather, his gentle, meticulous concern.

I frowned. "I suppose you're right." I glanced at the tray. "At least we have enough here. Would you like a muffin, Lizzie?"

She laughed. "No, thank you. I ate earlier. Babies tend to rise early, and I like to see little Paul before he starts his day."

I could tell from the increased animation in her face that motherhood suited her. More than it did me, perhaps. The depth of my love for Helen and now the boys had shocked me with its intensity. I hadn't expected to adore my babies quite so much because I had never been enamoured by children overmuch. My nephew Walter, a few others, but I hadn't deliberately sought their company or always welcomed it. But Lizzie had. She'd always loved children, sharing their games and secrets, and having one of her own, the first of many, I guessed, would make her very happy.

"How many times do you see him every day?"

"More than I should, some of society believes." She grinned. "Not that I care."

"How about Paul?"

"Paul doesn't care, either. He has enough respect and wealth that he doesn't need to, and he wants only to see me happy." Her smile widened. "Besides, he is as besotted by his son as I am."

"And you hope for another?"

She cast me a sly glance. "Actually, we might have achieved that. I'm waiting to discover. It's early days, and we mustn't count on events."

"Counting the days instead?" I laughed when she glanced at Nichols. "You can rely on my maid's discretion." I didn't have to look at her to remind her, I knew she'd say nothing. With the servant network as tight as the one above stairs, it was good to have two servants we could rely on to keep their own counsel, but it was rare. We had to assume that most of what we said in the presence of others would reach other ears sooner or later. In time, I'd find similar trustworthy attendants for my children. Allies were important.

Lizzie shrugged. "Yes, counting the days. I won't know for another month or maybe two. But we would love a brother or sister for Paul."

"Not three at once, though." I leaned back and helped myself to another muffin.

She shuddered. "I pray not. But surely it's because Richard's a twin—"

"And my mother was a twin, don't forget." Lizzie and I shared a father, but not a mother, although we had always considered ourselves full-blooded sisters. So Lizzie wasn't in danger of twins or even triplets, not as much as I, at any rate.

"You can't catch the tendency. Considering our histories, I assumed I would have twins. I never counted on triplets. I never counted on all of them living, either."

"Rose!" Lizzie lifted her hand from where it lay over mine to put it to her heart in a gesture of shock. Her bosom heaved under its covering of fine gauze and apple-green silk.

I waved my free hand in a dismissive gesture. "I don't mean it to sound like that. But both Will and I were very sick. If I'd woken from my fever to hear that my tiniest baby had expired, it wouldn't have surprised me. It would have added to my sorrows for sure, but I knew they wouldn't have told me about him when I was so ill. I needed you then, Lizzie, someone who'd tell me the truth, but Nichols was under orders not to, and Richard and Carier wouldn't have told me. Martha would have wanted to protect me too. So only when I was better did I trust them, and then I insisted they bring my babies to me every day. I love them, Lizzie, never doubt that."

Lizzie bit her lip, sharp teeth digging in, before she spoke again. "I did hate them for a while, I have to admit, once I heard of the birth and how ill you were. I wish I could have come, but it was too soon after Paul's birth and they wouldn't let me."

"But you wrote, and I had them read your letters to me before I was well enough to read them for myself. They brought me a lot of comfort. Thank you."

"I'm just glad to see you better." She picked up the plate. "Except that Richard is right. You're too thin. Have another muffin."

I laughed and took the last one.

It was so good to talk to my sister again. Her humour and her practical common sense countered my more romantical nature and brought me a different point of view I could trust.

Despite her ethereal, angelic beauty, Lizzie had always had

a hard head on her shoulders and never allowed anyone or any event to carry her away. While I'd dreamed of knights in armour and dukes and earls, she had set her sights on a solid, productive marriage with a local member of society, or even a wealthy merchant. As events turned out, we achieved something closer to my dream than to hers. Strange how life plays tricks on us sometimes.

As I pushed the plate aside for Nichols to take, the door to my room opened to admit Richard and Carier. Lizzie turned, startled, and made to scramble off the bed, but Richard stopped her with an outstretched hand. "Please. You make a charming picture, the two of you. In fact, a painting of you both in just this pose would make a fascinating conversation piece."

"If an unconventional one," Lizzie said, laughing.

"All the more charming," he insisted.

Carier closed the door quietly and glanced at Nichols. That one look told me we had trouble ahead of us. I braced myself for whatever was to come.

"Only you partook of the lemon cream at table, my lady?" Carier asked.

"Yes."

"I would have had some, but I was full from the dishes I had before," Lizzie confessed.

Without realising what I was doing, I stretched my hand across the bed to Richard's side. Immediately he was there. He sat down and took my hand. "Carier said he had something of import to tell us, but he needed privacy. I've set one of our footmen outside to ensure it."

Carier nodded, and his already thin lips thinned still more in a small demonstration that the news he was about to impart wasn't trivial. "Unfortunately, when the dish returned to the kitchen, the cook deemed that it had to be eaten right away due to the unseasonably hot weather. Three maids partook of the treat, and all fell ill. Ma'am, I'm sorry to have to tell you that one has died."

Cold shock arced through me, and Richard's hand tightened in mine. "There is little room for error," Carier continued steadily. "I believe that dish was poisoned."

An appalled silence fell. I dared a glance at Richard, and as I feared, his face was set and steady. He was concealing what he felt. Whether it was because of Lizzie's presence I wasn't sure, but I hoped that was the case. Otherwise he might be trying to hide his emotions from me again. I would not allow it. I counted it an advance that he'd not tried to shield me from this information.

He made an effort to release my hand, but I wouldn't let him. "So my falling ill had nothing to do with my recent health," I said. At least I had that.

"Nothing at all, my lady."

My sister found her voice. She cleared her throat. "Who died?"

"A housemaid by the name of Micaela Botelho."

Her lovely face clouded over with incipient anger. "Why wasn't I told immediately?" Typical of my sister, to be in touch with her household and ensure it was efficiently run. It would be unusual for her not to be aware that the girl wasn't at her work.

A flicker of a smile threatened to break Carier's composure. If I didn't know him well by now, I would never have noticed. Lizzie certainly didn't. Her belligerent blue stare met the steely gaze of Richard's principal supporter. "Because, my lady, she has been late for work twice this year and the housekeeper had threatened her with dismissal if she did it again." Lizzie nodded. She knew. "One of the other servants did her duties for her, trying to cover the girl's absence. She is—was—a popular member of the staff because of her cheerful nature."

"And her never-ending stream of off-colour stories," Lizzie added. "They think I know nothing because I had to learn the language when I first arrived. So they assumed she was still abed?"

"Indeed, my lady, until a maid went to investigate her absence after she had finished her morning duties. They found her ill, and ordered her to rest. The maid she usually shares her room with is away at present, so she was left alone to recover and someone brought her gruel and tea. She was discovered dead a matter of ten minutes ago. I have ordered discretion, but more than that is not my place."

"A pity," Richard commented. He had given up trying to release my hand and instead kicked off his shoes, moved my breakfast tray and swung his legs up on the bed to sit closer to me. Perhaps he thought I needed comfort. Or perhaps he did.

I was made of stronger stuff than that. My body might still reveal some weakness, but my mind was as resilient as ever.

Richard sighed. "May we trust your servants, Lizzie?"

"They're an ordinary household," she replied waspishly. "Not like yours."

"But we have brought some of ours with us," Richard assured her smoothly. "What makes you think it's poison, Carier, rather than a simple matter of the sweet going off?" Milk poisoning carried off a number of people every year.

Carier glanced at Nichols, who stood silently by the door to the powder room, but at his cue, she stepped forwards. "My lord, I've seen cases of food poisoning before, and there were a few things about my lady's illness that didn't appear quite right. It was why I insisted on purging her completely."

"I didn't know that." From the smooth, silky tone to his

words, I knew Richard was angry. "I prefer to be informed of these things immediately."

"I had no proof, sir." Nichols lifted her chin. "It was merely a thought, and I did the right thing and ensured her ladyship was free of the problem. I confided in Mr. Carier, and he agreed with me that best be safe than sorry. The symptoms weren't enough to be sure, just to be alert. He promised to inform you if he discovered anything."

"So matters got ahead of us." Richard frowned. "You should still have told me at once." His tone softened when he addressed me directly. "I will not have you in danger. I take it most of your domestics are resident here?" Lizzie nodded in answer to Richard's question. "In any case, we may be too hasty to assume the worst. I'd rather wait until we know for sure. It could be a simple matter of cream going off."

"We will know, my lord. I appropriated the remains of the dish. There wasn't a great deal. However, the rat catcher for the estate caught a particularly fine specimen last night in the gardens, and I persuaded him to leave the creature in the trap instead of killing it."

"How did you manage that?" I said.

He shrugged when I raised my brows. "I was in the military long enough to pick up a smattering of Spanish. Although it isn't the same as Portuguese, I made myself understood. I will give the creature a portion of the dish and watch its reaction carefully. I'll know from that what to do next."

Richard glanced at me. "He knows his poisons." I already knew that.

Lizzie got to her feet. "I must see to the household. I'll put it about that the dish was bad, if you please, and I'll reprimand the cook and the dairymaids. But since you say it might not be their faults, I won't dismiss them. Not yet, anyway." She kissed my cheek and bustled away, closing the door quietly behind her.

Richard glanced at Carier. "We will go through the possibilities methodically, if you please. You had the servants here investigated before our arrival?"

"I did, my lord. They were all trustworthy, and none are particularly new. Most of them come from local families." Servants would sometimes work for a single family their whole lives, particularly in the country, but higher domestics moved from post to post to advance their situations. A lady's maid might move from a baroness to a countess, for example, and advance her status considerably. But that only accounted for upper servants.

"I will discover what I can," Carier said. "I may have some success asking in the kitchen." Craggy-faced Carier had considerable success with maids and wasn't above using his attraction to gain answers when we had no luck above stairs. Perhaps that would work this time.

"We have discounted all but the one we must look at more deeply," Richard said. "Barber, the merchant."

Carier sighted. "He is not there, my lord. I went to investigate his room this morning, and found him gone. At the time I assumed he had business to see to, but I thought it bad form that he had not left a note, but I did not then know about the maids and I had not yet connected my lady's illness with a possible poisoning. I only retrieved the remains of the lemon cream after I heard of the maid's death."

"Then it's probably the merchant."

I'd already come to the same conclusion as my husband. One of the advantages in living in the country was that strangers coming and going were noticed, and Carier would have told us if that had been so. We needed that merchant, and our priority would be to discover him.

Carier nodded. "I fear so, my lord. He has, of course, left no trace. He took nothing with him that he didn't arrive with."

I voiced what they were thinking. "His object wasn't burglary, or to tell us about the boy Crantock. It was to gain ingress to the house for long enough to administer the poison."

Richard frowned. "We must be discreet. I don't want it known that it was poison rather than bad food. I don't want anyone alerted to the fact that we know. Let them believe we still think it was accidental food poisoning."

A picture was forming, one that became increasingly sinister. I summed up, ticking the events off on my fingers. "Someone attacks the boy on the ship because he did something, or knew something, or could recognise someone. When the attempt to kill him by throwing him off the rigging fails, they follow it up and strangle him. Then Barber arrives here. He excuses himself from dinner, pleading a mild illness, but one he knows Richard won't wish transmitted to me. That also gave him the opportunity to poison the lemon cream. So either Barber, or someone he is working with, wants to harm us."

A name lurked behind my mind, but it was far too early to try to drag someone half a world away into the picture. After all, Richard had assisted the Fieldings of Bow Street on more than one occasion. Among them, we might have made more enemies than we knew.

"I want the children guarded day and night," Richard said. "Our best men. And Rose and myself, although I will be with her as much as I can. When I am not, I want a footman with her."

Carier nodded. "I will search for the man, sir. If he returns to Lisbon, we know where to find him. If we can catch him, we will. In the meantime, I will go and observe the rodent. My lord, my lady." Carier bowed to us, and at a nod from Richard, he left the room, Nichols following him. Utterly trustworthy, she would form my main bodyguard. I would ensure I was armed from now on until we got to the bottom of the problem.

It said a great deal that Richard didn't immediately get off the bed, putting himself out of temptation. Although last night hadn't been the unqualified success that I'd hoped, it was a step in the right direction, and I was confident we'd progress even further, given time and patience. He was already more relaxed around me.

I loved that he didn't move away from me. Every time he had done that in the last few months he'd sent a shard of pain through my heart. What was worse, he'd known it. I could tell from his expression and his tightly controlled movements, the way he'd avoided me. It made both of us unhappy.

Now I reached out and took his hand, unwilling to push him any further, but to my delight he leaned over and planted a gentle kiss on my mouth. "You promise to stay here?"

Reluctantly, because I didn't want to spoil the mood, I shook my head. "Richard, when you've spent as much time in bed as I have recently, spending further time here is the last thing I want to do."

The lace of his sleeve ruffle scraped against my hand as he moved, but only back a little so he could see my face. As always, the sight of those clear blue eyes close up took my breath away. So much beauty, soul and power were encapsulated in their depths, I could never understand how he managed to hide it all in public. But he did.

He could turn those depths into mirrors, surfaces that reflected only what the onlooker wanted to see. He had never hesitated, but dropped the curtain for me from the first day we'd met. I loved him for his bravery, for his recklessness and for his care of me. And for everything else.

"Then promise me you'll listen to your body. You'll rest

when you need to; you'll demand food when you need it. And you won't mind the two footmen who will accompany you."

I had a duty to take care of myself, if not for me, then for him. "I promise. I may be impatient sometimes, but I try very hard not to be stupid."

He kissed the tip of my nose. "And you're extraordinarily successful at that."

I gave him a deliberately enticing smile. "Sometimes it's good to appear stupid."

"True enough. Or so obsessed with clothes and fashion that there's no room for anything else."

We laughed, and the sound born of impulse, untrammelled and unconfined, rang around the room.

I enjoyed our visit to the gardens later that day. The babies lay in the straw cradles that my sister had acquired for them, and my daughter was adorable in chinchilla and blue velvet. I wore the shawl Richard had given to me over a summery gown of lemon silk. I successfully ignored the two burly footmen who stood close to us, ostensibly waiting for orders, but in reality were there to protect us. My sister brought out her son, and although he could barely toddle, being a few months younger than Helen, our daughter played very carefully with him.

"I shall not," I murmured to Lizzie, "be arranging any future matches between my daughter and your son. I would have hated such an obligation when I was younger. Though they do look sweet together."

"Their temperaments complement each other." Lizzie smiled and leaned forwards to unclasp her son's hand from her arm. He had a tendency to cling, but most children did at that age. "But I agree. Far too early to think of matches. You have done very well indeed, though. Four children, and three at once. Is your mother-in-law pleased?"

I laughed. "Yes and no. Yes, she's delighted that I succeeded in giving birth to an heir and two spares, as well as a daughter. Helen is useful currency for future business negotiations, as she sees it. But I think she was put out that I had the temerity to live."

"Oh, Rose, surely not!" I had forgotten that Lizzie hadn't witnessed the worst of my mother-in-law's behaviour.

I could see no reason not to tell her. "Oh yes. Look at it from her point of view. If I'd died, they would have had their heirs and Richard could have added to the family coffers by making a more advantageous and influential second marriage."

Lizzie, my most practical sister, was nevertheless shocked by the matter-of-fact way I delivered the comments. I had learned to live with Lady Southwood's dynastic ambitions, so it came as no surprise to me that she had probably wished me dead once I'd outlived my usefulness.

Not that she had ever voiced such a wish. Just the sight of her frozen features when she first visited me as I was recovering persuaded me. I saw the flicker of disappointment in her eyes when I told her I expected to make a full recovery. And she meant me to see it too. I wouldn't put it past her to be the agent of my destruction here, except that it was not as yet clear that I was the victim, even though I had fallen ill. Our suppositions were bound together with threads as thin as spider webs, and just as fragile. We needed more information. And I would not distress Richard by telling him my private suspicions.

"She means nothing personal," I tried to explain now. "Lady Southwood doesn't believe in personal feelings. She doesn't wish me evil. But she sees the advantages in Richard being a free agent once more. It's obvious that Gervase will never marry, although she's tried to encourage him to think of it." Richard's twin preferred the embrace of my brother, Ian, and together they made a far more devoted couple than many I could think of, but that wouldn't have stopped Lady Southwood had she considered a suitable match for him.

At the moment their sister, who preferred these days to be addressed by her second name, Georgiana, rather than her first name of Maria, was the subject of her matchmaking ambitions. Richard had left Gervase in charge of checking their mother's more outrageous schemes, such as arranging a match between an aged, wealthy duke who happened to be close to eighty years old. It was fortunate that Georgiana's father doted on her and had witnessed some of his wife's more elaborate obsessions, so he would care for Georgiana too.

Lizzie swallowed. "How do you manage?"

I smiled and shrugged. "I avoid her company as much as I can. She has hurt Richard enough. She will not do so again."

"Even if you're not here?"

"It's one of the reasons I fought so hard to live. I wasn't ready to leave. I have children to care for and a husband to love." I was no longer shy of explaining my love for my husband. I left it to him what to say to others, but Lizzie knew how he felt about me. How much he needed me.

Lizzie had a loving relationship with her husband, so I wouldn't have expected the flush that mantled her cheeks now. But she had ever been the practical one. She had expected to make a comfortable match, not a passionate one, and I guessed she might be still coming to terms with what that meant. Thanks to servants' gossip, I knew she and Paul customarily slept in the same bed, much as Richard and I were wont to do.

Thinking of that, I broadened my smile. "Your strategy worked, Lizzie. Although my illness might not have helped, I won't let him draw apart from me again."

"I'm so glad. I take it you're reconciled?"

"Yes." We would be completely together, very soon. I was certain of that. Perhaps tonight. The thought sent an illicit thrill through me.

"And you're feeling well again?" She bit her lip, her pale blue eyes vivid under the shade of her broad straw hat. "I'm so sorry, Rose."

"It happens to the best of cooks." I brushed aside her concerns for me. "How is the maid? The one who—" It was my turn to redden.

"Died?" Lizzie finished for me, a note of bitterness in her voice. "I have to visit the poor girl's parents. Her mother will be distraught. It's fortunate she has other girls, since she depends upon them for a living." Typical of Lizzie to find out all she could. I would wager if the woman had no other means of support, Lizzie would have seen that she didn't want. "A hard-working, honest girl, despite her propensity to sleep in. As were the other two. They are still abed, but recovering. Weaker than you were."

"I ate less," I said. "If they ate most of the dish between them, they would have had considerably more."

She sighed. "I suppose so."

A shadow fell over me, and I turned to see Carier. "My lady." His unsmiling gaze held a query.

"Yes, Carier, I think the children should go in." I motioned to the nurses and glanced at Lizzie, who nodded. I gave her an apologetic smile. "I should have noticed before. Helen is visibly dropping." In fact she wasn't, but it wouldn't be long. The nurses should have time to get her to bed for her nap before she grew irritable, her invariable habit if kept awake for too long.

I kissed my children, paying special attention to little Will, but he gurgled at me and I could have sworn he smiled. Such a beautiful baby, eyes as blue as the summer sky and a fine complexion, with a fragile appearance belied by his more robust brothers. They would need to be put to the breast. Once again I felt a pang when I recalled that I would not be feeding these children and never had the chance. I would never have the chance again. Life is full of farewells.

I glanced at Carier. "Should I go in?" I was asking him if he minded if Lizzie was privy to the news he was so obviously ready to impart.

"Not unless you wish it, ma'am."

Richard approached, carrying a tray containing tall glasses. Their faceted surfaces glinted off the cold sun. He'd have brought a servant, but I knew he would want privacy. He presented the glasses to us with a smile. "Wine mixed with pomegranate juice."

"A popular beverage here," Lizzie told me.

After my first sip, I understood why. The pomegranate gave a rich, fruity flavour to the young red wine. A refreshing drink and one I'd remember when I returned home. It would make an interesting offering at my afternoon salons.

Richard settled on the couch next to me. Lizzie had ordered two comfortable couches brought out from the house, made of woven basketwork, covered with large cushions. They made an excellent garden seat, and far more easy than the stone seats I was used to at home.

Richard waved the footmen back. They stepped out of earshot but remained on duty. No doubt I'd see them a lot in the weeks to come. I could put them to use when we went shopping in Lisbon again, as we planned to do soon. Once we resolved our current mystery.

Richard took my hand and turned it palm-up in his. "You feel well, still?"

I didn't like the anxiety in his tone. "I'm fine. I've had a light meal and everything is as it should be."

Lizzie got to her feet. "Indeed she shows every sign of recovering well. I don't scruple to tell you it was a great shock knowing you were ill, especially after your—trouble." That was one way of putting it. "But I have ordered the dairy scrubbed out, and the kitchen too. That will keep the maids busy." She shook out her skirts. "If you will excuse me, I must take little Paul to his father. He likes to see him every day at this time, and in any case, I think my husband has been about estate business for too long." She laughed and held her hand out to her son, who toddled unsteadily to her. She picked him up and smiled at us. "I'm glad you're here," she said simply, before she went away.

We watched her leave, her pink skirts lifting in the light breeze, her essential elegance as apparent from the back view as the front.

Carier motioned to our attendant footman who obligingly moved a little farther away. By that alone I knew he had news. Carier spoke the words I was dreading. "It was poison, my lady. There's no doubt."

I wanted to know everything, nothing held back. "Tell me."

"The rodent died." His mouth thinned. "It was not the fault of the cook, or the dairymaids. The lemon cream had an extra topping that someone added between the dairy and the dining room. The dish was made and then put in the dairy to keep cool until the time to serve it. That was probably when it was contaminated." I swallowed but said nothing. "I gave the creature the whole item then noted a glistening substance on the surface. It appeared to be sugar. But I took some of the crystal and gave it to another creature the gardener provided me with. It convulsed and died."

"I noticed a new topping," I said. "I thought it was sugar,

143

but it didn't taste particularly sweet." I turned to face my husband. "When I vomited, Nichols didn't like the shivers or the spasms my body went into. That was when she decided to purge me, she said."

"She could have saved your life," Richard said.

"I didn't eat much, so I might have merely spent several more days in bed like the unfortunate maids."

"Or died, like the more unfortunate maid." Richard would face that first. His voice was steady but low toned. "I think we have to face the fact that someone tried to kill you, my love."

Chapter Eleven

I wanted to throw myself into his arms and let him hold me until I could face this ugly thing. I wanted to turn my back, run away, get away from the horror that had infected me. But I forced myself to remain calm. I couldn't add to his burdens now by behaving like a hysterical female. "How do you know it was me they wanted and not Lizzie?"

"We don't. Both of you have professed a fondness for the sweet," Richard said. It relieved me that he could admit the possibility, that he hadn't immediately surrounded me with more safeguards than I could cope with. "I doubt anyone intended it for the maids, though. Not specific enough, and there was no probability of the dish returning to the kitchen uneaten. You could have consumed it all at the table."

"Did you ask her ladyship about the sequence of events, ma'am?" Carier asked gently.

Lizzie had volunteered most of the information. I hadn't had to ask her, but I had committed what she told me to memory. "She said that she was running late, so she went down to the kitchen instead of having the cook come to her with the menus, as she usually does. They were preparing breakfast, so that would be at around half past ten. No later than eleven, because the maid hadn't yet got out the eggs. Paul likes scrambled eggs with fish and rice, so they provide a dish every morning for him." A ghost of a smile flickered over my lips at this reminder of the way Lizzie liked to control her household. "She discussed the menus with the cook then, in the main kitchen. Because they were preparing breakfast and beginning dinner preparations too, the kitchen was full, but none of the upstairs maids should have been there. They would be elsewhere."

Richard sighed. "A well-ordered household is a wonderful thing. Perhaps you could ask Lizzie to make a list of the servants who should have been in the kitchens at that time, and perhaps those who also might have the opportunity to be there and overhear the orders. Footmen running errands, perhaps, or the butler checking the wine list."

"But do we really need to know all that, if we think we know the identity of the poisoner?"

"I want to know everything, my love," Richard said. "All the details."

"I believe I should befriend the cook," Carier said. "He will be particularly distressed that a guest fell ill after his food. I will emphasize the importance of careful vigilance of the items between kitchen and table."

Richard glanced up at him. "A good thought." His perceptive gaze fell on me, and he stretched out his hand, concern crossing his face. Without hesitation, I moved closer to him. He settled my shawl more securely over my shoulders before he took my hand. "I will discover who did this and why. Not the agent, who we're fairly sure of, but the enemy we are undoubtedly facing. Any ideas?"

"At least we know the Drurys haven't sent an assassin." I shuddered at the reminder. "A terrible business."

Our old enemy Steven Drury had retired to the country with his father-in-law, trying to rebuild his fortune after his late wife, Julia, had dissipated it in search of a high social standing and influence over matters of state. As well as trying to kill Richard and me.

One enemy remained, and it was time to speak his name. I

kept the possibility of Lady Southwood close to my chest. I had no reason to suspect her. She had never attacked us in that way before, and I couldn't allow my dislike of her to colour my thinking now. "John Kneller is in the Colonies," I said. Someone had to say his name, but a chill crept over my skin at the words. "A new enemy? An old one returned?"

Richard exchanged a telling look with Carier, who stood behind the sofa where I'd recently sat. "We know that someone wanted to do you harm, my love, that's for sure. We are fairly sure we know who could have done it, but we don't know if he was working alone or with someone else."

He paused, thinking, before he voiced his suspicions. "It would have been a simple matter for Barber to go to the dairy, either before he made his presence known here or just before dinner." Activity in most dairies was confined to earlier in the day, when the milk was collected and processed. It was left closed after that, to keep the contents chilled until they were needed. "Dairies are customarily built against an outer wall of the house, or in a separate building, to facilitate the coming and going from the fields, and theirs is no exception. That means there is only one door between the dairy and the outside world, unlike the rest of the kitchen area. Easier to find a way in." Now his face was so rigid with control I felt sure anger simmered inside him. "Either Barber is a new enemy, or he is working with an old adversary. I want him found."

"I have put matters in train, my lord. We will do our best to track him down."

He gave Carier a brisk nod. "I know you will, Carier. But there is another possibility. Barber would have known an elaborate dish like the lemon cream was meant for table that night. He might not have known it was a favourite of either Lizzie or Rose, though he could assume that you had a good chance of taking it." He paused and leaned forwards, his eyes gleaming. "But think for a moment. Assume that Barber wasn't the culprit, and he left early to attend to business in Lisbon. Several other people in this household would know Lizzie's partiality for lemon cream. They heard her discussing it in the kitchen, or they knew it already. We cannot disallow that possibility. Who else would want one of you dead?"

The word simmered in the air, but nobody spoke it.

Silence fell. A bird sang in the distance, but other than that, the only sound was the breeze in the box hedges. And I knew why Carier had come out to me and then Richard had followed. We weren't overheard here.

I took a deep breath and said the name we were all thinking. "Joaquin. He ordered the dish and he knows Lizzie likes it. He might also have known that Lizzie may be *enceinte*, and decided to—to get rid of her before she produces any more possible heirs to bar his way to the title."

I caught my breath. Lizzie loved lemon cream as much as I did, and whoever poisoned the dish might have known that. Joaquin was responsible for the dish being made. He had ample opportunity to poison it. And if Lizzie were dead, he could control young Paul more easily, or even get rid of him in time.

Richard gripped my hand. "I don't want you put in any more peril. If an accomplice knows we have realised the sweet was poisoned, and it wasn't a simple case of food going bad, he or she will be on his or her guard and likely to do something in a panic. It will make our task of uncovering the culprit much harder. I want us to go about as if we didn't suspect a thing, as if the poisoning were an unfortunate domestic incident, no more. You must keep your trusted servants close about you. And we will institute a new regime for mealtimes, although I doubt the perpetrator will attempt to use that avenue again." Richard paused. "It shouldn't be for long. Hopefully there will be traces to follow. How many people know of your experiments with the rats, Carier?"

"One, my lord. The gardener's boy whom I bribed to supply the creatures to me, instead of disposing of them in the usual way. I didn't tell him why I wanted them, only that I wanted to try an experiment. I disposed of the corpses myself."

"We should assume that the gardener's boy gossips," I said. "It doesn't do to underestimate the servants' network. If he said nothing, all well and good, but if he did, someone might wonder."

Richard released my hand and reached for my glass. He took a reviving draught. I thought he was probably relieved that he could do something. He had me safe here, and he would do his best to track down whoever was attacking me. And through me, him.

"An excellent point, my love." Richard handed me my glass with an apologetic smile. I kept his attention long enough for him to see me take a drink from the same spot on the glass that he'd used, and he rewarded me for my gesture with a smile and a definite thaw in his gaze. "You will, sweetheart, keep Nichols, Carier or one of those two footmen over there with you at all times. That's when I'm not with you." However gently he put it, I didn't mistake the command for a suggestion.

"So I won't want for company, then." I smiled, trying to make light of the situation. But I saw the sense of it. Despite valuing my independence, I didn't cavil at the restrictions. To do so would have been foolish and headstrong.

Anger simmered through me, heated my blood. I wouldn't have my life so constrained that I couldn't live it properly. I wouldn't allow anyone to do that to me. "I want this cleared up quickly. I'll do everything I can to sort out this matter, then I want to go back to enjoying my visit here. It could be a grudge, something small, an idiot servant. Anything." We had defeated our worst enemies. Surely nothing else so bad awaited us. But deep in my heart, the events spoke of a conspiracy, someone who bore more than a casual grudge against us.

"I agree." Richard's touch on my hand was warm and reassuring, but I saw the edge of anxiety in his eyes, an expression I'd do anything to dispel. He turned his head to confront his valet's patient gaze. "What kind of poison do you think it was?"

"I suspect it's a mixture, my lord. You can buy poisons to take almost any effect, and you can get them on most street corners. It won't help us catch whoever has done this thing."

Exasperated, I put down my glass, stood and brushed my skirt down, more for something to do than from a real need. "I'll go inside and ensure the children are settled. Nobody goes near them but the nurses and their guards from now on, and everything they eat is to be tasted by someone else first."

"You won't allow me to have that done for you and yet you insist on it in the children?" Richard got to his feet and held out his arm for me to take.

"They are smaller and in more danger if someone should decide to strike at us through them." I grimaced. "I would rather we went about the business discreetly and quickly."

"In that we are totally in accord, my love," he said.

Back in my room that night after dinner, I washed, and with Nichols's help undressed and climbed into bed. When she left, I dragged my night rail over my head and tossed it by the side of the high bed. It was higher than the kind we usually used. It had interesting possibilities.

I was contemplating some of those possibilities when I heard the connecting door open, and I glanced up to see Richard, sumptuously robed in a dark blue banyan decorated with a riot of oriental figures, enter the room. He responded to my smile somewhat mechanically, but I was delighted to see that he had nothing on under his robe.

He undid the froggings at the neck, unhooked the inner fastenings and discarded the robe on a nearby chair, the white lining flashing a reminder of the surprising nature of inner secrets. He let me view him, and I took the opportunity to scan him thoroughly, just to ensure everything was there and in the right place. As I watched, his cock stirred. A good omen of future loving.

He smiled and climbed into bed, using the little footstool set by the side. Interesting to watch the play of his muscles on his arms and chest while he did so. He caught me looking, and his gaze met mine. He froze, one knee on the mattress, the other still on the footstool. He touched my chin, the only part of my face he could reach across the expanse of sheet.

I flicked my tongue over his finger and loved his responsive shudder, which he made no effort to hide. "Tonight, my love," he said, "we finish what we started. I have to stay with you now, else I'll get no sleep at all, and I can't be with you without making love to you. Not now." He groaned. "It kills me, but I can't resist you anymore."

He lifted his body onto the high mattress without effort. His nipples were already peaked, as were mine. I sat up and let the sheet slide down my body, enjoying the sensation when it caught on my nipples before it fell to my waist. He reached for me, grasping my waist and tugging me flush against his body.

"I'll never tire of the way you feel against me," I told him. "You feel so strong, so, well, *masculine*." I laughed. "I'll never make a poet."

"You hold all the poetry I'll ever need," he assured me, his lips so close to my temple that I felt the air pass between us as the words left him. He punctuated the sentence with a kiss, and

151

when I lifted my head, he pressed a gentle salute to my lips. His eyes, half-lidded as he stared down at me, darkened as the pupils grew with his arousal. "So beautiful. A world in a world in a world."

"What do you mean?" We shared a love of John Donne's poems, but I couldn't recall that line in any of them.

"Your body is a world to me, all the world I need. It sustains me and gifts me with its presence. It contains your soul, a world inside. We're in this bed, a world of its own. We're inside a room, inside a house—"

"Inside an estate, inside a country..." I laughed. "I see. You are my world too, my love. All of it." I thought of the children, people we had created from our love and now beings in their own right, and I remembered Helen's delight in the garden today. Not very romantic, but so much a part of married life that it seemed natural.

I didn't voice my thought, but he must have seen something in my eyes, for he laughed too. "Tell me. It's about the children, isn't it?"

"Just that I thought of you today. Helen scrambled towards a bush, one I'd already moved her away from because it had prickly leaves, and the glance she gave me, to see if I was attending to her—it was pure you."

He raised a brow. "In what way?"

He wasn't letting me off lightly, then. "The mischief and the calculation. That girl is already working out how far she can push us. And it's likely she'll push you further than she should."

"Highly likely, my love. How can I deny her anything? Just as I can't imagine refusing you whatever you want." Trouble put creases between his brows. "You understand why I'm so careful with you?" He touched his lips to my nose, and then my mouth, but released me so I could answer. His arms remained cinched around my waist.

"Of course I do." I couldn't imagine his tender care ever leaving me. "You're afraid for me. There's no need. We brought the highest level of servant with us, didn't we? And it's too early to jump to conclusions. Not until we know where John Kneller is. I imagine he's having a fine time abusing slaves and bedding plantation owners' wives and daughters."

He *tsk*ed. "I hope not." He drew me closer, so my breasts pushed against his chest. "It whirls around my head sometimes that I've done wrong. I had to let him live, to give him a chance. He had so much potential and he's young yet. He could prove a great man, if he overcomes his tendencies for revenge and retribution."

"Don't." I smoothed my hand over his cheek, feeling the stubble gathered there. Sometimes he shaved before coming to me, but I liked the stimulation of the short hairs on occasion. They could hardly be seen because of his fair complexion, but now they glinted in the starlight and the light of the two candles I'd left burning, set in the holders above our heads. I wanted to see him, to glory in his male beauty as we made love. Now I saw his concern, and although I wanted nothing more than to soothe him, I rejoiced that he felt secure enough in our love to hide nothing. It had taken him some time to learn that. I wouldn't let that go. "Don't think of it. Don't think of him. Concentrate on the facts, what is happening, until we know for sure."

He sighed. "You're right. I worry for you, and now I worry for our children too. I think it's become something of a habit, and I have to unlearn it. Maybe here, in this lovely country, without the duties I'm usually subject to, I'll find a way to relax." He smiled. "I have the most beautiful woman in the world in my arms and the best family in the nursery." His smile broadened, but I saw the trouble still lurking in his eyes. "I'm sure I'll learn to live with any imperfections."

When his lips touched mine, I let them open, let him tilt his head to increase the connection between our mouths. He tasted me, his tongue flicking around my lips, then deeper, rimming my mouth and touching my teeth in a sensuous caress that made my skin prickle under him. My nipples hardened further, pressing against the hard muscles of his chest and I moaned, wanting more and now.

His tongue delved, and I met it with my own, stroking, caressing, pressing closer so I could suck on it with a delicacy that wouldn't last long. He opened his mouth wider, urging me closer. The muscles in his back flexed against my open palms as I swept my hands up and down the length of his body, eager to experience and share every part of me with every part of him.

Finishing the kiss, he kept my gaze with his as he laid me on the crisp sheets, my hair tumbling against the white pillows. He grasped a handful of it, let the unruly curls sift through his fingers. Lifting them so the candlelight gleamed against the strands, he watched them fall against the linen. "So beautiful. None of the silk in all China compares to this." He rubbed his nose against the waves, inhaling as he did so. "I love the way you rinse with lavender and rosemary. I never experience that particular scent without thinking of you. It brings you to mind, like this." He gazed at me, drinking in my curves and my skin. "Lying back, waiting for me to share my body with you, to love you. And I do. So much."

"I love you too." It was all I could find to say, but it sounded inadequate to my ears. I wanted to say so much more, but words failed me, so I showed him instead.

When we were first together, my innocence was only matched by his eagerness, but he'd taught me to be unafraid, unashamed. We brought so much to each other now, and I knew him so well that he said we met as equals these days. However true that was, I don't know, but I loved that he said it and I tried to bring him all the honour he did to me. I wouldn't show him any reticence. So even though my body wasn't what it could be, even though fine silvery lines marked some places and my curves were less ample than they used to be, I knew I still gave him pleasure, so I wouldn't hide from him. Ever.

The evening being mild, I threw back the sheets and kicked them aside. No doubt we'd need them later, but not now. The light caressed his sleek curves and the powerful lines of his body like a lover. I traced the highlights with my fingers; his broad shoulders, usually so carefully disguised by his coats; his slim waist and hips, the bones perceptible to my hands; and his shaped muscles, firm with exercise and health. He remained still for me, leaning on one elbow and his hand, half-covering my body, watching me take pleasure in him.

When I touched his shaft, he sucked in a harsh breath. His cock was ready, hard, the smooth, silky skin damp with his essence, the drops he gave me as tribute to ease his way into my body. He braced his hand against the mattress, ensuring he wouldn't fall onto me. I gazed at the stiff evidence of his desire for me and grasped him before working my hand along his length. Mine, all mine. Every bit.

Slowly, he lowered his body until my nipples grazed his chest, and he stopped. Moved, stimulating the already sensitive tips to almost unbearable sensations. "You feel more there, don't you?"

"Yes." My voice came out trembling. I wanted so much, but he'd taught me the exquisite pleasure to be gained in waiting. I would feel even more soon. "I feel you touching me."

He lifted one hand that braced his body on the mattress and cupped a breast. That breathtaking display of strength, balanced on one hand only, his body steady above mine, might have surprised some of his enemies. But it didn't surprise me. I had ample proof of his power. He took my nipple between thumb and forefinger, caressing it with almost unbearable tenderness, slowly increasing the pressure until I arched my body up towards him, trying to feel it all, take it all.

His low chuckle told me I wasn't the only one affected here. With a swift, decisive movement he bent and sucked my nipple so that I cried out from the unexpectedness of the move. Retaining my hold on his cock, I used my other hand to clutch the back of his head, hold him there. He played, twisted his tongue around my sensitive flesh, tickled the very tip until I begged for mercy. He gave a devilish laugh and turned to the next one while his breath cooled on my skin.

He drew hard and let the nipple out of his mouth, then blew on it. I squirmed; he held me in place. "They're more sensitive, aren't they?" He hummed at it, his breath gusting across the tip he'd already stimulated to screaming point. I wondered if the nurses could hear me and decided I didn't care. As long as I didn't wake the children.

When he licked the underside of a breast, he activated a new area and invited it to join the riot taking part inside me. His hand slipped down my body, shaped my waist and cupped my hip before heading inexorably lower. His soft kisses on my stomach made me shudder, and he only paused at my cleft to tease, tickle my entrance with his finger, then slide around the opening without entering before delivering a long, slow kiss to my clitoris. Then my thighs, before he raised his head and met my gaze. I could hardly believe the level of eroticism from seeing my husband between my legs resting his chin on the curls that protected my mound.

The corner of his mouth quirked in a smile. "Ready for me yet?"

"More than ready," I managed. Barely. "I want you so

much. Please, Richard."

"I want you more," he growled, and finally came up on his elbows and made his way back to me. His shaft pressed against my stomach, hard and needy, leaving a wet kiss behind when he lifted again and put a hand between us to guide himself into my waiting body.

The pause that followed went on too long. I gazed into his eyes, smiling, ready, but my smile faded as distress entered his blue gaze. "Richard? What is it?"

"Rose. I don't know, I—I—"

The hesitation was so uncharacteristic of him that fear grazed my arousal. I reached up, grasped his forearms. "What is it?" For a moment, he didn't speak. "Richard, please, you're worrying me. Tell me."

He groaned and swung off my body to lie next to me. He covered his eyes with the back of his hand. "I don't understand." With a savage gesture, he swept the sheets off his body so I could see him down to his knees.

His cock was no longer erect. It lay lax and at ease on his stomach, taunting me with its inactivity. But I couldn't feel as bad as he did. I couldn't hesitate, couldn't give him any reason to doubt me or my love. I leaned up and over him, touching my lips to his in a gentle kiss.

He moved away. I followed, urging him back to face me. If he'd wanted, he could have wrenched away from me, but he did not. He gave a resigned sigh, dropped his arm and opened his eyes. Drenched in sorrow and confusion, he gazed at me. "I don't know what happened. I'm sorry, Rose."

"No. It could be any manner of things." I searched my mind, frantically wondering what it could be. He was so close—I could almost see his shield forming, protection he'd used against the world for so long. Not against me. Never against me.

"You're tired, worried, maybe you wanted me too much." That sounded good, and it would be something for him to think about, though I couldn't entirely believe it myself. "You wanted and wanted, and then went over."

"I didn't come." He shook his head. He looked so much younger like this, without his wig and furbelows, without the lace and the powder that made him so much a man of the world. Here he was himself, the essential Richard. "I wanted you, Rose, but something went awry. I don't know what it was or why it happened."

I rolled over him, lying on top of him so he couldn't get away. My nipples were still furled and hard, a travesty, but I wouldn't hide them. I remained wet, which no doubt dampened his thighs, but I wouldn't hide that, either. He deserved honesty, and I wouldn't stint in giving it to him. Within limits.

I couldn't rush into it. Now he needed reassurance and love, not doubts. Doubts would, I was sure, make everything worse. "It doesn't matter. We're together, we're not sleeping apart. Not ever again."

He gave a wry smile. "I won't leave. I promise." He smoothed the hair back from my temples, holding it clear of my face so he could see me properly. The light flickered over his features, sending shadows chasing across his high cheekbones, his bright eyes. "I'm sorry, Rose. I'm tired, that's all."

Yes, that was it. It had to be. "You cared for me and the children so much you didn't take care of yourself. Now it's my turn to care for you. I need to eat and rest, nothing more. I feel fine now, just weak. I know I have some ground to make up, and I promise I'll be good and take care of myself. Now we have to care for the children together and make sure they have what they need." If a child reached its fifth birthday, that was a good sign it would live a long and prosperous life. I wouldn't allow anything else to happen.

I shifted against him, and immediately he put his arms around me and held me safe and close. Always in my care. I could adore him for that alone. After a lifetime when nobody particularly cared, although I was loved as part of a robustly large family group, to have the devotion and care of one person was like having my very own pasha. "You're worried about the children."

"And amazed. I look at them in wonder sometimes." He grimaced. "Even more, now. That I could have made them when I can't even—"

I touched his lips with my finger to stop him saying it. "Once, my love. Just once. After a long journey. I've rested, but you have not. And we have this new problem, the poor maid. In the next few days I think that matter will resolve itself. We'll discover it was a squabble between the domestic staff, or someone Lizzie has dismissed or scolded, even. You know we will." I knew we wouldn't, but if the thought gave him solace tonight, I would say it.

He kissed my fingers before I removed them, allowing him to speak. "I know no such thing, but I appreciate your concerns. I think perhaps I need to get the matter into perspective. On top of everything else, to have your life threatened in this way, I won't deny it rocked me. I thought we'd reached a haven of sorts. By the end of the winter, I'd have a healthy wife, happy children and I'd be able to return home to face my mother secure in the knowledge that I had a healthy, happy family." He paused. "Then out of the blue you fell ill. So ill Carier worried for you." He smiled at the surprised expression in my eyes. "I questioned them both thoroughly after you fell ill." He sighed. "I won't be protected from the truth, Rose. Ever."

"Neither will I," I reminded him. "Don't even try. I can feel the strength returning, every day a little more, and the sickness merely proved a minor setback. Please, don't keep me out of this. Share with me." He'd taken too much on himself in the last weeks. Perhaps that was part of the reason for tonight. As it was, it gave him something else to worry about.

"Very well." He drew me close and kissed me with such tenderness that it brought tears to my eyes. After that he had to kiss them away. "I promise I'll keep you involved, every step of the way. Will that do?"

"For now."

He swung me around, laying me down next to him and rolling over me. "In the meantime, there's no reason both of us should suffer." He kissed me again, drawing it out this time, taking his time to explore me and love me.

His member didn't respond. It remained half-erect, stubbornly refusing to complete its journey. But Richard wouldn't let me touch it, wouldn't let me try to stimulate him back to full hardness. Instead, he lavished all his attention on me. He kissed down my body once more, and this time he stopped at the seat of my pleasure, teasing and tasting. The first occasion he'd done that to me, my shock was only exceeded by the joy he'd given me, but now I knew this was a way for him to regain his mastery over the art he'd made his own—the art of making love.

He moved down and slipped the tip of one finger into me while he took possession of the pearl of flesh that brought me the most pleasure, flicking it with his tongue while he spread his free hand over my backside, holding me to him like he was consuming a special treat. He worked me, slowly pushing his finger into me then adding another and scissoring them open to caress every part of my inner channel. When he discovered the spot that made me cry out and clutch handfuls of his hair, he laughed and lapped up the tribute my body gave to him, waiting to take long, sweeping licks over my clitoris and then sucking it into his mouth once more.

I erupted, my body straining against him, giving him all the love I could, physically and mentally devoting myself to him. Whatever he was, whatever he did, I was his willing slave. But not one without a brain. I wouldn't allow him to sink into self-recrimination and doubt, and I was glad he'd made this decision, to make me the recipient of his attentions.

When he came back to hold me, he was still in no state to make love to me, but apart from aching for him, wishing I could do to him what he did to me, I was glad. By that action he'd accepted me, by showing me his current inability to remain hard, he'd let me in, decided to share his weakness with me instead of pretending he was all strength. It would bring us closer. It would make us stronger, I was sure of it.

Chapter Twelve

Richard's problem was not a single incident. On the next night and the night following, the same thing happened. But I retained my belief that this was a temporary state of affairs while remaining cheerful in his presence and worrying in private. We made love in other ways, rediscovered how to please each other by touching and kissing, and I truly believed it could help to bring us closer. Another storm to weather together, something else we would deal with as a couple.

Left to himself, Richard would have gone away and brooded in private. It wasn't a problem he could turn to anyone else with, nothing he could ask anyone else about, so we would cope with it ourselves.

It always happened when he was about to enter me. I could imagine how debilitating it was, and I was almost relieved when my courses came on me after the third day and we could abandon attempts to make love but still spend the night together.

The fifth day after Richard's first attempt to make love to me had failed, not that I was counting, I asked him to join me in the music room. The previous day I had tested the beautiful harpsichord and found it adequate for my needs. As I had suspected, while the workmanship on the carcase was of the highest order, it decorated an instrument that was mundane at best, but I would not mention that to either Lizzie or her husband, neither of whom were particularly musical and were proud of the item. As a piece of furniture, it worked extremely well, but I'd have far rather had something much plainer but better constructed.

Richard closed his eyes and leaned his head back against the top edge of the sofa where he'd chosen to sit, a place he could watch me play and we could exchange glances and smiles. When I looked at his face, I saw exhaustion there. He'd taken everything on himself in the last few months, and our recent problem would not have helped him to regain anything like his usual demeanour of confident strength. That he still exuded it spoke for his force of will. But I was pleased to bring him this solace, and should he wish it, I'd play for him all afternoon and make this mediocre instrument work for him. I'd make it sing and dance if it would take the worry from his shoulders. Too much trouble piled up had brought him to this pass, and I'd ease his burden somehow.

I continued to play, choosing pieces I knew well and alternating them with new ones that I'd have to pause for when I turned the pages. I didn't want him moving, and when he tried, I shook my head. I'd spent a lot of my time as a girl turning pages for myself, and I could almost make it part of the music. "Oh, Rose is practicing again," meant I didn't have to make polite conversation with people I had little in common with, or try to embroider neatly, or any of the other pastimes considered suitable for a respectable unmarried lady. Which I mostly hated.

If, in those days, anyone had told me that I'd find a man as essential to my well-being as breathing, that he'd be a leader of society, heir to one of the richest estates in the country, I'd have scoffed. For one thing, where would I meet such a scion of the superb, and secondly, why would he look at me when he must have women falling at his feet? Well he did, and here we were. And I still had difficulty believing it sometimes. Like now, seeing the perfect being, dressed relatively casually today, but in clothes some of my Devonshire neighbours would have donned for a dinner with the squire, sitting listening to what I could make for him.

I ended with a quieter piece, deliberately easing off as I reached the end, although I could do that better on a pianoforte. The rhythmic rise and fall of his chest told me he'd settled into a restful state, if he wasn't actually asleep. When I lifted my hands from the keys, I realised he was deep in slumber. He'd slept restlessly last night, so I was glad to see him in that state today.

But not, unfortunately, for long. The door opened on a knock with a decisive click, and the rap of shoes against the parquet made Richard open his eyes. He snapped from sleep into wakefulness with hardly a movement, only his head coming forwards, alert once more. He sent me a regretful smile. "Thank you."

Then he turned to confront our intruder. Carier. He must have something urgent to say since he hadn't waited for my summons to enter. Startled, he made to back out, but Richard held up a restraining hand. "Please, come in. Close the door."

I saw the figure of one of our burly footmen outside before Carier closed the door a lot quieter than he'd opened it. Still guarded, then. I knew what a precious jewel felt like, and it wasn't a good feeling, not all of it. Good to know people cared, of course, but not so good to know that someone knew my every moment, probably knew the number of times I used the close-stool and which pot I preferred. That part I didn't like at all. But I could tolerate it. Better than being dead.

And I had to face it, there was a real possibility, however remote, of someone deciding that I needed to stop breathing. As long as I was married to Richard I remained a prime target for some people.

"My lord, I have news on two counts. Both are relevant, but they point us in different directions."

"Unfortunate." Richard waved a hand. "Take a seat, if you wish." A sign that Richard recognised Carier was on company business. Thompson's business. He never sat when he was acting as Richard's valet, but he was a partner in Thompson's and occupied a subtly different position in the hierarchy at those times.

Carier bowed. "I thank you, but no, sir." He lifted a sheet of paper, one side marked with smudges, scribbles and seals, all the marks of travel. "I have heard from Mrs. Thompson. She wrote to us while we were at sea, not in response to our recent query. She tells us that John Kneller escaped the press gang. She came upon the information from her more unusual sources."

Richard growled. "So that itch on the back of my neck meant something after all." I exchanged a glance with Carier. "How did Kneller do it?"

"His usual technique. Deception and charm. They took him in London and he said he was willing, but he wanted a last drink before he went aboard. He had a good head for alcohol, if you recall, my lord, could drink many men twice his size under the table. And that was what he did. But those men had taken our money, so they owed us something. They pressed another unfortunate, took him instead, and later assured us the work had been done."

Richard struck his open palm with a clenched fist. "I knew I should have attended to the matter myself. So when we thought ourselves safe, he was still in London, no doubt planning his revenge?"

Carier scratched his head. "We stripped him of his fortune and his name in society, so he started again. But on his own terms. Since the fastest ways to make money are illegal, I assume he reacquainted himself with his old contacts." John Kneller had been adept at smuggling. He knew people, and he knew the most valuable cargoes to buy and where to sell them.

"His persistence is admirable," I said. "Or it would be, under different circumstances. Did he contact his sister?"

Richard started. "I wrote to Gervase when we became suspicious. I doubt the letter has reached him yet."

"It has probably not, my lord, but there is a letter for you from Mr. Kerre. It was enclosed in Mrs. Thompson's missive. She sent it by private courier." He handed over the missive, and Richard glanced at the seal, then broke it and unfolded the sheet.

He skimmed it. "He hopes we arrived in one piece and he makes some jokes about the yacht." Since Richard had once owned a similar vessel that had exploded a few years before, I could guess at some of the jokes. "Ah yes. I'll read this part out, if I may. He writes, *Something of import occurred that I think you should be aware of. For some years now I've done business with a man called Barber. Good, solid, middle ranking, a man capable of good judgment. A few nights ago his housekeeper discovered him dead in his bedroom. Strangled. Barber was a single man. He had several young friends and liked to sponsor them in the professions of their choices, and his housekeeper said he'd made a new friendship recently.*"

Delicately put, but I think we all got the meaning.

"*There is no sign of the youth, but several items were missing. Some of value, small, portable pieces of jewellery and gold, and a letter I once wrote recommending Barber to another merchant. That was when he took a trip overseas and I could introduce him to a businessman there. Barber kept that letter locked up with his jewellery, and it was inventoried.*" Such letters could be valuable. This one had proved so.

"Gervase thinks I should know because of the housekeeper's description of the young man. Slight, probably blond, although he wore a wig most of the time, but his skin

166

was very fair and his brows pale, so she guessed his colouring from that. His eyes were grey. He spoke well, and once, in her hearing, he spoke of the Kerres and his acquaintance with them." He put down the letter. "He put the matter in the hands of Mrs. Thompson. The Fieldings and Smith, the Bow Street Runner, are also investigating the crime."

My heart missed a beat as I gasped for breath, trying, as had become natural to me, to appear normal. But surely it would be right to show some distress in these circumstances.

"I can add to that account, my lord," Carier said. He picked up his own letter, the seal clinging to the edge of the sheet. "She immediately began investigations and will continue to do so. The young man used the name of a dead sailor. She has discovered little at the time of writing, but found out that the youth had hired his lodgings but two weeks before he made the acquaintance of Barber. He met him at a coffee house known for assignations of a certain kind. The youth had new clothes, a new lodging and to all intents and purposes seems to have sprung from nowhere."

Richard swore, long and fluently. My ability to curse had been better than average, as I grew up in the country, but I had nowhere near his ability to string all the words together. Finally he snatched up the letter again. "Gervase increased his vigilance over Susan, suspecting that if her brother was back, he'd try to get in touch with her. Susan had no desire to see him." Susan was John Kneller's twin sister, but had taken a completely different path in life and was now under Gervase's guardianship. "Their suspicions were confirmed, that John Kneller was back in London. He tried to get in touch with his sister. He sent her a letter and gave her an address where she could reply. He said he'd obtained honest work and he was doing his best to start again. He'd been corrupted by Julia Drury, he said."

I made a sound of derision. "He didn't need Julia to show him the way."

"True enough," Richard agreed dryly.

Carier nodded his agreement. "He may have been seeking an excuse. But Miss Kerre had had enough."

I quirked a brow. Carier explained, "Mrs. Thompson writes that she has recently decided to adopt the family name as a sign that she wishes to put her past behind her." She had a good chance of that. Her previous career had included a stint as a courtesan, but she'd had only a handful of clients, the last of whom had wished to marry her. Her chance at respectability was snatched away when the man withdrew his offer after the scandal about her brother hit the press.

"I would have expected Gervase to consult me about the use of the family name. Did he speak to our father?" Richard sounded mildly surprised rather than shocked or unhappy about the decision. I would have wagered my favourite fan that his mother felt very different about the situation.

Carier almost smiled, the grim lines around his mouth relaxing slightly. "He informed them, my lord. With all due respect, there is little Lord and Lady Southwood can do about the decision. Mr. Kerre is independently wealthy, and does not depend on their goodwill for his wellbeing."

"I wouldn't put it like that," Richard said. "My father has a great deal of influence. But while he lives, Gervase is safe, and when he is gone, I will ensure my brother's wellbeing in society. Our mother will not be happy, however." He grinned. "I wish I'd seen her face."

He didn't say it, but I could hear it in the air. Lady Southwood would have to accept it, that one of her sons lived with another man and took his brother's bastard into his home as his own. A cosy household, Gervase with his lover, my brother Ian, and Richard's bastard daughter, Susan.

Of course, the fortune Gervase had made while he was in exile in India helped to reconcile society's hurt feelings. Gervase had taken to flirting with young ladies recently while making it clear they could hope for nothing from him but amusing conversation and the occasional escort. My brother was too serious minded to follow his example, but it wouldn't hurt Ian to take life with a little less gravity.

I picked up the music I'd been using and tidied it, ready to return it to the rack, but held the sheets in my hands, more to have something to do with them than for any other reason. I was pleased to note that my hands shook only a little.

"So Gervase is on his guard. Good," said Richard. "What else do you have, Carier? Gervase breaks off there, tells me that he will send more when he has it. He says he is glad we are out of town and out of reach." He put the letter aside, and gazed at us, eyes grave. "I'm not so sure of that. What we've done is give Kneller more familiarity with maritime affairs, if he needed them. After all, he began his chequered career by smuggling in the north."

Carier sighed. "He is being very careful and we don't have his whereabouts. However his sister received another letter, despite not replying to the first one. She gave it to Mr. Kerre. He gave it to Mrs. Thompson, who has copied it out for us, with Mr. Kerre's permission."

Richard glanced down and scanned the letter. "It says very little. Just repeats that he wants to see her and would she contact him." He looked up. "But it is dated after we left for Lisbon."

"We travelled at leisure, and we stopped and went ashore for a while when the crew fell ill," I pointed out. "He could easily have reached Lisbon before us. Or even left the letter to be delivered later, with a deliberately misleading date."

"I don't believe for a minute that he considered

169

apprenticeship or any other form of respectable employment," Richard said. "He'd have tried for another fortune, marriage, smuggling, forgery or just plain theft. Not an apprenticeship. That lasts seven years and leads to a situation as an honest working man. He wouldn't do that. Too impatient, too greedy. He wants the wealth and power without the responsibility."

That was his flaw. John Kneller considered himself a simulacrum of his father, but he was far from that. Only half of Richard, the public flamboyance without the underlying earthy power and the rock of dependability and hard work few people ever saw.

"I don't believe it either." The last time we'd seen him, he'd defied Richard, shown no desire to change. But I couldn't think why he'd send his sister such a letter. She'd be an idiot to accept his invitation, and she was far from that. "Even if Susan went to the meeting, she'd have taken ample protection with her. She has no reason to love her brother, save that of filial affection. And he killed most of that."

He sighed. "So Kneller murdered Barber and stole the letter of introduction. I had hoped I knew my own brother's handwriting. That letter went a long way towards persuading me to trust the man masquerading as Barber even as far as we did, since I knew that Gervase did not write those letters indiscriminately. We must hope that the unfortunate fake Barber is still in good health."

"So we can find him and get the truth out of him." The chances were that he wouldn't be in good health after that.

Carier nodded. "I thought it would be unwise to discount every other possibility, so I explored those too. I've made some good friends in the kitchen here," he said, not without a touch of smugness. "The news that I served in the military helped foster relations. Several of the footmen here once served in the Portuguese army, and ladies always have an eye for a soldier."

He cleared his throat and glanced at me. More than an eye, I guessed. "It didn't take much to evoke reminiscences, especially since the news isn't a great secret in this household. My lord, Joaquin is actually the older brother."

I blinked. "How can that be, if Paul is the marquês?"

Carier glanced at the paper he held, as if to refresh his memory. "His mother's marriage to his father was declared invalid by the courts at the request of his father, who wanted to be free to marry the present marquês's mother."

"They have different mothers?" I felt like my head was stuffed with padding. "I had no idea. I even spoke with him about mothers the other day, just telling him that my father had been married three times. He said nothing, although that would have been the perfect opening for him to mention the matter."

"He didn't want you to know," Richard said grimly. "For some reason he wanted to conceal it. You gave him the perfect opening, my love, but he failed to take it."

"Which means he didn't want to draw the matter to your attention, ma'am," Carier finished for us. "Perhaps he doesn't wish us to know that he resents his brother, if indeed he does."

"If matters were reversed between Gervase and me, I wouldn't resent him." From what he'd told me in the past, he'd have welcomed it. Richard hadn't wanted the responsibilities of the older son.

"But not all brothers feel that way," I said gently.

A smile flickered across his mouth. "No indeed."

"But to be replaced, and by the son of a foreigner, wouldn't he think he had cause?" I asked. Paul's English mother lived in her home country these days. Paul had spoken more than once of the affection his parents held for each other, so it had puzzled me that she hadn't spoken of Joaquin before. But a

171

different mother, and a respectably born one, might give her pause. She was a pleasant woman, though not an overpoweringly intellectual one or one given to much independence of thought. She would have accepted the status quo, if her husband had demanded it.

Richard frowned, putting one finger to his lips and pressing. The soft flesh formed a dimple, and I knew a need to touch him there. My body came on full alert, and I yearned to feel his on mine, over mine, in mine. My thighs dampened and my body longed for him. Not something I had planned, but something that happened nonetheless. An instant, unconsidered response that I did my best to quell as soon as it had arisen.

He looked up and caught me gazing at him with desire in my eyes. Too much to hope that I concealed it in time, although I returned my attention to the papers still in my hands, making a pretence of straightening the edges. I cringed inwardly. I had just made him feel worse. How could I do such a thing to him? The thought of what we could do in isolation had brought images to my mind that had nothing to do with the conversation and everything to do with my constant desire for him. A desire he couldn't fulfil.

I wet my suddenly dry lips and hastened to move the ostensible discussion on. "We should receive a summons to court shortly. If the Portuguese court is like the English and more especially the French, it lives on gossip. We'll hear all we need to know and more there."

"Indeed, ma'am. And until then, you should rest and restore your spirits." Carier wasn't just talking to me. He knew something wasn't right between Richard and me. He might even suspect what it was, given that we had spent some time sleeping apart. We should once more be presenting a united front against the world, but there were cracks in the façade, something I was trying desperately to mend.

"So," Richard said, as if the uncomfortable moment hadn't occurred, "Joaquin's mother was under the apprehension that she was married to his father, but his father later proved she was not, or someone paid to have it proved. Did her family have any influence?"

Carier shook his head. "She was a daughter of a hidalgo of great renown and little money. A soldier. Because her father was a national hero at the time, the late marquês married her. I don't know in what way the marriage was irregular, but there are many ways for an influential Catholic gentleman to obtain an annulment. An acknowledgement that the marriage wasn't valid and therefore the children of the marriage are illegitimate." He paused. "They can also be reversed, for a price."

I'd heard of such things but never encountered them in practice. "Why did he change his mind so soon after the marriage?"

Carier's voice turned softer, regretful. "It became an unfortunate marriage. The lady had given birth to Joaquin, and one other, a baby who died shortly after birth. The couple argued and then the lady's father retired and lost his fortune in unwise speculations. One of the servants, the head housemaid, remembers the arguments between them. She became a shrew. Then the marquês travelled to England and met Paul's mother. He fell deeply in love with her and determined to make it possible to marry her."

I sighed. "What an unfortunate series of events. And how sad for everyone involved. Is the first wife still alive?"

Carier shook his head. "She died of the smallpox fifteen years ago."

What a sad tangle.

"The marquês accepted Joaquin into the household after

her death and acknowledged him as his bastard."

"A kind act that could have added to the older son's resentment." Richard pressed his fingers to the bridge of his nose. "And since the marquêsa has never mentioned him, I presume she resented him or merely cut him out of her life. So to get back to the immediate point, Joaquin had cause to put the poison on the lemon cream. Or had someone else do it."

"To harm Lizzie, or at the least rid her of the child she might be carrying by making her ill. But she has a boy already." I frowned.

"Easier to get rid of the baby with the mother gone. Children die all the time." Carier cut his words off abruptly, the knowledge of what he'd said urgent in his eyes. "I beg your pardon, my lord, my lady."

"Nothing to forgive when you speak the truth." Richard leaned back and sighed. "What is set aside can sometimes be reinstated, if there is no impediment like a living heir. Or sometimes a court will reinstate a title in another person. So while, as matters stand, Joaquin could not inherit, he could be invested with the title after the death of his widowed brother. What if Paul confided in him that he and Lizzie thought they were pregnant again? What if Joaquin decided to rid himself of a problem before it became worse?"

"We cannot forget that. But we must remember that there are two suspects," I said. "At least. Barber could be a tool of Joaquin, just as much as he could be one of John Kneller's minions."

In the short silence the very air tensed, as if it would snap. Richard broke it.

"We are isolated here. If the danger comes from inside the house, not outside, we might be better in a place we can guard more securely. Somewhere we have ultimate jurisdiction over the comings and goings. While we did not suspect anyone inside the house, I felt reasonably secure here, but these new revelations give Joaquin a stronger motive to rid himself of his sister-in-law and her child, or children. If his mother brought him up to resent Paul, as appears likely given her history, it would strengthen his determination to become the next Marquês de Aljubarrotta."

He got to his feet. "Above all, my love, I want you and our children safe." I knew what he meant. He wanted men of his own choosing in place to ensure our safety. His next words confirmed my suspicion. He glanced at Carier. "I want to send you ahead to the house in town to ascertain everything is in place. It may become necessary for us to remove there sooner than we thought. We may staff a smaller establishment with people entirely of our choosing. I won't leave Rose alone in the house with someone we suspect of murder."

"What about Lizzie? We can't leave her here, surely?" I put in.

"She may come with us, and bring young Paul with her," Richard said.

I nodded.

Carier scratched his pate, leaving his wig slightly askew when he drew his hand away. "I'll make sure the Lisbon house is staffed with Thompson's people, my lord. We brought some with us, and I'll discover others."

"In Portugal?" I asked.

For the first time in what seemed like forever, Richard smiled. "Yes, my love, even in Portugal. We will manage and I will have you and our children properly protected. Perhaps then I can sleep at night."

And maybe he could make love again.

Chapter Thirteen

At dinner he didn't broach the subject of our removal to town, or the possible danger that remained here, even though every forkful of food that I brought to my lips came under his close scrutiny. He took care to have a glass of wine from the same decanter I used, and sipped it before I had any from my own glass.

His anxiety was almost palpable, and I couldn't do anything to dissipate it. Except to allow him to take control, for his own sake, if not for mine. I hated the necessity, but I had learned that sometimes it was best to give way while at other times taking a firm stance was more acceptable. If anyone had told me that before I'd met the fascinating, complex person I married, I'd have laughed them to scorn.

Lizzie noticed, but Paul did not. After dinner Lizzie and I went to the drawing room alone, and Joaquin excused himself, saying he had some business letters to write, while Richard stayed with Paul, probably to broach the subject of leaving. I tackled Lizzie.

"We'd like to spend some time in Lisbon, Lizzie. We don't want to cause any more trouble, and in any case, I should like to do some shopping." I hated that she felt so responsible for the trouble we'd had in her delightful house, especially since there was a strong probability that we'd drawn the trouble here.

She handed me my dish of tea before she laughed. "Really, Rose? You weren't always so keen to shop."

I took a sip of the refreshing brew. "I didn't have as much

to shop for, then." I glanced up at her. "Nor as much to spend."

As I'd hoped, that roused her to more laughter. "I do admit, that is one of the more appealing aspects of shopping these days. And you did have some time deprived of the pleasure." To Lizzie, that would have been purgatory, but shopping was the last thing on my mind when I'd lain day after day in bed waiting for my strength to return.

"I love seeing new places. Lizzie, I never would have imagined that, but I do enjoy it. Lisbon is so different to anywhere else I've visited, I want to explore it. And I need to ensure that my court gown is properly set out. I didn't order it sent here to the *palacio* because there wouldn't be much point. There's only one place I'll wear that mantua, and that's at court. It's so unwieldy, I don't know how they managed to wear them all the time in the old days."

"Is it the same one from your presentation?"

"Yes, with a little judicious alteration. I can't say to bring it into fashion, because it was never in fashion to begin with, but to add a few touches. I ordered it put on a figure and pressed, so it should be ready for me. Is there any word on our appearance at court?"

"No. You can see the palace without seeing the king, you know."

I smiled. "I'd like that. To find my way around before I go on show as one of its exhibits. Is it a beautiful place?"

She considered, one finger pressed to the dimple at the side of her mouth, as she often did when thinking. "It's very grand and full of works of art, but I have to confess I don't like it overmuch. I've discovered a passion for the smaller, more intimate places." She laughed merrily. "I know, who would have thought that my sister preferred the grandiose and I the intimate? But it's only in buildings, my dear. Palaces intimidate me. Clothes do not."

I took my time perusing her pale blue silk gown, worn over a flounced white petticoat. Triple lace ruffles adorned her sleeves and the lace at her neckline was equally fine. "I can see that."

"You still feel reticent sometimes, don't you, Rose?"

I couldn't deny it to the woman who knew me so well. "Sometimes. But Richard helps and so do the grand costumes. If I'm feeling particularly nervous, I dress very grand. Richard knows that."

"Does he do it himself?"

I took a sip of my tea. Despite his openness with me, Richard preferred to keep his private life and thoughts exactly that—private. I wouldn't allow even my sister to cross the line in that respect. "No. It's the way he was reared. To expect to always be in the public eye, to keep something of himself inside. Surely Paul does that?"

"Yes, in a way, but not the same way Richard does. I don't know what your husband is thinking half the time, and sometimes he behaves one way when I know perfectly well he's thinking something else. He's always very kind to me, but inside, I'm wondering if he approves or disapproves, and why I should care. But I do. I find myself desperate for his approval."

I couldn't understand how people would feel like that, why they should care, but like Lizzie, they did. Undoubtedly. He had people fawning around him, people he couldn't help financially or socially, people who had no reason to court him, but they did. Difficult for me, because I loved him, and different rules applied with love.

But I was never in any doubt how he felt, what he thought, not because he always told me but because I could almost sense it. I knew. I shook my head, trying to understand. The heavy earrings he'd given me recently swung against my cheeks, reminding me that he was always with me in some

178

form, but not in a menacing way. He just was, as I was with him. "He is a private man, underneath all the extravagance and display."

Lizzie knew that already, she must, from the way he behaved in public gatherings.

We finished our tea, and I watched Lizzie carefully. She wasn't sure about my lighthearted words, my reasons to visit Lisbon. My sister had never been foolish. I was proved right by her next words. "So you want to go to Lisbon to replenish your wardrobe? Or is it something else?"

It hurt me not to tell her, but I was in no doubt where my loyalties lay. "I want to see the city. We'd love to return here, with your permission, but it's obvious Paul will have to investigate the sad death of the maid, and we don't want to intrude on you at this time."

"So you don't think the death had anything to do with you after all?" Lizzie shot me a shrewd glance. She was too close.

"Tell her." The voice came from the door. Richard, firmly stating the facts. He entered the room with Paul and closed the door behind him. "She needs to know. I have told Paul some of it, and we agreed to come in here to discuss the matter with you."

I sighed in relief. Richard must have persuaded Paul she had to know, and I wanted it too. Her child could be in danger, even if only as a side effect of an attempt on us. I waited until he came to sit beside me. Paul took a seat in an armchair set between our sofas, which faced each other. I glanced at Richard, who nodded.

So I told her.

"John Kneller didn't get on the ship that was supposed to take him away," I said. "Richard arranged to have him pressed, but they lied. Took someone else after he escaped. We've only just discovered that. After the events of the spring, he might have decided to give up his plotting. He barely got away with his life that time."

Lizzie gasped. "So he's back?"

Richard didn't put his hand over mine—he joined me on my sofa and curved his arm around my shoulders. "John could be here, or he could be in London, directing the affair. We're trying to find out for certain."

Tension tightened my stomach. I stared at Richard, and he met my gaze with a solemn one of his own. He knew I was thinking of his son, the man who wanted Richard destroyed above all men in the world. Not just dead, but *destroyed*, so it would be typical of him to attack Richard's loved ones first.

He had the same thought as I did. "That request I made of you? Now it's a command. Until we clear up this matter you are to go nowhere, in or out of the house, without company."

I would do that for his sake. "But it has to go both ways. You must agree to it, or I will not. The children will be guarded at all times, of course, but I reserve the right to move about at my own discretion."

He knew more and he hadn't told me. I wouldn't allow that.

"You really think Kneller is capable of committing these crimes? Going to these lengths?" My sister had met him when he'd visited Devonshire, our home county, and tried to charm our sister Ruth to his side, as well as threatening my life repeatedly. She should know from that experience what lengths Kneller would go to.

"It's like him," I said. "It's his habit to attack his enemies at their weakest point, and I am Richard's weak point. As are the children."

Her gasp echoed around the shockingly silent room. I could understand her reluctance to believe the lengths John would go to, to get his way. Until faced with the cold, hard reality of the man Richard had fathered, it was hard to believe anyone would do this. But Kneller delighted in controlling people, being the puppet master. Privately, I thought he was aware he was missing something, natural affection, the ability to link and communicate with people. So he despised them and thought of them merely as ciphers, not equal to himself.

"We thought we'd sent him to the navy, across the ocean," Richard said. "But he has considerable personal charm and a wiliness of character that people don't expect in one so young. He sometimes works through agents. He has done it before. He has caught many people out. His crowning glory is his ruthlessness. He will kill without hesitation." He paused. "It's what makes him so dangerous. That and a willingness to sacrifice anything for revenge. Including, I'm guessing, his own life."

An appalled silence fell again. I felt obliged to break it. "He could have decided that revenge isn't worth the candle. He's spent his fortune and someone else's trying to achieve it. Perhaps he's finally realised it's not worth wasting his life on." A desperate thought, but if Kneller had considered power and influence worth pursuing, rather than revenge for something that had not been Richard's fault, then he might give up his campaign against us.

Richard shook his head. "I doubt it. We know he evaded the men sent to press him. We know that the real merchant, Barber, was killed and the letter stolen along with a number of other items. So I want John's whereabouts confirmed to me, and I want to repeat what I tried to do before. Only this time I will make sure of it. Personally. But until we know, I want my wife closely guarded."

"How much time before we know?" I demanded.

"About three weeks to get a reply from London, I think," he

said.

That sounded reasonable. "Very well, for the next month I promise to take special care and only go about accompanied." It seemed fair, to allay his worries, and he would have more liberty to investigate the murders. "But you must promise to take care too."

"I promise." We exchanged a long look.

I narrowed my eyes. He'd given in too easily. Richard hated being trammelled, and on the few occasions I had insisted on it, he had responded with an uncharacteristic irritation. Well, he could learn to bear it, and so would I.

Paul turned to Lizzie. "You too. I do not care if he regards you as collateral or as a prime target, you will not allow yourself your usual freedoms."

Lizzie laughed. "The arrogance of husbands!" She straightened in her chair. "I will take every precaution, of course, but I won't allow anyone to curtail my freedom. And I will not cower from danger."

"But you will take care," he persisted.

Her voice softened. "Of course I will. I swear it."

Paul's lips quirked into a smile. "Thank you. English women have a reputation for forthrightness and an independence of thought. It was what first attracted me to them. Now I have one of my own, I don't intend for her to get away from me easily."

"I want to go to Lisbon," Richard said. "To ensure the house we have there is properly set up and guarded. I'll check every door, every window and only my own servants will wait on us there." He glanced around, at the large windows that could be flung open in summer to catch every stray breeze. "This *palacio* is very beautiful, but not very defendable." His level of anxiety was understandable. He was not merely taking care of us, he was taking care of himself.

"So once you know we are safe, you can set about finding him?"

"Exactly."

"So we are to prepare ourselves for a journey." I forced a smile, but I felt my lips tremble.

"You want to be somewhere you can control." Lizzie sighed. "I understand. But come back when you know, won't you?"

Paul put his hand over hers and squeezed. "I will have to call the authorities and inform them of the death. Otherwise rumours will spread. I want them to consider it an accident, for now, and I've presented it as such. Bad cream in the sweet." He glanced at Richard. "So what are we left with?"

Richard sighed. "We have several possibilities." He ticked them off on his fingers one by one. "Barber. John Kneller through Barber. A series of coincidences, something I consider extremely unlikely. But the lemon cream was poisoned, and two people in this house are known to be particularly fond of that dish." *Was fond,* I thought, but I said nothing. Richard continued. "When my wife and children are involved, I take no chances. While I'm almost sure Kneller is responsible for this recent attack, we can't discount other possibilities."

A moment of fraught silence ensued, one I had no inclination to break.

Paul spoke first, his tones frigid as ice. "You suspect Joaquin?"

"We know of his history," Richard said gently. "That he is your elder brother. I also know that the Catholic church can be somewhat *flexible* when it comes to marriage decisions. Rose may not have been the principal target of the poisoner."

If that was so, then the accident on board could be considered an accident, and the strangling due to something else. Falling out between lovers, greed or something else. But if the poisoning was not of Joaquin's doing, then the series of incidents, plus even the sickness on board during our journey, could form part of a sickening chain. I wanted Joaquin guilty, God help me.

Paul rose to his feet. In his glittering clothes, the colours darker than the ones Richard preferred but no less magnificent, he stood tall and forbidding. "I would not have thought that you, above all people, would have doubted the bond that exists between brothers. Joaquin is without question innocent of this." He crossed the room to the window, turned and came back, the only reason for his perambulation, I suspected, to regain control over a temper I had not suspected him of possessing.

Lizzie watched him carefully, but not with an apprehension that might have indicated that she'd been the recipient of his anger at any time. Concern for him showed in her gaze before she turned her attention to us.

"Believe me, Joaquin did not do this, or have any knowledge of it. He doesn't wish to be marquês. That was his mother, whose bitterness and ambition eventually drove him away."

Paul returned to the sofa and took her hand, gazing down at his wife in a manner that revealed his love for her. "Joaquin has no wish to usurp my position and was the first to congratulate us when our child was born. He was relieved. His mother wrecked his early life, and while I understand what she did, Joaquin has steadfastly refused to challenge the decision of the courts." When Lizzie tugged his hand, he sat next to her once more, a little closer, retaining her tight clasp. "I am sure enough of him to know that if you investigate, you will find nothing. I will even help you, should you wish it."

I was astonished. For Paul, a man of good sense, to say this, he must have good reason. We had to trust him in this matter. Richard liked him and so did I. Paul was a man of honour, and a man who didn't take his responsibilities lightly. He'd known Joaquin for most of his life. It was enough for me.

Richard shook his head. "From what you say, it won't be necessary to investigate. Would you trust Joaquin with the care of your wife and children?"

"I not only do, but I have done so in the past. I have no compunction in leaving Joaquin to ensure her safety. He has engaged personal servants for us, offered the hospitality of his home. Any arguments you may witness between us are because we are both hotheads."

That came as news to me. I had never thought of Paul as a hothead. At one point, I didn't think his cold reserve boded well for a marriage with my passionate sister. "You concur, Lizzie?"

She nodded. "He is a man with a deep sense of honour. He's spoken to me of his mother. It grieved him to leave her, but he could not allow her to speak of his family in that way. True, his father did wrong in having his marriage put aside, but Joaquin didn't want to usurp Paul. He saw the responsibilities associated with the title, and he agreed that Paul was more suited for the role. He has little patience with court affairs. He cares only for his vines and the development of good wines. You have heard him speak of his passion. You know this."

Richard glanced at me, and I inclined my head. I would trust my sister, a woman in which deep passion and shrewd common sense held a perfect balance. "Then we will not pursue that line of enquiry." A man's word was his bond, and both Paul and Richard had just given theirs.

"I want that merchant brought to justice," Paul said.

Richard nodded. "As do I." He lifted his head and gave Lizzie a piercing look. "That revelation has just made things easier. I still wish to remove to the Lisbon house until we have resolved the matter, but this gives me a chance to ensure the house there is ready to receive us, and to further my enquiries. I will go tomorrow."

"I would come with you," Paul said. "I know the authority you have in your own country, but I have authority here. Portugal is a land where the formal approach is preferred. I can open doors and command attention."

Richard didn't pause for a moment. "Then I accept. Thank you. But I don't wish to leave my wife and children unprotected."

"Joaquin," Paul reminded him.

Then there was a pause, but only while Richard bit his lip, frowning. "We may come back the next day, the day after tomorrow."

"That is Sunday, All Saints' Day. It is an important day in the calendar. Everyone will be at church, and some will not travel or do any work on that day. It wouldn't look well if I didn't attend at least one service, also."

Lizzie turned to him with a rustle of silk, immediately concerned. "Should I come? Do you wish to be seen with your wife at your side?"

"It's not essential, and I would rather you stayed here, where you are safer. I think you can be slightly unwell and attend a service here, if you wish."

Lizzie had converted to Catholicism. As she said to me at the time, "It doesn't matter to me in what way I worship God, and it would make things much easier for Paul. Why should I worry if they burn incense or not?"

Of course the matter was far more complex, but trust my sister to see through all the politics and the scheming surrounding the various religions to find the truth of the matter. Turning Catholic would ally her with the Jacobites, for one thing, and I would wager they had been in touch with her.

Since Culloden, they'd been desperate to reclaim some kind of power in Europe. But my sister would claim to have no interest and send them away.

"I doubt I'll be attending with you," Richard said, "but I might seek out an Anglican church. It would be a good idea if I nailed my colours to the mast." It would indeed. It would save us a heap of Jacobite petitioners calling at our door, thinking they had some ingress.

I had never felt the need to attend church every day and twice on Sundays, being content with a single attendance on the Sabbath, but I would forego the pleasure this time. "I shan't be attending," I told him, "so I need to be very good until I can reach a church, do I not?"

Richard burst into laughter at the arch smile I sent him. "Minx," he declared with wholehearted conviction. "You will be very good indeed and take care to obey your husband in every way."

Paul brought us back down to earth. "It is a shame, because officials will be at home with their families. We may have to stay until Monday at least."

"If we don't achieve what we want to tomorrow." Richard made a decision, firm in his resolve. "We'll leave early and try to get the business done in a day. I want to check the manifests for the ships in port, and I want to find and hold Barber, by whatever means I can."

"Then I will request the presence of my largest footmen. I have some authority to hold prisoners," Paul said.

"So we may question him as we would," Richard replied.

"Exactly." Paul gave a grim smile. "I am sure we can get the business done faster that way."

"I will miss you," Lizzie murmured.

Paul turned to look at her, and his expression was for a

moment unguarded, adoring her, and with a promise in his gaze that I understood only too well.

The moment took me by surprise, and when I dared to glance Richard's way, his slight smile told me he'd noticed. Hot blood coursed under my skin, and I tried to ignore the fact that my sister had a particularly faraway expression. I changed the subject hastily. "You trust us to stay here and be safe?"

He gave me a wry smile. "I plan to leave Carier behind, as well as the largest of the men we engaged in Lisbon. Also, you will promise to lock yourself in at night." Carier would sleep in the bedroom between mine and the nursery. And he'd station servants at the doors.

After an evening at cards, in which Richard and I cheated outrageously and Lizzie and Paul merely watched our efforts with bemusement, we went up to bed in much better spirits.

I had hopes for that night.

They were dashed yet again. But as he lay on my body, heated with his efforts to please us both at the same time instead of to bring me to climax and leave him behind, I thought I felt the wet trace of a tear.

I would not have that. I pushed him up so I could look into his eyes.

Sorrow clouded them. "I love you, Rose, so dearly. I have no idea why this has happened."

"You're worried and tired." I paused. I wouldn't think of any other possibility, but the traitorous thought occasionally intruded. What if his condition proved permanent?

Nothing. In that case, nothing. I would still love him, would still want him with me at night, would still take pleasure in having him with me. I would never allow him to sleep apart from me again when we were in the same house. Ever.

Some days were made for naps, and the next day seemed like one of them. I missed Richard, who had left that morning for Lisbon, and I worried, even when I decided to sleep away the afternoon. Dreams disturbed me, and I woke crying out, though ten minutes after the experience I couldn't remember what it was about. A lingering aura of terror remained with me, so I elected to read.

Returning on my own to the bedroom later that evening, I reflected on the ease with which Richard and I had taken to sharing the same bed again, despite our other problems. It was our natural state, as natural as breathing, and although I had spent most of my life sleeping alone, I found it difficult to get used to once more. I wanted to turn over and feel his arms close around me. I wanted to snuggle up to his heat and the comfort of his body. Consequently, I slept badly. And woke to a note.

He must have sent it overnight. It was dated the previous day.

Rose,

Know that you have brought me the greatest happiness I have ever known. It is more than love, it's companionship, friendship and a shared life. I have joined with you, truly become as one. Whatever lies ahead for us, remember that, and remember that I do what I do for your health and security. Living without you doesn't bear contemplating. I will not consider it.

Richard

He'd signed it with his usual flourish, but with a few extra crosses. Kisses I would make last until his return.

No wonder some people thought us foolish. But I can't say that I cared much for their opinion in this instance.

Meeting for dinner that night seemed terribly uneven. Just Joaquin and us. With Richard's permission, Paul had brought him up to date, and although he was understandably anxious, we spoke little of the business. We could not do anything to help, so we tried to relax, as much as we could.

Chapter Fourteen

I woke with a suddenness unusual to me. My eyes snapped open, and I stared up into the pleated silk of the bed canopy. Something had woken me, but I could hear nothing now. I glanced towards the window. It was still night, pitch dark outside.

A rustle made me turn my head to where the connecting door joined my room with the sitting room.

Carier stood there. I recognised his silhouette immediately. I sat up in bed, drawing the covers with me. "What is it?"

"I've apprehended the merchant, ma'am. He is ranting, and I thought it best to rouse you since you asked to be apprised of developments. He tried to get back in through the dairy. He must have stolen a key or had one cut. But we were waiting for him."

I appreciated that he respected me and my opinions enough to consider me an adequate substitute for his master. "Where is he?"

"I have him secured in the dairy. We captured him as he entered. I have told no one yet. Do you wish me to rouse the household?"

"No, only Nichols."

Nichols appeared as if conjured by a spirit, noiselessly gliding into the room. "I am already here, my lady. Please wait outside, Mr. Carier."

She already had a loose robe ready for me, and she helped me into it with the minimum of fuss. I paused while she put my hair to rights, pinning up my nighttime braids, although I had no idea why she considered it necessary, and I took possession of the sturdy pistol she handed me. I was a better shot than most people knew, and it remained my weapon of choice.

Carier returned. "What do you wish to do, ma'am?"

At last, something to do. I would not allow anyone to deter me. "Question him, of course."

"This way, ma'am." Carier led the way down the stairs and along a service corridor, past the large, well-appointed kitchen where servants would be slumbering, and past several other rooms. If this house followed the same pattern as the ones I knew, the dairy would be outside or in a room with an outside wall. The better to allow the dairymaids to enter and leave without disturbing the household.

We entered a small room with a distinctive chill. No doubt it was on the cooler, north side of the house and had thick walls to promote what coolness there was. The shelves mounted on the walls held a collection of large, shallow bowls, some of them covered with clean cloths.

Someone had pushed the large centre table aside, and in its place a man sat on a chair, secured to it with thick lengths of rope. His mouth was unbound, but a man stood silently by holding a kerchief and another stood at the door. They were both our footmen. Thompson's footmen.

The room was illuminated softly by two candles set in holders on the shelves with small mirrors set behind them. Enough light for me to see the man's expression of sneering hatred.

"Since we know you're not Barber, what do we call you?"

"Sweetheart?" His jeering mockery, using the name Richard preferred to call me in our private moments, jarred me. But I said nothing. He shrugged, or tried to, but he was too tightly secured to make a convincing job of it. "Jerry. Call me Jerry."

Carier stood by my side, Nichols at my back. I kept my distance. The chair wasn't fastened to the floor, so he could have made an attempt to jerk it forwards. "Well then, Jerry, tell me. Why did you kill Crantock?"

Jerry pursed his mouth. "I didn't. But he had to go. He saw too much and he'd failed."

"Failed?"

"That sickness aboard ship?"

Ah. That explained a few things. With the poisoned lemon cream, I should have thought of it before, but subsequent events had driven the seemingly natural events on board out of my mind. So the dessert had been the second attempt to kill us, not the first. And poor Crantock had died for it. That and his ability to identify the mysterious youth for us. A youth I was more than sure was John Kneller.

"You'll hang anyway, for knowing about the death and aiding the murderer. I'll make sure of that."

"So why should I tell you anything?"

"We could be of great help to you. If you're an accomplice, if you didn't kill Crantock, it might be transportation instead of hanging." But he'd caused the death of the maid. He'd hang for that. Not that I was fool enough to remind him of that now.

His expression changed, softened. He was considering our offer. If he was a paid accomplice, he'd turn coat for the chance of saving his life. "What do you want to know?"

"Who are you working for?"

"I don't work for anyone." But he lowered his gaze after a moment, and his mouth twitched an infinitesimal amount. The candles sent a sharp chiaroscuro onto his face, and we could see every movement.

"You're lying."

"Am I?"

I glanced at Carier. "The name," Carier said.

"And the description," I added. "In exchange for our word that you were not responsible for Crantock's death." Did he even know about the maid? He'd poisoned the cream, thinking that Lizzie and I would eat it, not that anyone else would suffer, and Lizzie had treated the matter with discretion. Barber—Jerry—was English, and might not know Portuguese well enough to find out from the villagers, some of whom were related to the dead girl.

Jerry tried to lean back, and the chair legs scraped against the stone floor. "An angel. A man so beautiful he took my breath away. And he loved me. But you can't pin him down like ordinary mortals. Strong, with a body that made me worship him. Fine features, grey eyes. He asked me to call him John. An angel's name." His voice gentled as he spoke, and his eyes grew dreamy, faraway.

The hammer fell, and finally we knew for sure.

John had seduced him into obedience. That was his way. Emotion could bind tighter than money, especially when he had none. No emotion, that is. John could always get money, by stealing, smuggling or even prostituting himself out to men or women. He had a seductive personality, made worse because he felt nothing himself. He could calculate to a nicety when someone was ready to fall for him and act on it without compunction, without guilt. That was something he didn't get from Richard. He presented a cold, heartless façade to much of the world, but underneath lay the heart of a sensitive man who cared deeply, sometimes too much. The two men were mirror images of each other. John, passionate and caring on the surface, frigidly insensitive about anyone but himself and calculating beneath, and Richard, exactly the opposite.

I needed no more confirmation. All our other speculation was useless. John Kneller was in Portugal and he wanted us dead.

"So you're doing this for love?" I asked.

"That, and for justice. Your husband has treated his son shamefully. He has never given him his due. That's all he wants."

Lies, but lies John had used to his advantage before. I should have let Richard kill him last year, but I couldn't bear the thought of a father killing his son. I should have done it myself. Carier would have helped me.

I didn't bother to respond, and when Jerry began to growl insults, I felt almost weary of it. I was so tired of hearing those stories. I glanced around. "We can't keep you here all night. The maids will want to use it in the morning. Carier, do we have somewhere we can keep him?"

"Indeed, ma'am. A secure cellar well away from the main part of the house."

At Carier's nod, our men untied him, keeping hold of his arms.

Jerry spat, the result landing in a sickening shiny spot on the well-scrubbed stone floor. "You think you have us, don't you? I might have failed in my mission, but the other plan is still intact."

"You were sent to kill me," I said wearily.

"And your children," Jerry added. "You're in adjoining rooms; that makes it easier. But he can finish you off after he's seen to his father."

I went still. "What do you mean?"

Carier clapped a pistol to the side of his head. "Tell me now or I'll drop you where you stand. That is not a threat. It's a promise."

Jerry shrugged. "I'd tell you anyway, just to see your face. He's set a bomb. Nothing you can do about it. It's probably gone off by now. I was to take care of you while he made sure of his lordship."

Panicked, I turned hurriedly to leave the room, no longer concerned with the foolish man, but filled with terror. I couldn't believe that was true. Not Richard, not like that. I had to tell someone, send someone after him. Even go after him myself.

I let my arm drop to my side, the one holding the weapon, and in my haste, I stumbled on a loose piece of flagstone. One of the men moved forwards to help me as I regained my balance. That was Jerry's chance.

Events seemed to speed up. I heard a shout as Jerry broke free from his captors in a vicious movement that spoke of the rookeries. He leaped forwards and grabbed my arm to pull me back against him. He dragged it almost out of its socket, then, as I landed hard against his body, he twisted it behind me. I cried out in pain, trying to wrenching away, but by then the wretch had my pistol. As I turned back to him, he pointed it at me.

The shot sounded like a veritable explosion in the confines of the small room. I barely had time to throw my body sideways, but I wasn't fast enough. Pain seared my arm. That, and the wet gush of blood, told me he'd hit me.

Pain tends to incapacitate by its very existence, but I'd given birth, I reminded myself. I could handle this level of agony.

I rolled towards the wall when I hit the floor, moving out of the way of the men struggling to recapture Jerry. By now, although my arm stung like the devil, I realised he'd only grazed me. Blood poured over me, but flesh wounds sometimes bleed the worst. It didn't spurt and I didn't feel the terrible coldness that presaged a severe wound. Jerry had no more bullets to use. That desperate bid to escape had finished him.

The smell of powder and singed linen filled the small room. The bullet had gone into the plaster of the inner wall behind my head. The pain had incapacitated me for long enough to prevent me retaliating immediately. I took some deep breaths, and then let the last one out noisily. The breaths helped me regain control, think straight. The last, noisy breath, I hoped, persuaded him he'd hit his target.

Shouts and screams filled the air from outside. Just what we needed. We'd roused the servants.

Another shot burst out, and I thought I was done for until I regained my senses. It took a few seconds for me to realise that the shot wasn't for me, and it sounded different to the first one. Our men were retaliating. My hair had fallen over my eyes, and I squinted through the tumble at the chaos around me, my mind in turmoil.

"My lady, my lady!"

"Lady Strang, ma'am!"

Not Carier. I opened my eyes fully and shook the hair away. Nichols leaned over me, her hair coming loose from its neat knot, a smoking pistol in her hand. She tossed it aside and touched me. "Oh God, oh God!"

One thing, I had to say one thing. "Go after Richard, Carier. You can get to Lisbon in two hours. Go now!"

"My lady?" He sounded torn. When I first married Richard, all his concern was for his master. He'd cared for me because Richard did. I heard a different note in his voice now, and I knew he'd stay with me if I needed him.

"It's a flesh wound, I swear. Carier, go!" He must know that I could distinguish between a slight wound and a serious one.

He jerked his head in a sharp nod and got to his feet.

The fumbling of a key in a lock and the slamming of the

outer door told me he'd obeyed my order. I didn't know if Jerry had been bluffing, but I wouldn't take that chance. Not with Richard's life.

"How is she? Should I ride for a doctor?" Joaquin's voice, concerned.

I swore and made it satisfyingly rich. "I'm fine, he barely grazed me. Help me up, Nichols." She grasped my shoulders, and I cried out in pain. "Well, not completely fine, but it's not as bad as it looks. Flesh wounds sometimes bleed a lot. What happened after I went down?"

"Barber grabbed your weapon and shot at you. Carier has killed him." This time she took more care helping me to sit. People filled the room, but not enough to obscure the grisly sight across the room from me. Jerry lay half-propped up against the opposite wall, a bloody mess where his head should have been.

Nichols tore at my robe and gown, clearing the wound. Then I heard her sigh in relief.

"I told you." The wound smarted, but it was in no way dangerous. Damn the man, taking a ridiculous chance for his lover. John Kneller did that to people—incited insane devotion. I could understand it, given that Richard was his father, but it was a blasted nuisance. I waved feebly at the gun lying on the floor and winced. "Don't leave that lying around. It's one of a pair."

I glanced up to see the worried, drawn features of Paul's brother-in-law. "What happened? How did he get in here?" he demanded.

I motioned with my uninjured hand to one of our footmen. "Tell him." The man rapidly brought Joaquin up to date.

Nichols didn't bother to try to unfasten my gown any further but found a small pair of scissors from the rubble on the floor and cut the sleeve off me. She used the remnants of the garment to press against the wound on my upper arm. "I can fix you up." She turned her head and addressed one of the servants crowding into the room. "Help me get my lady to her room and bring some hot water."

I tried not to flinch when they helped me to my feet because I knew I couldn't afford to be treated as an invalid. But it did hurt. However, I needed to stay in control and in full knowledge of what was going on. There was protection and there was smothering. I had reason to know the difference.

In my room, Nichols helped me tenderly onto the bed. Joaquin crossed the room and pushed aside the drapes. "It's as quiet as the grave out there."

At least he could make me laugh. Nichols found a plain dressing gown for me and helped me insert my undamaged arm into the sleeve. She carefully exposed the wound and nothing more, and I knew it as a sign that she was prepared to allow Joaquin to stay, if only so he could see my injury in clear light and ascertain for himself that it wasn't serious. She pressed a clean cloth against my arm, and I held it there while she went into the dressing room.

I wanted to move, but I knew if I did so I could set me to bleeding worse. "The children must come first. Set an extra guard on them."

"I've already done so." Joaquin said something vicious in Portuguese. I didn't need a translation to understand its import. "My brother left me in charge of the household in his absence, and I am ashamed that this has happened." His face twisted, his bitterness showing clearly. "I would not have this happen for the world. I should have set a better watch. Why was I not informed of this man's arrival?"

"I didn't want the rest of the house roused, but I should have had you called. I'm sorry."

Nichols returned with a bowl of hot water, cloths and soap and sat on the bed again to clean my wound. She worked in silence while I rapidly assessed the situation, forced the panic and terror from my mind, because that would not help Richard right now. I needed to secure my children and then attend to my husband. Nothing else mattered.

Joaquin paced, occasionally glancing at me while I brought him up to date with what Jerry had told us. He didn't interrupt more than uttering a few curses, but listened attentively. I told him all—Jerry's ridiculous devotion to John Kneller, his gloating and the bomb, which we only had his word for, but I had to believe, because if I ignored his warnings and they were real, the consequences didn't bear thinking about.

Nichols lifted the rag away. "It's almost stopped bleeding, ma'am."

"Then get me cleaned and patched up."

I heard a new voice from the doorway. "Oh no, oh God!"

I should have expected Lizzie to come, but I hadn't realised she was standing at the door and had probably heard most of my account. Had for sure, by the expression on her face. "I'll go to Lisbon," she said. "Paul is in danger too, and I won't wait tamely here for him to come back."

"When Nichols has finished, I'll dress and follow, with you. Carier is on his way."

John was in Lisbon, trying to ensure Richard's death. We were safe enough to travel, with guards, and I had been passive too long, allowing other people to take responsibilities I should have taken for my own.

With our enemies at last in the open, I could take this chance. And I would.

Nichols bound the wound. All the time, Lizzie watched. She had already dressed in a plain riding habit, and I ordered mine laid out. "Fasten the bandage tightly and I will do," I told my maid. But it took far too long before Nichols was satisfied. If I hadn't sent Carier on ahead, I'd be frantic by now.

Nichols fastened the white strip tight enough for me to get my shirt and jacket over the top, and loose enough to give me enough movement to ride. I was accounted a good rider, better than Lizzie, so between us we would manage.

I flexed my arm. Jerry had not delivered any long-term hurt when he'd wrenched it, only when the bullet had grazed it, so I could consider myself lucky, although I'd have a few bruises to remind me of the places where he'd grasped my arm. I felt stiffness only, and in a few days I'd hardly notice. Anxiety rode me, driving out pain.

We left the house as dawn was breaking, the pink fingers stretching across the sky. In normal circumstances I might have paused to admire its beauty, but now I was only glad we'd have adequate light for our journey.

I stuffed the large onion watch that had been my father's in my pocket and allowed a servant to boost me into the seat. I hooked my leg over the pommel, glad I'd had the foresight to bring my own saddle, made precisely for my measurements. I would be much safer and I could travel faster because of that saddle. Lizzie mounted a sturdy mare, and I had charge of a younger, piebald creature, a gelding in his prime. He would do. I'd ridden him earlier in the week, when I'd taken a gentle trot around the grounds, so I knew his paces. Enough to realize I could handle him easily and he could put on a turn of speed when he chose, or rather when I did.

I also took charge of two pistols, some spare balls and powder, and a couple of the wicked stiletto blades Richard always had about his person. He rarely travelled without a case of them, and I'd appropriated a couple before I left. Lizzie had a cane that looked suspiciously as if it concealed a rapier. My sister might have a more domestic, feminine outlook on life, but she'd grown up in the country, in the heart of a smuggling gang's heartland, so she knew the right end of a pistol and how to wield a light sword.

Two footmen accompanied us, two of the remaining Thompson's men. I wanted to take one and leave one behind, but Nichols wouldn't hear of it. "Even if he doubles back and tries to take us, we can hold him off long enough for Carier to find us. We've called the outdoor staff in and taken every precaution. Nobody will get in, ma'am. I'll stake my life on it."

I was torn between my children and my husband, but while I loved my children enough to put their lives above mine, I loved my husband more. Limitlessly.

We set a fair rate but didn't rush, since Lisbon was some twenty-five miles off and we needed to pace the horses. It would take two hours, maybe a little less, to get there, and then we had to work our way through the streets to the house. I had to curb my impatience. I wanted so much to set my mount to a gallop, to get there faster, to ensure Richard's safety. I checked my watch as we took the turn that would bring us on to the public road outside the estate. Nearly eight o'clock. Carier was an hour and a half ahead of us. Pray God he got there in time.

After the first five miles, we joined a major, well-maintained road, so we made better progress. We travelled some miles farther, with no incident, passing few people because of the holiday, I presumed, and the fact that it was a Sunday.

"Who is that?" Lizzie said.

Some fool stood on the highway, blocking our progress. Although we didn't let up our pace, he kept his position as we approached.

He had a pistol in his hand. Surely not a highwayman. What idiot would attack two riders with attendants on his own? His hat was pulled low over his eyes, and he wore plain clothing, a coat and heavy muffler, so he certainly appeared to be some kind of footpad.

He looked up and I caught my breath. Grey eyes met mine, and I knew this was no ordinary thief. I also knew that if we didn't stop, he'd shoot us. He didn't want our valuables. He wanted our lives.

We brought the horses to a halt, and he jerked his pistol, indicating for me to get down. Of course he did.

I glanced at Lizzie but did as he wanted. A footman alighted with me and stepped forwards, his hand on his belt. I gestured to him to stop.

Our aggressor looked like a young Richard. He wore uncharacteristically ill-fitting clothing but with his usual easy, athletic stance. He watched me, a smile curving his lips. Grey eyes fixed me with an unblinking stare.

"You look more like him now," I said, keeping my voice calm.

John Kneller pushed back his hat. "A shame I have the wrong colour eyes, otherwise I'd consider masquerading as him. Even so, the resemblance has stood me in good stead at times."

I fought to keep my voice calm. "You've used it recently?"

He smiled, the expression easy because he felt in control. His arrogance had been his downfall before. Maybe it would be again. "Only to make certain orders concerning the town house you hired. A pleasant place. But not now."

I yawned, covered my mouth with my hand and then returned it to my side, feigning polite boredom, but my heart was racing. "What do you want?"

"My father and I share one desire. You."

I needed to keep John talking. Pander to his vanity. "What have you planned this time?" I let my voice trail off, as if I found the situation tedious, scarcely interested in his answer. He'd

203

want to rouse my interest, make me pay attention to him. I needed to get to the town, to see if Jerry had told the truth.

"I've made certain that my father will never return from Lisbon. After all, it's a matter of pride now. I have little else left."

No, he'd have planned something for his own preservation. I felt it deep down. But I refused to let his threats cow me. "You have a long life ahead of you and a quick mind to make your fortune with. You should have gone into the navy. Letting you do that was merciful, otherwise you'd have been dead or brought to court and tried for murder."

"Ah yes." He stamped the ground, his booted feet creating a hollow thump. "But that case is over now, is it not?"

"You were tried in your absence and sentenced to transportation."

"I have a hankering for fresh woods and pastures new. When this episode is over, I do have plans to travel." Metal gleamed dully in his hand, the barrel of one of the pistols. "I might have known that idiot Jerry would botch it. I came to make sure the job was done."

Panic rose in my throat. I swallowed, trying to hide the movement by shifting my feet as if the morning crispness were chilling. "Why don't you just go? You must know you'll be hunted down for this. Killing me will not be an anonymous slaughter, like the many you've committed before. The authorities won't rest until they've caught you."

"They won't know." He swung his pistol up, idly glancing at the hammer. He hadn't cocked it, but it wouldn't take much. It wasn't the lethal but beautiful duelling pistols the like of which my husband and friends owned, but a serviceable weapon, gleaming dully. I couldn't reach him before he'd cocked it and fired, but perhaps that would be my only recourse. The men were too far away, although if I ducked to the ground they could try charging him.

Had he already killed Richard? If so, I had to live, and do it for the children. If he hadn't, I had to live, for Richard's sake.

No escape this time. *Keep talking, make him show his vaunted superiority. Give him the upper hand, let him slip in his arrogance.*

"You had three sons. A remarkable achievement, especially since they are all alive. Or they are until I get there." His face still showed nothing but smooth urbanity, but his voice held menace.

I ignored the threat. But I'd left them in the charge of a man I had only just learned to trust, and with servants, not all of whom were under my control. John worked through minions. Jerry had just been one more. He could have set one on the children. Fear filled my mouth with bile, but I kept my expression calm, all the while giving thanks to the man who'd taught me how to hide what I was truly feeling.

"It nearly killed me giving birth." That was common knowledge. I wouldn't be telling him anything new.

"And no doubt you'd do it again, if they died."

I decided to tell him the truth. It would make me less of a threat in his eyes. "I can't. I had childbed fever. That tends to make the woman infertile."

As I'd hoped, his smile grew. "You're barren?"

I bit my lip. "Yes." Let him think it hurt us instead of being a reason to rejoice.

"I saw you on the ship." So it was him on the rigging that day. "You weren't close then, were you? Have you outlived your usefulness?"

How could he think that, after knowing what Richard would do for me? But his vanity made him less sympathetic, less able to put himself in the shoes of others. He would discard a woman once she was of no use to him. He had done that with my sister Ruth, courting her to get close to us and then abandoning her without a backwards glance, only to try to renew the connection later. And she, poor fool, would have accepted him, had we not made that impossible.

I shifted, as if to get closer. He responded immediately.

"Stay there. Don't move any farther."

"What if I want to use the necessary?" I couldn't resist the taunt.

"Piss where you stand."

"I can manage, for now." I widened my stance to ensure my balance. Behind me a horse shifted, and I heard the creak of the harness.

"I said *don't move.*" An edge of steel entered his voice in a way I recognised because I'd heard Richard use that tone. Only my husband was more lethal and more ruthless than this young thug, but for vastly different reasons. John had to know that if he killed me and Richard lived, he'd signed his own death warrant. If he had killed my husband, Gervase would hunt him down like vermin. Was that what he wanted, or did he think he was clever enough to evade them?

I needed time to work out what to do or to give one of the men with us a chance to take him off-guard. He kept his weapon trained on me. I would die first, and that was what stopped the others from doing anything.

"Why are you doing all this? Why didn't you just go and start again somewhere else?"

He shrugged. "Justice. He turned his back on Susan and me, pretended he didn't know we existed. How does a man not know that?" He snorted in disgust.

"He didn't know about you. His mother spirited your mother away before she could tell him. Besides, he wasn't a man at the time, wasn't in control of his own destiny." I hated that others could hear this, but we had nothing to be ashamed of. And I needed to keep him talking.

"*I* was. From the age of fourteen, I was a man. I left my mother and sister and ensured I had what I needed to come after him." His face was a rigid mask of pain. I looked into his set features and knew he was telling the truth as he saw it. That he was the one wronged, that he deserved to seek revenge. Nothing else mattered to him. Not to him, the boy who had a chip on his shoulder that weighed so heavily he couldn't think properly anymore.

"What if I'm under Richard's spell? What if I'm another of his victims?" If I tried to distort his world, it might put him off balance. God knew the man wanted to talk, so desperately that he'd use any chance he had.

"Then you're better off dead." He tilted the weapon, and my blood ran cold. I tensed, ready to throw my body to the side, or forwards. It would hurt, badly, since my arm throbbed from the wound I'd already sustained. Once he'd discharged that weapon, he'd have to reach for another. That would give us the second or two we needed to rush him. Unless he was a better shot than I remembered, in which case I was dead. But it was the only chance I could think of right now. I daren't even look at my sister, in case he saw that as a weak moment.

He regarded me with an expression that looked like disbelief. "This is the last time before I turn respectable, so I'll get on with this. Anything else you want to know?" He sneered the last words.

"How do you plan to get away this time?" Behind my back, I gestured to my men, pointing to the ground to my right. I would fall there, if I needed to.

"They'll have too much to do after the explosion to worry about me."

My heart missed a beat. The bomb at the house. After that,

Kneller would escape, or he would die. I knew, from his reckless behaviour here, that he didn't much care. But he'd had to vent his spleen one more time. John would hit someone with that first shot, and he had enough pistols stuffed into his wide leather belt to ensure he could shoot more. Not that I'd care by that point. I'd be dead.

He *tsked*. "You should know I'd have everything planned." But his planning was sometimes careless, too engrossed by the overarching scheme to worry about details. I had to pray this would prove to be the case now.

He lifted his weapon and I tensed, ready to make my move.

The ground under me shifted. That was the best way I could describe it. The earth truly moved. What kind of explosion had he set? Did he mean to destroy half the city?

Lizzie screamed. "Earthquake! Get on the ground!"

I took my chance and fell, tumbling in an untidy heap, and I heard a shot, but no chill, no pain.

This was no man-made explosion. This was nature taking its part in our little drama.

"Dismount!" I cried. The horses would likely bolt. John stared at me, wide-eyed, his pistol smoking, and I knew he was as shocked as we were. He turned and ran towards his horse, staggering but making progress.

Lizzie obeyed, and our attendants. We stared at each other. Lizzie opened her mouth to say something. Then the earth moved again. Much harder, much more shocking. I fell forwards, flat on the ground, clutching at the vegetation under my hands, and my horse shrieked. I came away with a handful of grass. Around us, ominous rumblings attested to the power of nature.

I lay on terra decidedly unfirma and knew it was no support. Nothing was. I recalled stories of the earth opening up and swallowing people, and I wondered what I had done to deserve such terror, if this was God's way of telling me I'd done something appallingly wrong. Perhaps John was in the right, after all.

I fought down my panic and waited, trying to assess what was happening, what it would mean, and how we could use this situation to overcome John. The trouble was, we were all in the same boat. The sky clouded over, and what had been a fine, sunny day became so overcast it was as if the greatest thunderstorm in the world was about to begin.

Someone touched me. It took me a moment to realise it was my sister. We clung to each other, our only safety in a world that seemed to be shifting on its axis. "They have earthquakes here, though nothing like this. Nothing like this!" Her voice shook, echoing the turf under us.

It stopped and I waited a moment, expecting it to start again, not trusting that it was over. I pressed my hand flat against the ground, which was once again solid. Then I made to get to my feet, looking around for the horses and footmen, and John.

Another rumble drove me back down once more, grabbing more handfuls of grass and earth. Lizzie gripped my skirt, her knuckles white against the crimson fabric.

I closed my eyes tight, unable to take any more, and I saw a moment from my past. That flash of bright red took me back to the sight of a man in a cobbled, broken courtyard, standing as if he were in the middle of St. James' Palace, staring about like a sightseer. He lifted his quizzing glass, an elaborate confection of gold and crystal, and stared at me, then turned to his brother and murmured to him.

My first sight of Richard, wearing red, dressed for court rather than for the ruin of a once-great house and its crazy inhabitants. He always said he'd fallen in love with me in that first moment, recognised his fate in my eyes. To my shame, and his constant teasing, it had taken me a little longer. A day longer, perhaps. He had always loved me for longer than I had loved him, but if this day had consequences I hardly dared to contemplate, I would love him for much longer.

No. That couldn't happen. Not after everything we'd been through. But I recognised that this earthquake was serious. Buildings would fall, and fissures would open in the earth.

I started to pray.

Chapter Fifteen

I opened my eyes. The sky was still overcast, more like dusk than morning, but at least the ground had stopped its infernal vibration, apart from one or two gentle rumbles, which were like an infant's teasing next to the adult fury of the main quake. At its worst, I didn't know if I should hold on to my sister or just lie flat. We were in the open air, with some trees and foliage at a distance. One tree sloped drunkenly to the side, but otherwise everything appeared much as it had before. I drew a deep breath, then another.

Our attendants stood a little distance away. I got to my feet and stamped, needing some kind of reassurance that the ground wasn't about to move again. Not that we could be sure of that. Or anything else, for that matter.

John was gone, but that was the least of my concerns now.

Lisbon, where buildings crowded around the busy port, would suffer more damage. And the house too where the children were, could be in danger.

I made a decision. "You go back to the house, Lizzie, and secure the children. Make sure they're safe and protected. I'm going on." I had no way of knowing which road John had taken—to Lisbon, or on to the house. They would need to know at the *palacio.*

"You can't!"

I could. It was the only thing I *could* do. I was torn between my children and my husband, but he would need a strong horse to get him to safety. We were closer to Lisbon than the house, and I was in a position to help. His horse would be stabled in the mews, and who knew what had happened there. I fought down the terror that rose like gorge in my throat. No time for that, no time.

I remounted without the help of the footmen, who were still standing around helplessly, and motioned to one of them. "You can come with me. White, isn't it?"

The man nodded wordlessly, a sign of his extreme discomfiture. He should have bowed and verbally acknowledged my order. I was a little startled at his response, but in a moment he'd collected himself. He vaulted on to his horse and followed me. Time was of the essence now. I'd have to take my chances with John, but I kept a pistol ready at hand, just in case.

We set a brisk trot, the fastest pace we dared take. We had to have time to stop if we came across an obstacle in the road. This was the main road on this side of the city, and I expected to meet people, the ones who might have been in church services, or at home, celebrating the holiday quietly. We raced past a stricken tree a little faster, in case it should not be safe, but slowed again.

We got closer to Lisbon. Carriages lay with splintered chassis and wheels by the side of the road, bringing painful memories back to me of the time Richard had been in such an accident and nearly lost his life. As it was, the wound he'd sustained had drawn us closer together. Would we be so fortunate this time? We had to be. I couldn't think of anything else. Wouldn't think of it.

People milled around, crying, some clutching injuries, but I would not stop to help them now. One other person had all my attention.

We had to slow down, to preserve the horses and to avoid the obstacles on the road, and at that point another tremor shook the ground under us.

We pulled up the horses and dismounted, trusting them to stay by, and as before, flung ourselves down. We were about half an hour away from Lisbon now. I checked my watch. The tremor had lasted barely a minute, and when it was done, I fetched my horse and remounted, using a fallen tree to help me up, and motioned to White, who was, like his name, pale as a ghost. But he remounted and joined me.

People waved to us in warning or asking for help. My heart went out to them, especially the wounded, but I couldn't spare the time.

I shouted to them to get out of the way, but I didn't stop. They couldn't help me, I couldn't help them. The urge to reach my husband consumed me. John Kneller could take as many shots at me as he liked—I wouldn't stop this side of death.

White and I paused when we reached a crest, from where we could look down on the city and harbour.

We gazed down in silence, as did some others, who were either leaving the city or arriving, or just staring, too shocked to make any decision. Neither of us could think of anything to say, bar a few low-voiced expletives from my companion.

The city lay in ruins. Jagged remains of buildings jutted up into the air like defiant fists, others sharp like daggers, stabbing uselessly into the sky.

Parts of the city appeared intact, like the palace, close to the harbour. We weren't near enough to see or hear the responses from the inhabitants, but on the highway, people were already streaming out of the city on horseback or simple vehicles, carts and gigs. Probably traders who had their vehicles tacked up and ready to go. They might have been delivering in the city and turned around at the first sign of danger. The more affluent residents would try to salvage what they could and would likely try to commandeer any vehicle they found. Soon it would be total chaos down there.

As we stared, I discerned scattered spots of colour racing around the streets. People. They hurtled towards the harbour, probably to take ship, but the city did appear more intact in that direction. I could imagine the shouts of terror, officials trying to keep order, demands of the more self-important. And I wanted my husband.

Kicking up my horse, I headed down the slope towards the city.

Only to stop once more as I caught sight of something out at sea.

It looked like a wall, but this was a wall of water. It reared up like a living thing, or as if some deity had summoned it, like a conductor ordering a crescendo. The grey-green mass surged inexorably towards the shore.

At our cries of dismay, people stopped to look behind and their cries joined ours.

We could do nothing but watch as the huge wave rode the sea towards the shore. People raced in the opposite direction, and I thought I heard their calls, lifted on the wind.

Terror seized me, freezing my bones. I was glad my sister couldn't see this. Enough that one of us had to witness it. If our husbands had survived the earthquake, this great wave might well finish them off. Dear God.

I could do nothing but pray. Paul should be in one of the churches, while Richard would remain in the house. Would at least one of them be safe? God help me. God help them.

The wave crashed over the town, swamping everything and everyone in its wake. The only good effect was to kill some of the fires that flickered around the city, but they could have been dealt with in a much less destructive way. I prayed for Richard most, but I remembered all the inhabitants and visitors, everyone I saw who flowed through the city, and pleaded with God to save them all.

"My lady!"

The cry didn't reach my consciousness at first, and he had to repeat it, raising his voice over the cacophony of wails around us.

I jerked my head around to see if my ears were telling me the truth. They were. Carier cantered towards me, on a horse whose sides heaved with exertion. This was the main road out of this side of the town, so he would head for it to get to the *palacio*.

"Where is he?" I demanded.

Tears shimmered in his eyes. "You can do nothing down there. Come away, ma'am. Now!"

"No, I will not. While I can do something, I will stay."

He moved closer, so our mounts nearly shared breaths. "You can do nothing, believe me. But you can save your children. There are mobs down there. If he has survived the disaster, he doesn't need to concern himself for your safety. You've seen him in a corner. He fights with no thought of giving quarter or gentlemanly behaviour. He needs you safe to do that. If he has to think about you, he's dead."

Nothing else would have persuaded me. But the reminder of the children, and Richard's protective nature towards me, demonstrated how well Carier knew his master. And how well he knew me.

I waited for him to move clear before I wheeled my horse around. It would have traversed forty miles by the time we reached the house. It couldn't be helped. If it dropped under me, I'd have to find another. I'd rest it, let it drink, and hope for the best.

I glanced over my shoulder at the ruined city, sending my

heart there for Richard to touch. If I couldn't be there, then something of me would remain to encourage him. While I was alive, he'd continue to fight.

The ride back was necessarily slower, but we exchanged few words. I wanted the full story, not one recounted briefly, and I needed time to absorb what we'd seen. Terrible things, sights I wouldn't wish on my worst enemy—who was perhaps still at large, making mischief. He would see this disaster as an opportunity, I was sure.

Richard would return; I would consider nothing else.

Back at the house I was relieved to find it in one piece, though wondering at the chances of it, a mere twenty-five miles away, surviving. I had imagined sleeping in a pavilion on the grounds, but it seemed that wouldn't be necessary. I brushed off concerns from my attendants, relieved to discover no lassitude pulling at my muscles. Not yet, at any rate. I'd make the most of it, before my body decided it had had enough.

Lizzie met me at the door, but I brushed her fussing away. "I have tea," she told me, the first thing she'd said that held any interest for me.

"Order more."

I had to make sure my children were well, see them for myself. I lifted my skirts high and took the stairs two at a time, then ran to their nursery. The nurses were feeding them, and after, they would sleep. I kissed the babies, hugged Helen and left to find Lizzie waiting for me outside.

"Under Nichols's direction, the servants took them into the gardens when they felt the first tremor. Before they brought them back inside, Joaquin insisted on having every part of the house scrutinized. They found a few cracks, and we've lost some of the stucco and pilasters, but the building is sound. We are safe here."

I thought of the people streaming away from Lisbon. "There are many people about, much more than usual. Lisbon is gone, Lizzie. Destroyed. I didn't get down into the city, Carier wouldn't let me. He told me the mob was about, and Richard would need to keep his wits about him. That's all I know. I saw—" I broke off and shuddered, "—terrible things. But those who are able are leaving the city."

"I've set people at the perimeters and around the house." She closed her eyes as the import of what I told her took hold. "No news?"

I shrugged.

I followed her to one of the smaller salons at the back of the house. Glancing out the window, I saw the garden no longer had its almost military precision. Now it seemed almost dishevelled, some of the cleverly cut hedges and bushes drunkenly askew.

I motioned Carier in. Nobody questioned me, although Lizzie gave me a quizzical look. Joaquin had stood at my entrance, and I had no compunction in taking the chair he led me to.

I glanced back at Carier. "Come and sit, man. You'll fall over if you don't."

Lizzie cleared her throat.

I had no patience for the proprieties right now. "He has news. He's ridden all day, and he needs to rest so he can tell us what he's learned."

At once, Lizzie found another dish and poured an extra serving of tea. She didn't object any further when Carier found a chair and sat. He'd have to be exhausted to contemplate doing so. He refused the tea, but I took it from my sister's hands and pressed it on him. "Don't be foolish. Drink, and then tell us. Consider it Thompson's business, if it helps."

He gave me a grateful smile and drank. He didn't stop until he reached the bottom of the dish, then he handed it back to Lizzie with great care.

"I fear I have no good news, my lady."

I knew that. "Tell me he's not dead."

"Not to my knowledge. He was living when I left."

"Then why—?"

"Why did I leave him? Let me tell you in order, ma'am. It will make more sense that way." He glanced around, but he needn't have done so. He had our complete attention. He frowned. "You're sure this house is safe?"

"Perfectly," Joaquin said. "Some repairs are needed, but it won't tumble down, unless we have another earthquake."

"Ah God, don't say that." It spoke for the way Carier had taken the disaster that he would even display such weakness. He buried his face in his hands. "I've served in the army, I've followed my master into the bowels of hell, but I've never seen anything like this. I knew something was wrong when the rats came out." He lifted his head, staring at us from suspiciously watery eyes. "Rats always know when something is wrong. There were far more in the streets than you would expect to see."

He paused, but not for long. I could see determination in his granite features, a decision to tell his story to the bitter end. I prayed that it wouldn't be too bitter.

He didn't look at me, or at Lizzie, making me fear the worst, but addressed Joaquin who sat quiet and still, all his attention fixed on him.

"I didn't let up until I got to the house, at about twenty past eight, but Kneller had beaten me to it. He had only one purpose in mind—to cause my lord as much harm as possible. To hurt him and kill him. He had a lock of hair he claimed was your daughter's, and he'd contrived to bloody it. Probably by using his own gore. He had the master and the marquês at gunpoint. My lord didn't twitch, didn't move when I entered the room, and I would have put all right, but the marquês looked in my direction and the—Kneller turned on me. He shot, I ducked and then fell, feigning injury. But there was no blood on me, so he told me to get up.

"By then my master was on him. Kneller had other weapons tucked into his belt, and my lord grabbed one and tossed it to the marquês. We had him. Or so we thought.

"I told my lord what we knew, that the boy had mined the house or rendered it unstable in some way. Kneller laughed my notion to scorn, but then I would have expected that. He struck a theatrical pose, and drew his final weapon, which he'd had hidden, holding it to his own head. That gesture affected my lord deeply, though I suspect nobody present knew it but me. Most of the servants in the house had already left for early service at the church, so the house was nearly empty. 'You'll never know,' the boy cried. 'And I will die before I tell you!'" Carier made a scornful noise. "Kneller should have stopped then. Shot them and got away. Thank God he did not.

"The marquês told him to drop his weapon, to no avail. My lord turned away, feigning indifference, and the boy lowered his weapon, aiming it at my master. I could do nothing, since I lay too far away to get to him before he fired. I should have moved faster, I should have done something, but I thought the best way was to wait and to choose my moment. I didn't know we had so few moments left." With a visibly shaking hand he accepted the second dish of tea Lizzie held out to him and drained it like a man dying of thirst.

Joaquin rose to his feet. "I'll get some brandy." Carier was obviously in deep shock.

Carier shook his head. "In a while, sir. Let me get this out first. Please." He would get blind drunk if he wanted to, but not before he'd told us.

Now Carier met my gaze. "I failed, my lady." He took a deep breath, pushing the air into his body. "Kneller forced us out of the room and towards the kitchen stairs. There was one servant down there. He shot him. The kitchen is below the ground, a small window at the top letting in air, but it was hot there, as hot as hell because of the kitchen fire blazing away.

"I think the boy was half mad, confronting his—my lord in that way. I made my move, stumbled and came up with a small weapon I'd hidden about my person. He responded, but he switched pistols almost immediately and had a fresh one ready. I ducked, but Kneller leaped over me and into my lord, who fell the rest of the way down the stairs, collecting the marquês on the way. The gun went off, but it hit the wall. Kneller must have known they could overpower him and he ran.

"I couldn't do anything but race up the stairs after him. Then I heard the explosion behind me. The bomb had gone off. It rocked the house. Windows exploded out, and I was lucky not to be hit by flying glass. People screamed, but the house stayed upright, although there were great cracks in the outer part. It was sturdily built, but when I went inside, I discovered some of the inner walls had fallen in, and I couldn't get to the steps down to the kitchens. I needed help. I ran to muster some likely men, but it took too long. I had gathered half a dozen and we had returned to the house and were assessing the damage. I had every expectation of digging them out.

"Then the earthquake struck. I'd felt the ground move under my feet once already that morning, and it confused me. The shifting ground made me fall. I saw buildings falling, like paper houses, not bricks and mortar. I ran up the street and found a horse, a good mount and saddled ready. It would have charged—its ears were back and I could see the whites of its eyes—but I took the bridle in a firm hold and let it know I was master and it was safe with me. The sound was terrible, roaring and crashing as buildings fell. I've been in the heat of battle and nothing was as bad as that sound. I'll hear it to my dying day."

His voice shook. "When I returned to the house, it was gone. Just a pile of bricks and glass."

Lizzie gave a cry and clapped her hand to her mouth. I stared at him, just stared, my mouth open but no words emerging. "Then he needs digging out," I managed eventually. "There is no time to waste."

Carier shook his head. "I mounted the animal and raced off for help. People ran by me, heading for the harbour. I tried to call to them, followed some, cried out. But I was calling in English and they were yelling Portuguese. If they'd ever known English, they didn't now." He sighed and dropped his chin, staring at his scuffed and scarred shoes. "I saw enough to know I could do nothing, so I decided to ride for help. With a few likely footmen we could set to and dig out their lordships."

I sprang to my feet. "That sounds like a good plan. What are we waiting for?"

Carier rose immediately, a little slower than I had. "Ma'am, you're forgetting. The great wave."

My blood ran cold. I could feel every rivulet, every tiny blood vessel, and I swear it all ran completely icy in an instant. "Still, we must go."

"We can do nothing, ma'am. They were trapped belowground." He touched my arm, and I was so shocked I didn't shake it off. "I will go back and with men to help, but you must swear to stay here. One of you must stay alive. For the children. You know that, ma'am."

"Gervase—" I couldn't bear it. Everything we'd planned and discussed meant nothing now. I would not stand by and do nothing.

"Besides, you can do no good there. Only attract the lower orders, the mob. We would be protecting you, not searching for their lordships."

I heard the sound of muffled sobbing and realised it wasn't me, but Lizzie. I was too numb to cry. I wouldn't weep, not yet. I wouldn't give up.

Waiting would be the hardest thing I'd ever done in my life, but Carier was right. He would get on better without me, and I should stay with the children. If the mob came this way, if the country turned lawless, we'd have to get out to safety. Thanks to the great wave there was little opportunity of our getting on the yacht. That was probably in pieces at the bottom of the harbour.

Nothing could have survived that wave. Nothing and no one.

I refused to think that way. I nodded. "Bring him back, Carier. Send me word as often as you can, even if it's no news, or worse. I want to know as soon as possible, so I can take the appropriate steps."

"My lady, I swear it. I will not return without him. One way or the other."

Chapter Sixteen

I put down my pen and dusted the letter with sand. So much had survived the earthquake in this lovely house, it seemed a travesty that so much else had not a mere twenty-five miles away. The sander was made of fine crystal and not a chip marred its deeply cut surfaces. I ran my finger over the sharply incised pattern, wondering if my lord would ever feel anything similar again. I'd refused to let my mind wander too far that way over the last few days, but sometimes I found it impossible.

I still hadn't wept. I wouldn't, not until they brought him back.

After three days of searching, the men we'd set to dig out the house still hadn't found Richard and Paul. Not for want of trying. Fires raged now in the ruins of what had once been one of the most beautiful cities in the world, some accidental, started by open fires and upset candles and lamps, and others deliberately by the rampaging mob. What had survived of Lisbon was now destroyed in flames. Carier and his men had fought the destruction, but he wrote that he despaired of locating the correct house. The area appeared so changed. He sent notes via the men who had worked themselves into exhaustion, men he sent back to sleep and eat before they returned. God knew how Carier managed. Probably the same way I did, on hope and prayer.

Lizzie had spent most of this day in the chapel, praying for her husband's soul. We didn't talk much, unless in the presence of our children. I spent as much time as I could with them, especially Helen. Before I came into this quiet boudoir to compose the letter, I'd played with her, romping on the floor among the large cushions the nursemaids used to help her retain a sitting posture, to break her fall if she tumbled, as she did often, getting up again with a merry laugh.

Before I left, she said one word. "Papa?"

I stared at her, eyes wide, my hand clapped to my mouth as I gasped. Right there, my heart broke in two.

An appalled silence fell, breached only by the cry of a baby. My baby. Edward, the stoical, quiet baby, had sensed the mood changed and didn't like it. I crossed the room and took him from his nurse, glad of the distraction.

The room regained its normal tone, and I set to comforting my child. I held his sweet-smelling head to my face and kissed his soft baby cheek before I rocked him and sang him a song my sister-in-law Martha used to sing to her babies at night. One that most Devonshire children had heard. Because that was part of their inheritance too. Not just the fashionable, high society, exclusive and expensive part.

I would take them home. Perhaps I'd buy a house near my brother's and let them grow to adulthood in peace, visiting London and their relatives enough to let them become comfortable with their future station in life.

If Richard was—if I never saw him again in this life, I'd sell the Oxfordshire house. I wouldn't want to see it and recall the memories we'd left there. I might want to remember him, but not to torture myself with what I couldn't have.

I just wanted him back.

Setting my jaw against tears, I glanced through the letter. I'd couched it in formal terms, telling Lord and Lady Southwood that we were safe, but Richard's fate was not yet decided. I'd put off writing it for days, every minute hoping that some news would arrive, the kind of news I needed to hear. But nothing had come, except exhausted men, here only to rest before returning to the area where the town house had once stood.

I put it on top of the letter I'd written to Gervase. That was more personal and had nearly moved me to the tears I'd sworn I wouldn't shed until I knew for sure if he lived or died. If I was a happy wife or a grief-stricken widow. I wouldn't weep for him before I knew. And I *would* know, I was determined on that.

My life would be over. I would live for my children then pray for death.

That sounded so dramatic, but it was the raw truth. Without him, I had nothing except my duty, which I would execute meticulously. I would have been a fool not to make plans, because once his death was confirmed, I feared I wouldn't know myself for a time. I drew a sheet of paper towards me and started writing. This was for my maid, my manservant and Gervase, who would do what I needed him to do.

I wish to move to a quiet house in the country for a time. I want to buy a moderately sized establishment close to my brother's house in Devonshire. I do not want to live with my brother or with anyone else. I will start my new life as I wish to live it. Alone. My existing children and servants will come with me, and unless Carier desires otherwise, I wish him with me too. He will become my steward. Unless he wishes to retire, that is.

That was all. I knew Gervase would see it done. I signed it and sealed it, putting, *In the event of Richard's death* on the outside. I enclosed it in the letter for Gervase. I told Gervase not to come to Lisbon until I sent word. Then I would need him. I would come home with the children and I could trust Carier to make the arrangements and keep me safe. We would have to wait until after the funeral. I would take Richard home, to his

225

family chapel in Eyton, and he would rest there, as was his right. Alone, until the blessed day when I would lie by his side once more.

I wasn't sure when the letters would reach England, but it was my duty to write, and I couldn't put the melancholy task off any longer. Word about an earthquake of those proportions must be flying around the Continent and England. They might even have felt the tremors, however slightly. And they would worry and send for us, if I didn't inform them. Gervase would be frantic. I'd send the letters by courier. They'd go overland until they reached a safe place on the coast, so it might take three weeks for them to arrive.

I called a servant and entrusted the missives to her care. She assured me they would leave the house that very day.

Now I had nothing more to do. Should I go to the chapel and share my sister's vigil? I hadn't known she was so religious—she'd never shown signs of it before. Perhaps she wasn't, perhaps she was seeking solace anywhere she could. Both of us knew that if we gave way, we wouldn't be of any use to anyone. This from my sister, who had merely looked for a suitable marriage. She had fallen as deeply in love with her Paul as I had with Richard, and on this visit I was beginning to see why. Paul's generosity to his tenants, his kindness and a sense of humour that could take a person by surprise, all demonstrated his love for life and for his home.

I wondered if Lizzie had written to Paul's mother. I would ask.

When I left the study, planning to take a walk on the grounds, I saw what looked like an old man, bent over with care, his short gray hair clinging to his head in damp spikes, his gait uncertain.

Carier had returned. I hurried towards him, holding my hands out. I needed human contact. "Tell me," I said.

He shook his head and lifted his gaze to mine. In the bloodshot depths, I saw despair. Not grief. Perhaps he was too exhausted for grief. "We haven't found him, although we dug through the remains of a kitchen earlier today. But all we found was an unfortunate boy, someone left behind when the servants from that house fled. That boy had drowned when the tidal wave overwhelmed the building."

I knew what he was telling me. If Richard had survived the house collapsing on top of him, he would have drowned afterwards.

But I couldn't believe it. I had heard that people, gone in grief, refused to believe the truth, that their loved ones had gone beyond recall. They would see them in the street, even chase them, only to find perfect strangers. I stared at him, and I felt— nothing.

"He's not dead," I said.

Chapter Seventeen

"Ma'am, I'm more sorry than I can say, but there is no point searching for anything but their bodies."

I didn't waste my breath. "Then search. But do it quickly. He is *not dead*, Carier. I'd know it. Or rather, I'd know if he *were* dead." My hands curled into fists. "Oh, I don't know, I can't explain it properly, but, Carier, he is *not* dead. Go and look. No, go and rest. *I'll* go and look."

He opened his mouth, but I wouldn't let him deny me this. "If he's dead, then I need to see it, to know it. If he isn't, I want to be there when we find him. You say it's dangerous—I'll carry a weapon. Several. We have men to guard me, men we can trust absolutely."

He glanced at me. "There is something else. When you were recovering, the first night after we learned you would live, he ordered me to put your life above mine." He made a sound, a cross between a laugh and a growl. "As if I hadn't already. You mean everything to him, ma'am."

"As if you had to tell me that," I said, echoing his words deliberately. "But did you notice something else? You said 'mean', not 'meant'. We have to do this, Carier. If you want to protect me, then fine, you will. But I am going, now I know the children are safe. You will not keep me away."

He promised to eat and rest. I had to swear to wait for him, but it nearly broke me to make that promise. Every minute counted. Only Carier's assurance that the men wouldn't stop digging until they found him gave me the patience to prepare.

Four hours later, I was ready, wearing a riding-habit jacket and shirt with a pair of Richard's breeches, hitched up at the waist by a broad leather belt I'd filched from one of the gardeners. I wouldn't have passed any arbiters of fashion, but I could clamber over rocks and walk through piles of rubbish. I rarely wore breeches, and they felt strange. I had thought of wearing a skirt and employing an old trick used by the women at home in Devonshire, pulling the tail of the skirt through my legs to the front and fastening it at the waist, but breeches would do. I had a spare pair in a small pack, with a towel and a blanket, and a basic medical kit. I might have to sleep there because privately I determined not to return here until I knew, one way or the other. Until we found him. Them.

My mind had reverted to a primitive state. I no longer thought about the others buried with Richard, dear though one of them was. *He* was all that mattered. Nothing else, no one else.

When the door opened, I expected Carier, but I got Lizzie. Dressed in sombre colours, dark blue, which happened to become her exceedingly, she stopped when she saw my unusual attire. "You meant it? You're going?"

"I can't stay. He's not dead, Lizzie."

"Oh, Rose!" She heaved a sigh and crossed the room to me. I took her hands. "You have to face it, love. The chances of them living are remote." Her voice shook, and she bit her lip, hard, denting the soft flesh with her sharp teeth. "You need to see him, I understand that, but you have children to care for."

"They're safe here with you and Joaquin. They won't be any safer if I stay here. But I know Richard, I can almost *feel* him. I don't know, Lizzie, but I have to do this. Or live with the knowledge that I didn't for the rest of my life. I have to go."

"It's not safe."

I indicated the breeches. "Thus I will bundle my hair up

229

under a cocked hat, and while I won't pass as a man in polite society, nobody will be looking at me particularly, and so they won't bother me. Besides, I have a few extras." I patted my pocket, allowing the knives to clink. "He taught me how to use them." With a great deal of love and laughter. I had my pistols in each pocket too. One in each, so as not to weigh me down unevenly. I had food packed in saddlebags, durable stuff like cheese and apples, and I had three tinderboxes. A comb was my sole offering to the goddess of vanity. And my old *necessaire*, the battered one I'd had when I met Richard, the one I wore to my wedding and had with me at all times. It would come in useful, if only for me to touch, to reassure myself some things in the world remained constant.

My love for my husband and my children, my loving family and the talisman I took everywhere.

Nichols entered the room. My stately, middle-aged maid had found an old riding habit, and she too had chosen breeches in preference to skirts. She stood silently, hands folded before her.

I gave her a wry smile. "You want to come."

"I can hardly leave you to do this on your own, ma'am."

I had never heard a sweeter demonstration of loyalty. Nichols, tight-lipped, the woman with a wonderful way with hair and clothes, impeccable taste, but who dressed more like a kitchen maid half the time. And she wouldn't leave me.

"Without you, I shall have to seek another position, my lady. It's in my interest to ensure you are cared for." A glimmer in her eyes, the slightest of twitches to her mouth, told me she felt more than employer loyalty. She cared for me.

The consideration rocked me. Maids didn't have that kind of relationship with their mistresses—everything militated against it. They might come to an understanding, and most employers would balk at any sign of affection from a body servant, but now it warmed me. It was what I needed. Someone to support what I was about to do, not fight it.

Lizzie half-screamed, "How could you even consider it? We have so much to prepare for, and with Lisbon in ruins, few people to call on to help. I have to secure the estate here, and the others. Joaquin and I need to discuss what we should do next, and I want time—time to remember him." Her lip trembled and she bit it again, this time hard enough to draw blood.

"I'll bring him back, Lizzie. I swear it." I didn't say if I'd bring Paul back alive or dead, because I didn't know. But Richard wasn't dead. I knew it. I wouldn't believe it until I saw his body laid out before me.

He was alive.

"Ma'am, Carier says he has the horses ready downstairs. If you're ready."

"More than ready." I seized Lizzie's shoulders, dragged her to me and kissed her on both cheeks. "I trust you to do what is right. But if there are any problems, if I don't come back, I've written our wishes out for you. They are enforceable by law. I want you to keep the children safe until their guardian arrives to take charge of them. And in case you had any illusions, that guardian is Gervase. Under no circumstances are you to give them up to my mother-in-law. Keep them in Portugal if you have to, but don't give them to her. Understand?"

Lizzie smiled, though it was strained and watery. "I can at least do that for you."

The road to Lisbon was more ordered than I'd seen it before. People straggled out of the city, and some were going in, but not many. The authorities had taken control, it seemed, because I saw a few officious-looking people around. I didn't approach them and I kept my hat brim pulled low.

Riding astride was the worst part. I hadn't done that since I was a child, and what came naturally to me as a woman, didn't in my male attire. It took some getting used to. I wanted to avoid unnecessary attention, which could include notice from marauding mobs, so I made the effort. Nichols took to it better than I did, but by the time we reached the city, my thighs were aching. I gritted my teeth and hid my discomfort.

Fires still raged, but most were extinguished. Of the royal palace, very little remained. Carier told me that there were rumours that the mob did it, rather than the natural disasters that had devastated the city. Looters were, luckily for us, concentrating their efforts on that area, by the harbour, rather than here, deeper in the city, although some had picked over the houses nearby.

Men were digging. A lot of men. I'd brought gold, sewn into my clothes and in purses, and I would pay them as long as they continued to work, but some looked exhausted.

Carier set to, and I realised the identity of the canvas rolls he and Nichols had brought in. Tents. Rudimentary, but once erected they formed an adequate shelter. He tapped the men who'd slowed down almost to a crawl and pointed at the tents. They left. Carier had pitched the tents on the grounds of one of the houses.

Here, a few walls and buildings stood, but some lurched in a drunken way, proclaiming their unsafe nature, and others were interior walls, fireplaces and shelves clinging to the wreckage. The remains of a civilised society, all that persisted after nature had decided to take things in hand and deliver a lesson. Though what the lesson could be, I couldn't tell. Innocents had perished along with the guilty; the poor had lost everything along with the wealthy. Priests and sinners, all fell before this tide of destruction.

The pervasive stench didn't belong to one thing alone. Cesspits had been disturbed, food was rotting in the kitchens underground and so were people, trapped below the buildings, dead and decaying. I breathed normally, hoping I would grow accustomed to the stink soon.

The ground was uneven with rubble, and when I kicked a stone aside, it was damp underneath, a remnant of the wave that had come so close on the quake. It would have swamped the cellars, the kitchens.

Carier was right. If Richard survived, it would be a miracle. But I couldn't stop now.

I set myself to helping in the ways I could do best. I patched up grazes and scrapes sustained by the diggers, ensured they had food and fresh water, and wandered around. The worst of it was that we didn't know where, precisely, the house had stood. We hadn't been in it long enough to know for sure which one it was—we couldn't recognise the details of the garden or the décor. And there were few landmarks left. This had been a terrace of fashionable houses, all similar to each other, built to the same pattern, many of them on short-term leases to people visiting Lisbon for the season or attending court.

Now gone, tumbled into the street like houses made of cards.

I had tethered my horse to the remains of a tree in one of the gardens. Only the lower branches remained, but they were enough to ensure my beast stayed there. That and the grass that it cropped. Carier and the men had pitched the tents close-by, on the softer ground where they wouldn't have to dig.

A cry came from one of the men, and the sound of stones and bricks being tossed aside stopped. "Listen!"

I hurried over and heard it for myself. Scrabbling. Something, someone, was alive below that pile of broken bricks

233

and timber. The men gathered around, passed the bits from hand to hand to join a pile they had begun in the street. Something scrambled out and hurtled away. A rat, big, black and fat. I wanted it dead. It had no right to survive when I—

Without pausing to consider, I dragged out my weapon, cocked it and fired. The rat screamed, and its body flew into the air, tail whipping up, before it dropped to the ground.

I shrugged. "One less to eat the dead." It had to have grown fat on something. I moved, but as I did, I saw a glint reflected from watery beams of the sun. It was overcast, as it had been every day since the disaster, but the sun had done its best to give us some light today. Something sparkled, a cold, clear light. I knew what that meant. Crystal, glass or...

A moment later I had my answer. Ignoring the body of the rodent I'd just dispatched, I plucked an item from between what looked like the undisturbed stones and bricks. A pin, a diamond pin. I turned it over. I couldn't be more sure. "Here! Drop everything else and come here!"

Carier was the first to reach me. I held out the pin on the flat of my palm, and he stared at it. "His lordship's solitaire."

Richard's favourite ornament, the one he used to secure the folds of his neckcloth.

The world stood still, and all I could hear was Carier's quickened breathing. With a visible effort, he straightened and waved to our four helpers. Two were resting, but at his cry of "Here!" their heads appeared between the folds of the tents, and they emerged to share in the renewed effort.

I didn't stand by, and neither did Nichols. We tossed bricks and stones aside, on to the new pile the men had begun. I understood the necessity to be methodical. Other people, engaged in similar pursuits to ours in different parts of the street, ran over to help. Soon we'd cleared a patch of ground, discarded the shattered remains of a door and started on the opening to what was clearly a flight of stone steps leading down.

Richard was here, I knew it, I felt it. Carier organised the men. Either they were too tired to protest, or they had worked long enough to recognise they needed to keep order. If too many of them had stood over the cellar, it could have caved in. So we formed two lines, radiating away from the stairs, and passed buckets of rubble hand to hand, slowly clearing the area.

One step appeared, then two, but no sign of a person. After the third, Carier glanced up, exchanging a brief smile with me. Reassurance and hope. I had made him do this, and I was right.

The fourth step, and then someone cried out. I left my place in the line and raced forwards, falling on my knees to see what they'd uncovered.

A hand. A hand that moved. It had pushed through a gap in the stones, and the fingers twitched as we stared in stunned disbelief.

They cleared a space around it, and we heard a few stones fall under our feet. That meant a cavity, an opening. An air trap. Or a place that could fill with water.

Once we realised that, we stepped even more carefully. Two lines thinned to one, and it fanned out over the street, not the spot where the kitchen must be. We'd tramped over that point, clambered over the pile of rubbish to get to other parts of the area. Had we made it worse, pushed more stones into the space?

I remained, standing to one side, hopefully where the wall that supported the stairs had been. I couldn't leave him. Not now. I talked, not knowing if he could hear me, but I needed to, babbling nonsense, promising him a good meal, a bath, my love, anything, uncaring what the others thought, only that he should hear me and come back to me.

They cleared the person, brushing away the choking dust, and as soon as they could, they hauled him up.

Paul. It was Paul. His dark hair tangled about his face, clogged with brick dust and filth. He moaned. Alive. I blinked, forced myself to concentrate. He needed help. But I couldn't move.

Carier put his hand on my arm. "I'll see to him, ma'am. Stay here. He'll need you when we bring him up." He didn't mean Paul.

The men climbed down the stairs, disappearing into the stinking depths below. They brought out a man, bloated with water and death. Not Richard. They placed him some distance away. We'd see to him later, but he was beyond our help, had been for days.

Then they brought Richard out.

Chapter Eighteen

His hair was almost as dark as Paul's, matted with filth and blood. His limbs were limp, his eyes closed. They carried him over to the tents and laid him on a bed of blankets that they made just outside them. I sank to my knees by his side, heedless of the stones digging into my flesh, and I grabbed his wrist. I held my breath.

Small, erratic thuds against my forefinger rewarded me. He was alive. Oh, thank God, alive.

My senses rushed back, blood coursing through my veins once more, and my damned-up emotions threatened to break free.

I caught my breath, forced myself to calm down, to think. The last thing he needed was a sobbing, hysterical woman. He needed help, not tears.

His clothes were soaked through—they needed to come off. My hands steadier now, I stripped off his clothing and grabbed the damp cloths and the dry ones that Nichols handed me. I should have realised she'd be there, waiting to serve me. His body, so pale and defenceless, lay on the dark blankets. For a second I realised I could have been laying out his corpse, and cold chills chased through me. But I wasn't, I wasn't.

I scanned him, searching for any irregularities. Hands, limbs in awkward positions, indicating breaks; unnatural swellings, indicating something wrong under the skin. I turned him on his side, and passively, he went.

I wasn't surprised to find Carier with me. "Nothing," I

concluded, laying Richard on his back. I lifted the edges of the blanket and wrapped it around him. He was covered in bruises, purple and livid against his pale skin.

Carier went to his bare foot, which was sticking out of my extemporised cover. "Except this." He'd seen something I missed, most likely because tears misted my vision, the tears I'd fought back for days now. He probed, and I felt Richard wince, but he said nothing. He was barely conscious, but I guessed he'd been floating in and out of awareness. "It's a bad wrench," Carier said. "Nothing else." His voice was completely steady, almost a monotone, a sign that he too was keeping his emotions rigidly under control.

Richard opened his eyes. His gaze went straight to me. I stared in amazement when he smiled. "I knew you'd come."

I tried to smile back, and again amazed myself by succeeding. "Of course you knew. Why would you doubt that?"

He was alive, I was alive. In the middle of terrible devastation, we were happy. Later I'd feel regret and horror for the almost total destruction of a city and many of its inhabitants, but now all I could feel was blessed relief and a desperate need to thank someone for sparing the person who made my life real.

I looked up, my eyes blurred by the tears I'd refused to let fall. And then, at a short distance, I saw John, his blond hair glinting in the light of the sun, his grey eyes steady as he took aim.

I didn't hesitate. I dragged a pistol from my belt and shot. John fell forwards like a stone. I knew he was dead, I felt it. And I couldn't be sorry.

"My lady?" a man close to me asked.

I tossed my discharged weapon to the ground. "Just another rat. Ensure that's reloaded, would you?"

Numbness enclosed me. All I felt was a slight relief that another threat had left us. Perhaps the shock had rendered me unable to feel anything more, or maybe the natural disaster had put the machinations of one youth back where it belonged—into obscurity. I wouldn't make myself care. I had more things to concern myself with now.

"My lady, we have to see to the marquês." Carier's gentle words reminded me that there were more people to care for, and I had the skills to assist. By his lack of reaction I knew he cared as little about John's last act as I did. Hardly worth discussing when we had more important matters at stake.

I squeezed Richard's hand, very gently, because bruises and scrapes marred the knuckles and flesh. Richard returned the pressure and turned his head to one side so he could watch me. He wouldn't willingly take his attention away from me now.

Paul lay a little way away. A man knelt by his side. Unlike Richard, Paul was unconscious. The man had stripped and cut his clothing off, so he lay naked, under our scrutiny. No place for modesty here. When I scanned his body, my horrified gaze remained on his foot, which was sickeningly twisted to one side and limp.

It was swollen, dark with bad blood, and when Carier touched the sole of the foot, nothing happened. He should have responded to the touch, even unconscious. Even though Paul's skin was of an olive tone, the foot was darker, with streaks of red marring it. I swallowed. Both Carier and I knew what we had to do if we were to save Paul's life. Those streaks contained poison that would infect the rest of his body and kill him if we didn't act quickly and decisively. I had helped in a similar situation years before, when a man had fallen on a scythe, sustained a relatively minor injury and bound the wound lightly. Days later, he came to us, too late to save the limb, but in time to save his life. Not that it helped him later, when employers refused his services.

Now Paul was in the same physical condition. And the same solution rode us. I glanced over to where Richard had rolled on to his side so he could watch me. He nodded, very slightly but I saw it, and it gave me the courage to say what I had to. "It has to come off."

"Can you assist, ma'am? I'm sure I can find someone to help if you feel you cannot," Carier asked.

"Yes, I can help. Let's do it now, before he has a chance to wake. If we do this while he is conscious, he'll perish from the shock."

Carier set his mouth to a firm line. "Likely as not. Yes." He nodded to someone behind me. One of the Thompson's men, who handed him a roll of canvas, which I knew from past experience held his medical supplies. Carier handed the man an iron, which the footman took away to put in the fire. We'd have to cauterise the wounds, or Paul would bleed to death. But it would take hours to get back to the house, and by then the infection could have spread, and he'd lose more than a foot.

I will not go into the details of the operation. Suffice it to say that we had the foot removed and the stump cauterised, the blood vessels tied off and the wound bound in clean linen as quickly as we could. Carier and I had worked together before, and one-word comments sufficed. We trusted each other's abilities, and we did the job as cleanly as possible, given the circumstances.

Paul lost some blood, but not enough to endanger his life if we were careful. All through the procedure I felt Richard's gaze on me, steady and stronger than he should have been. I knew it was for me. Someone had brought fresh water to him, and some bread. They must have starved these past four days. He drank and ate, all the while watching me.

To our relief, Paul didn't regain consciousness while we

were operating. But we had to get him back to the house and awake to assure ourselves that he was, apart from his injury, ready to recover. We had sent word back to Lizzie for carriages and more help, and the welcome news that we'd recovered them, alive. No more.

We rested. I lay next to Richard, and we curved blankets around us and fell into a light doze, too tired to do more than clasp hands. Nevertheless, it was enough.

Hours later, I don't know how many, I was shocked to see the vision of my sister. She climbed over the rubble, a servant in attendance, holding her skirts high to prevent herself from stumbling on them. She looked fresh and clean, an angel visiting the poor rabble in the streets. Of which I was one. Dirt streaked my hands, together with the blood from her husband. We had saved the fresh water for the people who needed it most, and I wasn't a priority.

As she sank to her knees beside Paul, I turned my attention back to Richard. He fought his hand free of the blankets that covered him and reached for mine once more. Grasping it, I felt the stress and sleeplessness of the past few days sweep over me like the great wave that had devastated Lisbon. The rare hours of snatched repose were nowhere near enough. I wept, and he watched, too weak to hold me. But he understood. He murmured words I could hardly hear, but his musical tones were enough.

Nichols touched my shoulder. "Come, ma'am. We've found a door to lift their lordships. The men will carry them to the place where the carriages wait."

I swiped my sleeve over my eyes and then blew my nose, again on my sleeve, since I wore no petticoat and handkerchiefs were an unheard of luxury in this place. Like the urchins in the street, suddenly I understood that their ill manners weren't necessarily because they didn't know any better. It was because

241

they didn't have the means to follow them. Etiquette could only work if one was rich enough to follow the edicts. An odd thing to realise now.

Little revelations as well as big ones. While I couldn't stop my tears overflowing, I could feel the burdens leaving me. If Richard fell ill over the next few days, I had it in me to care for him. I wouldn't have to worry about him alone, needing what I could bring him. I didn't have to worry about a future life without him.

I stood and only then saw the two bodies laid out on the ground. The unknown man, who must have been the cook Carier had spoken of, had obviously been dead for days. I didn't approach his corpse. I could do nothing there.

The other hadn't been dead as long. I stared down at the body of my husband's firstborn son.

His hair gleamed gold, an echo of his father's, and the face, now in repose, appeared its true age. Young. So young my heart went out to him. He'd never see twenty. A pale, flawless complexion, with the clever, clear-cut features I saw in his father every day when I woke. He was lithe of limb and beautiful, even in death. I knelt by his side and prayed. They were the only prayers his body was likely to get, and I hoped they'd help to speed his soul to heaven. So full of promise, he'd destroyed it all by his vicious, driving ambition, that ambition that had urged him to commit acts a boy of his age shouldn't even know, much less take part in.

I recalled what Richard's life had been at that age. He'd lost his brother, Gervase, to exile. He was abroad with Carier, meeting Gervase in secret before his twin left for India, doing the Grand Tour, teaching himself to be the immaculate, heartless man who the world saw when he returned home, the brilliant leader of society and inventor of vice, determined to make society pay for the destruction it had helped wreak on

Gervase.

Freed of its constraints, the rigid ruts I'd forced it into in the last few days, my thoughts ran riot, and too tired to stop the process, I let them go. I returned to my husband, stumbling in my fatigue.

The men loaded Richard onto a door and carried him the mile to where the carriage drivers had found a place to wait and guard the vehicles. Already people were converging on them, but the men Lizzie had hired to accompany us rode around the vehicles with loaded weapons, prohibiting access.

It was a tragedy that we couldn't offer more help, but the carriages would hold us and our patients, and the footmen who were returning with us. We left two to clear up and follow in short order. They would bury the bodies as well as they could. Then we'd leave the site to its sad fate.

Chapter Nineteen

"Rose."

The sound, soft as it was, woke me from exhausted slumber. I lay on a truckle bed in the bedroom, unable to leave Richard now that I had him back.

Immediately I sprang to my feet. It was dark, the curtains drawn, but a glimmer of light showed through the cracks.

Oh God, he must be frantic, waking up to find that. My husband had always hated being closed in, and after the experience he'd just gone through, must hate it even more.

"I'm sorry."

I crossed the room, but before I reached the windows, he spoke again. "It doesn't matter. Come here. I need you, not the light."

Obediently I went and stood on the side of the bed. The floor was chilly under my feet, but I repressed my shivers. The morning was cold too.

He threw back the covers. "Get in."

"I shouldn't."

"I want to hold you. Get in."

Unable to resist the temptation, I climbed in next to him and snuggled close, letting him slide his arm around my waist. "I'll get up today," he said.

"You're not well."

"I'm perfectly well. I've lain here for three days now, and if I don't rise and see to business, I'll go mad. My foot is nearly healed, and I can bear my weight on it." He held me more firmly when I started. "I visited the necessary while you were asleep, using the cane Carier thoughtfully placed within reach. I'm sure it was to strike the wall or the floor if I needed help, but it supported me well enough. I've eaten, drunk, rested, even greeted our children yesterday, and now it's time to start living again."

He touched his lips to my forehead. It felt like heaven. By instinct, I lifted my chin, and he dropped a kiss on my mouth. It turned into something neither of us expected, and we shared a long, leisurely kiss of love and welcome. I had come home, truly come home.

"Sweetheart, I want to make love to you. I want to prove that I'm alive, that you're here with me and it's not another fevered dream. My love, *mi adorata*, I can't go another minute without it."

I was worried about him, but the entreaty in his eyes let loose the restraint I'd been holding back for so long. I wanted him so badly. I wouldn't let myself think, not about anything.

I reached up and sealed our mouths together with the kind of kiss I wanted to give and receive.

He touched my lips with his tongue, traced their shape. My frantic urgency seemed lost on him because he took his time, easing into my mouth with a luscious richness that melted my concerns away and forced me to concentrate on the moment. He could do this for weeks, months, years and I'd never tire of it, always want more.

He devoured me, as if we'd been apart for months, and in a way, we had been. This time we wouldn't stop.

We both wore nightwear, but not for long. His bruises had faded to greenish yellow, but he wouldn't let me soothe them. He tossed our nightwear aside and leaned up to look at me. "So beautiful, and all mine." He glanced at the light bandage that

245

covered the gunshot wound Jerry had given me.

When he lifted his gaze to my face, I smiled and shook my head. "An inconvenience, no more."

He touched his lips to my mouth, then down to the hollow at the base of my throat, a place he knew drove my senses to high alert, and down farther. He covered my breasts with his hands and took a nipple between thumb and forefinger. "I love the way they peak for me. It tells me you want me, that you can't resist me. As I can't resist you. I don't intend to try." He bent then and sucked a nipple deeply into his mouth, releasing it to move to the other and give it the same treatment. Short, intense, like a steel needle to my nerves, he roused me to almost unbearable levels. But he wasn't done yet. Sliding his hand down my side, from my breast to my hip and my thigh, he did it again. "A delicious curve, made for a man's hand."

I reciprocated. "And this. Masculine and mine." His muscles swelled under their covering of satiny skin. Despite the bruises, it still felt the same. His touch was addictive, as always, and I would never get enough of holding him. If I lost him—

He must have seen my sudden fear because he stopped his caresses. "Look at me, Rose. Look at me." I lifted my gaze to his. "We are here," he said. "This is now, and that is all we have. We only have this moment, this time, and we should live it. That's what I got back in those days in the cellar. The immediacy of *now*. Think of nothing else but us, you and me, here in this bed, loving each other. Can you do that?"

I swallowed and understood. "Yes, I know, I understand."

"Then touch me and know that I'm here."

I was only too willing to obey him. His sex stood hard and ready for me, and I wanted him. A bead of moisture gathered at the tiny opening at the tip, and I touched it, smoothed it over the shiny head.

He groaned, and his fist clenched in the sheets by my side. "Not too much, my love. I want to get inside you first."

With a wry smile he swung his body over mine and settled between my thighs when I opened them for him and drew up my knees. I clasped his narrow hips between them, loving the way he pushed my thighs wide and caressed me with his shaft. He slid down my wet crease, lifted and slid again, catching the pearl of passion, which, he told me, was correctly called the clitoris. I preferred pearl.

Richard had expanded my vocabulary in a most lascivious way and encouraged me to show him everything I wanted to in the privacy of our bedchamber. And occasionally elsewhere too. He'd unlock the door and add the spice of possible discovery to our trysts. He wanted me with an eagerness I could only respond to with equal need, and his honesty forced me to drop any pretence at maidenly modesty. Or any other kind of modesty.

Now, naked as nature intended, we explored each other's bodies with a greed born of abstinence and a reconnection spiced by rebirth. He stroked me, slid his fingers deep into my body and found the spot that drove me wild. Mercilessly he stroked, murmuring my name and how much he wanted me. "You will come, Rose, and then I'll come inside you. We're not stopping this time, my love."

I poured a litany of pleas and begging, alternately wanting him to stop and then do it more, not stop until he caused that explosion that came to me new-minted. My senses lifted, became aware of the scents of our bodies, the slightly foreign perfume of the soap we'd washed him in, not his usual one, and the musk of his arousal, so yearned for, here with me now. My sharper aroma rose to wreathe us in a sensuous perfume of our own making. His skin slid against mine, creating a friction, an embrace that was wholly Richard, one I'd know anywhere. From now on I could wake in the night and reach for him, and he'd be there.

I opened my mouth to scream, but he covered my lips with his own, taking me in a devastating explosion of mind and spirit. I pulsed around him, my body contracting in waves of magnitude, gripping him and then releasing. I lost my mind, coming to when he pushed his shaft deep inside me.

Then he stopped. Lifting his upper body, leaning on his elbows, he gazed at me, so that when I opened my eyes I found him there, waiting. He was smiling. "Sometimes I wonder, why you, why me? How did we meet all that time ago? If I'd found you after you'd come to London, if you belonged to someone else, I would have moved heaven and earth to get you, broken every law there was if I could have you. But we got there in time. If not for your trust and your generosity that day when you offered me everything you had, I might have missed you, might have done something stupid, like sacrifice myself for my family honour. The family can go hang, then and now." With a low laugh, he withdrew and plunged back, taking me to heights he'd taught me to abandon myself to enjoy.

I thought I was worn out after the climax he'd given me. I was wrong.

I cried out helplessly, giving myself up to him. Everything I was, everything I could be, was in his hands, in his talented body, at present pounding into me. He entered, touched, retreated, thrust, until I lost count of what day it was, or why I should worry about him. Nothing. His strength surrounded me, as it always did, as it always would, and then, in that moment of stillness before my body exploded with our passion, he said, "I love you."

I gasped his name, panted that I loved him, and then we climaxed together, his hot essence jetting into me, as I gripped him, cried his name over and over as if it would save me.

As it had.

When he finally drew away, he gave a chuckle and touched his forehead to mine. "We're ready to turn the page and begin again." He rolled to one side, taking me with him. I curled in, wanting contact with him all over me. I felt his firm, warm body next to mine and knew it was enough, for now. Until the fever of passion took us again, and it would, in the not-too-distant future.

I hadn't realised how exhausting worry could be, but I knew now. I knew that must have added to Richard's burden when I had fallen ill after the birth of our sons, and recognised the size of the weight he had unstintingly carried for the last few months.

I glanced around. The light filtering through the drapes was brighter now. Day had arrived. "Should I draw the curtains now?"

He chuckled. "No. I honestly don't mind them being closed. I seem to have overcome my fear, although I would have wished to do it some other way. I had too much to think of at first, and by the time the confines of our imprisonment had borne on me, I was too concerned with other matters to give it much thought. I want to be close to you, and being enclosed like this adds a certain intimacy to our situation. Don't you think?"

"Yes, I do." Unlike Richard, I had always enjoyed the privacy afforded by small spaces. I had shared bedrooms for most of my life, with my sisters, and the luxury of a space of one's own could never be overestimated in my opinion. "Can you sleep better like this?"

He chuckled. "With you in my arms? Indubitably. But I seem to have done nothing but sleep during the last three days.

That and eat." He kissed me, lingering over my lips like a dish he was reluctant to leave. His expression turned grave. "I'm ready to talk about it, if you want to hear."

"Are you sure?"

He pressed his lips against my hair before he answered. "Yes. While it's fresh in my mind. It was a nasty experience, and I have a feeling that the mind, which likes to forget the worst parts of everything, will discard it as soon as it can."

"I'll make sure your account is recorded. Tell me, Richard. If you want to."

"I want to." His voice, strong again, but low, created a cocoon of intimacy between us that I never wanted to end. He drew a breath, kissed my forehead and tilted up my chin once more so he could watch me while he spoke. "Carier was there at the start. I presume he told you. Forcing us down into the cellar actually protected us from the explosion. John must have set his bomb in the upper rooms. He showed me bloody hair, said the children were dead, and you were too. He wanted me to know so I'd die despairing. It only made me more determined to escape."

I shuddered when I realised how close I'd come to losing him in that moment, but he murmured words of comfort and stroked me until I felt better. Everything was fine because I had him now. I urged him to carry on.

"We were trapped, but we decided to wait, because help would undoubtedly come and we could make things worse if we tried to dig ourselves out. When the first tremor, the warning, happened, Paul realised that it was an earthquake.

"Then the second tremor struck. It brought what was left of the house down on top of us and a chunk of masonry hit the cook who was down there with us. John had shot the man, and we'd done what we could. He was badly wounded, but still alive. The blow killed him." He paused once more. "That would have been the time when I panicked. But I choked it down. What good would it do? I needed to keep my wits about me, if we were to get out of this situation with our lives. And it looked increasingly unlikely. Especially when the water came.

"I presume a great wave struck, one of those that often follows an earthquake. The disturbance to the earth must be the reason, I suppose. It filled the cellar, sent the body floating, and us too. It extinguished the kitchen fire, which I'd hoped to use in some way.

"We had a bare six inches in which to breathe, but we were relatively high in the city, so the wave did not completely submerge us. Eventually the water receded. The cellar had upper windows, and some of it escaped. Over the next few hours more drained away, but we were left with about a foot of water on the kitchen flags. The kitchen has drains, presumably to facilitate the ordinary cleaning routines, but the water had a way of escaping through the earth too." He sighed, staring into space, and I lived it with him, there in that small, stinking space, not knowing if help would come but never giving up.

"We couldn't risk missing our chance at rescue, so we slept in turns, and only for short periods."

"Did you eat?"

He shuddered. "We found enough to keep us alive. We found some food. Cheese, apples, but not much else. We were surrounded by spoiled food and water we couldn't drink. Bodies and sewage fouled it. But we found some bottles of wine." He grinned. "Never have I wanted water rather than wine so much. Just before you arrived to find us, we'd discovered a small barrel of beer."

His voice shook. I nestled closer. "You don't have to say any more. Not if you don't want to, or if it hurts too much."

Tears glistened in his eyes, turning the sapphire to a vivid cobalt. "Yes I do. I thought John would kill you. He escaped,

251

and my only hope was that Carier had caught up with him and dispatched him. But I didn't know and I couldn't make sure. I thought I'd go mad. You want me to say we made up our differences before he left, that I wouldn't have killed him, given the chance? I have to disappoint you, my love. Twice he made serious attempts on your life. He said he'd already killed our children and you, but I refused to believe him. I knew that, if you'd gone, I'd know."

I gasped. "I thought the same! That was why I insisted on going back to Lisbon to find you, even though others had given you up."

He drew me closer for another kiss, taking his time. He traced the outline of my lips with his tongue and then plunged inside for a brief but devastating caress. "We are one, my love. I hoped you felt the same, that you'd come and find me."

"I wouldn't let them stop me. They tried."

"I can imagine they did. I've set fierce guards around you, sweetheart. I was obsessed with losing you, especially after the fever nearly took you. But we have now. If we continue to live that way, we need not fear. I won't constrain you anymore, although I reserve the right to protect you. You are the most precious thing in my life. Nothing else comes close."

I accepted his gift now, for what it was. Not a threat, not a restriction and not something for me to be afraid of. He gave his life into my hands, and as long as I reciprocated, we'd have nothing to fear. "You mean the world to me."

He kissed me again, but drew back to watch me. "Should I send for some food, something to drink? You've cared for me without stint. Now you have to rest."

"I'm perfectly well. Better than well," I assured him. "I have back the part of me that was missing. I'll call for tea soon, maybe something to eat. But not yet. Finish your story."

He sighed. "Very well. I must, I know. We managed for the first day, and Paul and I slept one after the other. We made some efforts to shift the rubble over our heads, but it only brought more down. For all we knew the entire house had collapsed on top of the kitchens and only the beams lay between us and complete collapse. But it's hard to wait, and trust, and not do your best to escape."

"The second day, or the third, broke. Paul had his watch, but somewhere we lost track, and all we knew was what hour of the day it was, not if it were day or night. It grew very hot in that space, despite the chill of the water swirling around our feet. We built a kind of platform from broken furniture and fittings, and piled our food and drink on it, as well as ourselves. But it wasn't large enough for both of us at the same time, so we took turn and turn about. I donated my coat as a towel, something to dry our wet limbs on when we switched."

"How did you see?"

He smiled. "My practical love, trust you to think of that. The upper windows sent in a very little light, hardly enough to see by. We had candles, and a tinderbox, and we tore up Paul's shirt to provide rags. Most kitchens keep tinderboxes on a high shelf above the fireplace, and this was no exception. It had fallen into the water with the tremor, but we rescued it, and once we'd dried off the flint, it struck a spark well enough. Paul wanted to conserve the lights we had, but I couldn't see the point. The candles would last us as long as we needed them, one way or the other." He paused and gazed at me, as if gaining strength from the sight. I accepted it and returned it in full measure. I loved looking at him.

"We heard sounds from above, though whether it was people digging for us, or scavengers, we weren't sure. We had one weapon. We conserved that weapon and the one shot it contained. One of us had an easier way out."

He drew me closer. "The body of the cook had bloated, and it was stinking pretty badly. It had to be, for us to notice after we'd been living with it for days. On the third day, as near as we could tell, Paul slipped on the table and fell. It was a bad fall, and he trapped his foot in an underwater drain. One of his turns twisted it. I heard the snap, knew he'd broken something. I should have checked more rigorously, but he assured me it would do, and I believed him. I shouldn't have done that." He shuddered.

I held him close. Kissed his cheek, his brow, his lips. "Don't think of it. He's here, he's alive."

"I know."

"He's fine." Not more than that, not yet. Paul had lost a foot, and while he was sanguine about it, at least to us, an edge of suffering tinged his expression now. He knew he'd been lucky not to lose his leg, had declared his determination to walk again, once the estate carpenter had fashioned him something to replace his lost appendage. "He'll live and he'll be happy because he has Lizzie and his brother to help him. Joaquin will remain here as much as he can, but since much of the family wealth depends on the winemaking, he'll travel to the vineyards. He really loves that work. I misjudged him, Richard. He considers the making of fine wine and port akin to the creation of a work of art. It's his calling."

"We both misjudged him. He's a fine man."

"So are you."

"I've done many wrong things. Some of them I can never atone for. I would have killed John without compunction. You'd have forgiven me, then?"

I smiled and reached up to caress his cheek, rough with stubble. It glinted in the dim light, like powdered gold dusted over his beloved features. "It wasn't a matter of me forgiving you. It was you forgiving yourself. I would have remained with
254

you, supported you, even if you'd killed him in the spring. But you wouldn't have lived with that very easily. A man shouldn't have to make that decision. Neither should he have to live with it afterwards. John largely made his own future by seeking revenge at every turn. You did everything you could to make him see reason, but he refused. And now he's dead."

"How did he die?" He hadn't asked that before. We'd only told him John was dead when he demanded to know.

Now I had to tell him. "I shot him when they brought you out. He must have been watching all that time and not attempted to help us. I would have shot him for that alone. He aimed his pistol at you, and I'd had enough. No more, I decided. I've always been a good shot, you know that, and I got him in the head." I swallowed. "I'm sorry, so sorry. But I'm glad you didn't do it."

"Even after everything he did, so am I. It's wrong to kill someone of your blood. But I'm glad he's dead. He had his chances to make a new life and he refused to take them. He'd have always caused trouble, and his mind was dangerously twisted. He was obsessed with revenge."

"I think he was part mad, at the end." I stroked a hand over Richard's chest, down over his stomach. The muscles tightened under my hand in instinctive response. "But remember, Richard, you killed for me once. I've returned the favour."

"So we're even." His smile, at first grim, turned tender. "And we've come through our ordeals, we're alive and in love. What more could we ask for?"

What more indeed?

I reached up and kissed him. He threaded his fingers through my hair and held me close, making the kiss deeper, hotter, and just like that we created another conflagration. It wouldn't stop until we were both sated. Then we'd rest and return to the flame. It would always be like that between us.

Epilogue

Late spring, 1756

"I want to remodel the garden."

Richard looked up from the letter he was perusing. "Sorry, my sweet?"

"The garden. It's dingy. No colour. I want to remake it."

He reached a hand over the breakfast table, and I put my own in it. "You must do as you see fit. Are you missing the colours of Portugal? Shall we buy a house there?"

I repressed a shudder, recalling the events of the previous winter. "No. I can understand why Lizzie is so happy there, but she has reason to be. She has two children now, and her husband back."

Paul had recovered his spirits with his strength and as he'd promised, was learning to walk again, with the help of his wife and the collection of clever false feet the carpenter was constantly fashioning for him, refining the design with each new model. He had learned to use a crutch as soon as he could, when his wound had knitted sufficiently for him to try, and joked about having more in common with the sailors in Lisbon port.

Lisbon was busy rebuilding. A remarkable man had taken charge, one of the government, and he was rebuilding as fast as he could, replacing the beautiful city with one just as fine. Our help wasn't needed. But we received the government's thanks, for what we weren't sure.

This was where our life lay. Here, in London and in the

country, fulfilling the purpose Richard was born for, and living every day, as Richard had promised, for the moment. We could make plans and still remain with each other. Every time I looked at him, every smile, every time I lay in his arms at night, I thanked God for sparing us both.

We had nearly died in 1755, me in the spring, Richard in the autumn, and we both had the strong feeling that something had turned, the tenor of our lives had changed.

"I like it here," I told him now.

He laughed delightedly, his eyes sparkling. "I thought you dreaded London. Remember when we first married, how afraid you were of society? I told you that you'd come to lead society in the end, that you didn't need it, it needed you. And I was right."

He stood and came around the table to me, tugging my hand so I got up too. I eagerly met his lips and felt him caress me, his hand splayed over my back. "No stays? What a delightful surprise. While I sometimes enjoy the confinement, and the shape they convey to your body, nothing compares with your luscious self."

I had regained the weight I'd lost during my illness and he delighted in it. He was no longer afraid that he'd break me, he said.

"I have to go out later. I'm attending Mrs. Montagu's salon, so I thought I'd be lazy and dress properly after I'd eaten."

"Do you need to go to the salon?"

I looked at him quizzically. "Why?"

"Because I can think of something far more interesting to do." Just to prove his point, he kissed me, long and slow.

I drew away slightly, smiled, then laughed. "Richard, do you never think of anything else?"

"Not while you're in this world, my love. And that, I know, will be for a very long time to come."

Author's Note

It's the first time I've done one of these. While I always take care that I don't distort history for my own ends, this is the first time I've used such a cataclysmic event as the background to a story.

The Lisbon earthquake of 1755 was a natural disaster such as hadn't been experienced for centuries in Europe. While Lisbon had suffered earthquakes, this was a monster. Modern experts rate this at around 9 on the Richter scale, as powerful as the Japanese earthquake of 2011. I was writing this story at the same time as the Japanese earthquake, and the experience was a strange one. It really brought home how devastating these disasters are, and my sympathies go out to everyone affected by the terrible disaster.

The earthquake, tsunami and subsequent fires and lootings destroyed most of old Lisbon. It's not known exactly how many people died, but many were at church for the services of All Saint's Day. After the earthquake, several determined and gifted people drew services together to rebuild the city, which is now the beautiful city you can see today.

It says much for the resilience of the Portuguese people that they survived such a disaster. I read extensively about the subject, trying to do the people justice by describing it as closely as I could. For instance, the royal palace, close to the harbour, survived the earthquake but was destroyed in looting and fires afterwards. There are accounts of people surviving in cellars, although many of them couldn't be reached because of the rubble piled on top and the anarchy that immediately followed the disaster.

I always meant to end the story of Richard and Rose here. Right from the beginning I knew where they'd end up, and I worked all the dates to suit. Apart from that, the individual stories in the books were done as I got to them. I had no idea at the beginning of the story that Richard's chequered past would catch up with him, but it seemed right that he should be made to think about what he'd done in the past, and to pay for it.

I wanted to tell the story of two men in this series. One who had a sensitive nature hidden under a hard, uncaring exterior, and his mirror image, who was also, by a twist of fate, his son. But Rose needed her own conflict. She couldn't be the woman she grew into without that, so the Drurys were born too.

Where I've included historical figures, I've kept them as true to life as I could, relying on contemporary accounts for the most part, and many of the great houses in the books are also based on real-life examples. I based Eyton, Richard's family seat, on Chatsworth, a house I know quite well. The ruinous Hareton Abbey was based on Calke Abbey, an astonishing place with a nursery just as I described it in *Yorkshire*, and the rebuilt Hareton Hall, James's family seat, is based on the superbly elegant Saltram House. Admittedly Saltram was built a little later than Hareton, but I didn't use the Adam brothers, merely the layout and the idea of classical elegance. And it's in the right part of the country.

The *palacio* where Lizzie and Paul lived is based on a real-life example too. A very beautiful landmark that is today open to the public, it survived the earthquake virtually intact.

I can't imagine doing the series without the help of all the editors, cover artists and most of all, the readers. Your encouragement has pushed me to make the best I could for Richard and Rose, who I've come to know very well over the course of the ten years it's taken me to write their story. For which I thank you.

However, Richard and Rose won't completely disappear from my books. Richard makes a guest appearance in *A Betting Chance*, for instance, and I'm planning for him, and perhaps Rose as well, to make an appearance in other stories.

One final word. Thank you for coming on this journey with me. Writing Richard and Rose's story has given me more insight into the era I love and the chance to do lots more research. For all your emails, tweets and requests for signings, as well as the interest you've taken, thank you from the bottom of my heart. Richard and Rose might not be done, but they deserve a rest from their exertions.

However, watch for more adventures set in the wonderful Georgian era. There are so many more stories to tell.

About the Author

Lynne Connolly has been in love with the Georgian age since the age of nine, when she did a project about coffee and tea at school. One look at the engraving of the Georgian coffee house, and she was a goner. It's the longest love affair of her life.

She stopped looking around old houses and visiting museums long enough to go to work, fall in love for a second time, marry and have a family, but they have to share her with her obsession, which they do with good grace and much humor.

To learn more about Lynne Connolly, please visit www.lynneconnolly.com or send her an email: lynneconnollyuk@yahoo.co.uk.

Visit her Yahoo! group to join in the fun with other readers! (https://groups.yahoo.com/group/lynneconnolly). She can also be found at MySpace, Facebook and the Samhain Café.

In this game of hearts, winner takes all.

A Betting Chance
© *2010 Lynne Connolly*
The Triple Countess, Book 4

Sapphira Vardon needs five thousand pounds to avoid a cruel marriage and a grim future, and there's only one path for her. Don a mask and an assumed name, and risk everything to win at the gaming tables. First, though, she has to get through the door. Luckily she knows just whose name to drop.

Corin, Lord Elston, is curious to find out who used his name to gain entrance to Mother Brown's whorehouse and gaming hell. The enigmatic woman who calls herself Lucia isn't the sort of female usually found here. Behind her mask and heavy makeup, she's obviously a respectable woman—who plays a devilish hand of cards.

Sapphira is desperate to keep her identity a secret, but Lord Elston's devastating kisses and touches demand complete surrender. And once he learns the truth, there's more at stake than guineas. Corin finds himself falling hard for a woman who's poised to run. A woman who's about to learn that he only plays to win…

Warning: Hot action on the gaming table and in the bedroom might make you go looking for a time machine.

Available now in ebook and print from Samhain Publishing.

It's all about the story...

www.samhainpublishing.com

CPSIA information can be obtained at www.ICGtesting.com
Printed in the USA
BVOW070953130613

323234BV00002B/94/P